A NICE HOT BATH

The thief leaned over to pick through Smoke's clothes, then fingered the money belt. "Say, look what we got here. A bunch of fancy city duds and a big ole thick money belt."

Smoke's eyes grew cold as ice. Evidently the man was too stupid to notice Smoke's empty holster lying on the floor next to the chair. Smoke shifted in the water, steam rising from his bare shoulders. "Sir, I worked hard for that stake. Do you really think I'm going to sit here and let pond scum like you take it from me?"

The man stepped back, still holding the belt in one hand and his pistol in the other. "Well, Mr. City Dude," he snarled, "I don't see you have much choice in the matter. I think I'll just tie you up and head on out of town. By the time somebody finds you, I'll be long gone."

Smoke grinned, but the smile didn't reach his eyes. "I want you to think on it real hard. Is that money worth dying for? 'Cause I'm giving you one last chance to put it down and walk out of here. Otherwise I'll see that you're carried out on a board."

The man eared back the hammer on his Colt. "Maybe I won't tie you up after all, pilgrim. Maybe I'll just drill you instead."

Without another word, Smoke let the hammer down on his Navy and it exploded, blowing suds and gunsmoke out of the tub all over the man standing in front of him. The slug took him high in the forehead, blowing his scalp and half his head off and throwing him backward to land sprawled on his back, a pool of blood forming under his ruined skull. He was dead before he hit the floor.

Smoke carefully wiped his pistol on a towel before placing it gently on his clothes. Then he sighed and lay back in the water.

CREED OF THE MOUNTAIN MAN

William W. Johnstone

PINNACLE BOOKS
Kensington Publishing Corp.
http://www.kensingtonbooks.com

One

Smoke and Pearlie were leaning on a corral fence, watching Cal try to break one of the horses Smoke had bought for the Sugarloaf remuda.

"Ride 'em, Cal boy," Pearlie shouted, grinning from ear to ear. "Don't let that cayuse show you who's boss."

The boy in his late teens was holding on to the hurricane deck for dear life, shouting and waving his hat in the air as if he were at a county fair competition. The bronc was crow-hopping, swallowing his head, and generally giving the young man fits.

Smoke Jensen smiled and tilted his hat back. "I know Cal is pretty good with most horses, but I think this one has his number."

Just then, the horse bent almost double and gave a quick double jump and twisted sideways at the same time. Cal went flying head over heels to land in a pile of horse apples in the middle of the corral.

"He's forked end up, Smoke," Pearlie hollered as he quickly scaled the fence and shooed the still-bucking animal away until Cal could climb shakily to his feet and make his way over to the fence.

"Jimminy Christmas, Smoke, that there broomtail acts like he's got a burr under his saddle," Cal said.

He brushed the seat of his pants with both hands, grimacing as he touched areas bruised by the fall. After a moment, as if the idea had just occurred to him, he narrowed his eyes and glanced over his shoulder at Pearlie. "You didn't do somethin' nasty like that to me, did you, Pearlie?"

Pearlie sauntered over, holding his hands out in front of him. "No, Cal, I didn't put no sticker under your saddle." He gave a short laugh. "I didn't figure I needed to since there weren't no way you was gonna be able to stay in the saddle nohow."

"Whatta you mean, Pearlie?" Cal said, sticking his jaw out. "You think I can't break that hoss? Just gimme another try and we'll see."

Smoke said, "Hold on, Cal. We all know you're a pretty good rider, but breaking horses takes some specialized knowledge. Pearlie, show him how it's done."

Pearlie pulled his hat down tight and walked to the snorting horse, ignoring the way it was pawing the ground and looking walleyed. He bent down and picked up the reins, bringing the horse's head down toward his face. He grabbed its ear, bent it over, and swung into the saddle. As the mount kicked up its heels, Pearlie threw his weight forward, wrapped his arms around its neck, and squeezed and twisted the animal's ear almost double. It immediately quieted down, rolling its eyes back and trying to see what was happening. Pearlie dug his spurs in and made the bronc trot around the corral a time or two.

After a few minutes, he let go of the horse's ear and continued to ride in peace, the horse trotting as if wearing a saddle and rider was the most natural thing in the world.

Pearlie grinned, took his hat off, and swept it in front of him as he took a bow toward Cal while riding the now-docile animal.

"Well I'll be gosh-darned," Cal said, wonderment in his voice.

"That's an old-timer's trick, Cal," Smoke said. "The old trail hands used to tell the tenderfeet they were whispering in the horse's ear when they did that, but they were really just putting all their weight on the animal's neck and using the ear to cause it enough pain to make it forget all about bucking."

He shrugged, and inclined his head toward Pearlie. "It doesn't always work that well, but you had already tired the animal out enough that he was about ready to quit bucking anyway. Course, Pearlie's going to try and take all the credit for it—you just watch."

Pearlie trotted his mount over to the two men and said, "See, Cal boy, it's easy when you're an old hand at breakin' hosses like I am."

"That's bull an' you know it, Pearlie. I already had that crazy animal plumb tuckered out so's he couldn't hardly walk, much less buck you off."

"Okay, boys, that's enough jawing," Smoke said. "Let's get the rest of this sorry bunch of animals broken so we can get some lunch."

Pearlie, an acknowledged chowhound, grinned and said, "Yes, sir!" at the mention of food. He walked his bronc over to the gate and put it in with the ones already broken. He and Cal managed to saddle another of the wild horses, and he walked back over to stand next to Smoke as Cal once again tried his hand.

As the young man leaned forward on the horse's neck and twisted its ear, Pearlie said, "Smoke, I can't hardly believe the changes in Cal since Miss Sally brought him back to the ranch a few years ago."

Smoke's eyes crinkled as he smiled at the recollection. "Neither can I, Pearlie. . . ."

Calvin Woods, going on eighteen years old now, was just fourteen when Smoke and Sally took him in as a hired hand. It was during the spring branding, and Sally was on her way back from Big Rock to the Sugarloaf. The buckboard was piled high with supplies; branding hundreds of calves made for hungry punchers.

As Sally slowed the team to make a bend in the trail, a rail-thin young man stepped from the bushes at the side of the road with a pistol in his hand.

"Hold it right there, miss."

Applying the brake with her right foot, Sally slipped her hand under a pile of gingham cloth on the seat. She grasped the handle of her short-barreled Colt .44 and eared back the hammer, letting the sound of the horses' hooves and the squealing of the brake pad on the wheel mask the sound. "What can I do for you, young man?" she asked, her voice firm and without fear. She knew she could draw and drill the young highwayman before he could raise his pistol to fire.

"Well, uh, you can throw some of those beans and a cut of that fatback over here, and maybe a portion of that Arbuckle's coffee too."

Sally's eyebrows raised. "Don't you want my money?"

The boy frowned and shook his head. "Why, no, ma'am. I ain't no thief. I'm just hungry."

"And if I don't give you my food, are you going to shoot me with that big Navy Colt?"

He hesitated a moment, then grinned ruefully. "No, ma'am, I guess not." He twirled the pistol around his finger and slipped it into his belt, turned, and began to walk down the road toward Big Rock.

Sally watched the youngster amble off, noting his tattered shirt, dirty pants with holes in the knees and torn pockets, and boots that looked as if they had been salvaged from a garbage dump. "Young man," she called, "come back here, please."

He turned, a smirk on his face, spreading his hands. "Look, lady, you don't have to worry. I don't even have any bullets." With a lightning-fast move, he drew the gun from his pants, aimed away from Sally, and pulled the trigger. There was a click but no explosion as the hammer fell on an empty cylinder.

Sally smiled. "Oh, I'm not worried." In a movement every bit as fast as his, she whipped her .44 out and fired, clipping a pine cone from a branch, causing it to fall and bounce off his head.

The boy's knees buckled and he ducked, saying, "Jimminy Christmas!"

Mimicking him, Sally twirled her Colt and stuck it in the waistband of her britches. "What's your name, boy?"

The boy blushed and looked down at his feet. "Calvin, ma'am, Calvin Woods."

She leaned forward, elbows on knees, and stared into the boy's eyes. "Calvin, no one has to go hungry in this country, not if they're willing to work."

He looked up at her through narrowed eyes, as if he found life a little different than she'd described it.

"If you're willing to put in an honest day's work, I'll see that you get an honest day's pay, and all the food you can eat."

Calvin stood a little straighter, shoulders back and head held high. "Ma'am, I've got to be straight with you. I ain't no experienced cowhand. I come from a hardscrabble farm and we only had us one milk cow and a couple of goats and chickens, and lots of dirt that weren't worth nothing for growin' things. My ma and pa and me never had nothin', but we never begged and we never stooped to takin' handouts."

Sally thought, *I like this boy. Proud, and not willing to take charity if he can help it.* "Calvin, if you're willing to work, and don't mind getting your hands dirty and your muscles sore, I've got some hands that'll have you punching beeves like you were born to it in no time at all."

A smile lit up his face, making him seem even younger than his years. "Even if I don't have no saddle, nor a horse to put it on?"

She laughed out loud. "Yes. We've got plenty of ponies and saddles." She glanced down at his raggedy boots. "We can probably even round up some boots and spurs that'll fit you."

He walked over and jumped in the back of the buckboard. "Ma'am, I don't know who you are, but you just hired you the hardest-workin' hand you've ever seen."

Back at the Sugarloaf, she sent him in to Cookie and told him to eat his fill. When Smoke and the other punchers rode into the cabin yard at the end of the day, she introduced Calvin around. As Cal was shaking hands with the men, Smoke looked over at her and winked. He knew she could never resist a stray dog or cat, and her heart was as large as the Big Lonesome itself.

Smoke walked up to Cal and cleared his throat. "Son, I hear you drew down on my wife."

Cal gulped, "Yessir, Mr. Jensen. I did." He squared his shoulders and looked Smoke in the eye, not flinching though he was obviously frightened of the tall man with the incredibly wide shoulders standing before him.

Smoke smiled and clapped the boy on the back. "Just wanted you to know you stared death in the eye, boy. Not many galoots are still walking upright who ever pulled a gun on Sally. She's a better shot than any man I've ever seen except me, and sometimes I wonder about me."

The boy laughed with relief as Smoke turned and called out, "Pearlie, get your lazy butt over here."

A tall, lanky cowboy ambled over to Smoke and Cal, munching on a biscuit stuffed with roast beef. His face was lined with wrinkles and tanned a dark brown from hours under the sun, but his eyes were sky-blue and twinkled with good-natured humor.

"Yessir, boss," he mumbled around a mouthful of food.

Smoke put his hand on Pearlie's shoulder. "Cal, this here chowhound is Pearlie. He eats more'n any two hands, and he's never been known to do a lick of work he could get out of, but he knows beeves and horses as well as any puncher I have. I want you to follow him around and let him teach you what you need to know."

Cal nodded. "Yes, sir, Mr. Smoke."

"Now let me see that iron you have in your pants."

Cal pulled the ancient Navy Colt and handed it to Smoke. When Smoke opened the loading gate, the rusted cylinder fell to the ground, causing Pearlie and Smoke to laugh and Cal's face to flame red. "This is the piece you pulled on Sally?"

The boy nodded, looking at the ground.

Pearlie shook his head. "Cal, you're one lucky pup. Hell, if'n you'd tried to fire that thing it'd of blown your hand clean off."

Smoke inclined his head toward the bunkhouse. "Pearlie, take Cal over to the tack house and get him fixed up with what he needs, including a gun belt and a Colt that won't fall apart the first time he pulls it. You might also help pick him out a shavetail to ride. I'll expect him to start earning his keep tomorrow."

"Yes, sir, Smoke." Pearlie put his arm around Cal's shoulders and led him off toward the bunkhouse. "Now the first thing you gotta learn, Cal, is how to get on Cookie's good side. A puncher rides on his belly, and it 'pears to me that you need some fattenin' up 'fore you can begin to punch cows."*

As Smoke grinned at his memory of the day Cal arrived, his thoughts turned to his foreman, Pearlie, standing next to him.

Pearlie had come to work for Smoke in as roundabout a way as Cal had. He was hiring his gun out to Tilden Franklin in Fontana when Franklin went crazy and tried to take over Sugarloaf, Smoke and Sally's spread. After Franklin's men raped and killed a young girl in the fracas, Pearlie sided with Smoke and the aging gunfighters he had called in to help put an end to Franklin's reign of terror.†

Pearlie was now honorary foreman of Smoke's ranch, though he was only a shade over twenty-four years old himself—boys grew to be men early in the mountains of Colorado.

Sally, Smoke's pretty, brown-haired wife, appeared next to

*Vengeance of the Mountain Man
†Trail of the Mountain Man

him, breaking his reverie. "Howdy, boys. I thought you might like to take a little break and have a snack before lunch."

She was carrying a platter of still-steaming bear sign, the sweet doughnuts that cowboys had been known to ride ten miles for.

Pearlie's eyes widened and he let out a whoop. "Hey, Cal, Miss Sally's got some bear sign for us!"

As Cal looked over, he let his concentration slip and released the horse's ear. It immediately began to crow-hop and jigger around the corral, finally throwing Cal in a heap in a far corner.

The boy sprang to his feet, slapped the bucking horse out of his way with his hat, and ran to jump over the fence. "Boy howdy, I could sure use some nourishment, Miss Sally."

Sally laughed and handed the platter of doughnuts to Pearlie and a pitcher of lemonade and some glasses to Smoke. She shook her head and started back toward the cabin. "You boys don't work Smoke too hard breaking those broomtails. He's getting on up in years and may not be able to take it."

Smoke called out to her retreating back, "Dear, you notice I'm not the one sweating here. It's these two young bucks who're doing all the work. I'm busy supervising."

She called back, "Good, then that means they can have all the bear sign."

"Like hell," Smoke muttered, as he hurried to grab a handful before they were all gone.

Two

The day was finally over, and Smoke and Sally were sitting at the kitchen table, having a cup of after-dinner coffee. "Sweetheart," Smoke said, "I'm going to make a trip to Wyoming."

Sally put her mug down and stared at Smoke for a moment before asking, "Why?"

"Seven, the Palouse stud Preacher gave me, is getting old, and even though he's bred us some good crosses for our remuda, they aren't Palouses. I want to find some pure Palouse stock mares and maybe another stud or two and carry on Seven's line."

Smoke didn't have to say any more, for Sally to understand this was his way of keeping alive the memory of the man who meant as much to him as his father. Back when Smoke's name was Kirby Jensen, just after the end of the Civil War, he and his father came west from their crab-apple farm in Missouri with all they had strapped to one mule. Soon, they met Preacher, an old mountain man, who saved their lives from a band of marauding Indians. During the fighting, young Kirby killed his share of the attackers, and was given the name Smoke by Preacher, both for the thin trail of smoke from his Colt Navy .36 and for the color of his ash-blond hair.

After traveling with the mountain man for a spell, Smoke's father was killed by three men who had stolen some gold from the Confederate Army. Preacher took Smoke in and raised him for the next several years, teaching him all the lore of the strange breed known as mountain men.*

Sally asked, "What about Horse?" referring to the Palouse Smoke had been riding since putting Seven in his own pasture on the Sugarloaf to run free and enjoy his old age.

"I'd like to carry on his line, too. I ran across a trapper coming down from the mountains for supplies last week. He said the Nez Percé tribe that used to live there was gone. He didn't know where, but he'd heard there was still a small band of them camped up near Buffalo in northern Wyoming."

Smoke drained the last of his coffee and reached across the table to take Sally's hand.

"The Nez Percé are the ones who developed the Palouse breed, Sally, and they always keep a good supply of breeding mares and studs on hand. I plan to go to Wyoming before the tribe gets killed off, or mixes with another and loses their identity. I'm going to carry on the Palouse line here on the Sugarloaf, starting with Seven and Horse."

"But Smoke, it's the middle of winter. Don't you think this will wait until spring, at least?"

He shook his head. "No, I don't want to be gone during the spring calving and branding. That's too heavy a load to leave on Pearlie and Cal. I'm going to get on the Union Pacific Line train and take it all the way to Casper, a little range town at the foot of the Big Horn Mountains. From there I'll pack by horse up into the mountains north of Buffalo and see if I can find out where the Nez Percé are now."

He sat back and shrugged. "Then it's just a matter of doing some good old-fashioned horse trading."

Sally got the pot off the stove and poured him another cup of coffee. "I don't like the idea of you traveling halfway across the country in the dead of winter by yourself. Why don't you take Cal or Pearlie with you?"

*The Last Mountain Man

"There's too much work here they need to be doing." He glanced out the cabin window at their ranch. "Fences need mending, corrals have to be built, and the cattle have got to be taken care of." He hesitated, a slow grin crossing his lips. "Besides, do you think this old beaver is getting too old to make a trip by himself? You think I need taking care of?"

She stared at him for a moment without speaking, as if she *was* considering that possibility. Finally, she got up from the table and took the coffeepot off the stove, putting it on a counter to cool. She stoked the fire in the stove, sending waves of warmth through the chilly room. When she was finished, she took her apron off and began to walk toward their bedroom.

After a few steps, she glanced back over her shoulder and smiled. "Oh, I don't think you're getting old at all, but why don't you come to bed and show me how young you're feeling?"

And he did just that.

Three

Hubert Teschemacher and Frederic O. deBillier swung their identical gold-headed walking sticks to and fro as they approached the Cheyenne Club through a light snowfall.

They swaggered as they walked, tipping their top hats at other prominent citizens as they passed. Having come to Wyoming from Boston a few years back with five hundred thousand dollars to invest, they were well aware of their place in Cheyenne society as two of the wealthiest men in the state capital.

"Freddy," Hubert said, "we've come a long way since we roomed together at Harvard."

DeBillier glanced at his friend, a sardonic smile on his face. "Yes, Hubie, this western country is certainly different from Boston, wouldn't you say?"

Teschemacher shrugged. "Yes, of course. There is no culture at all out here, and the food is generally atrocious."

He paused, before grinning and smoothing his handlebar moustache with the flick of a forefinger. "But then, there is always the Cheyenne Club to relieve our boredom," he said with a wink at his friend.

DeBillier smiled back, adjusting his silk cravat as the two men entered the three-story Cheyenne Club, described in its charter as "a pleasure resort and place of amusement."

A doorman in formal attire took their overcoats and hats and walking sticks, saying, "Good evening, sirs. The others in your party are awaiting you on the third floor."

The first floor of the Cheyenne Club was the kitchen and storage area for the vast supplies of liquor and wine and other culinary delicacies the members maintained.

The second floor was the "communal" room, where the prettiest whores in the state would arrange themselves in various small cubicles and rooms, to play pianos or other musical instruments, sing, and otherwise amuse their wealthy clients. All of the girls were handpicked by Teschemacher and deBillier, who as co-founders of the Cheyenne Club, retained certain perks for themselves.

The third floor was the dining and meeting hall. Dozens of overstuffed leather chairs and tables were arranged around the room in the manner of the English men's clubs that Teschemacher and deBillier had seen on their travels abroad. In a separate room was a dining table made of carved oak, over twenty feet long, with chairs to seat forty diners.

Butlers and maids were everywhere, and the floors were connected to the kitchen by a series of dumbwaiters, so the members were never without food or drink for very long.

As Hubert and Frederic climbed the stairs, Hubert said, "Now remember, Freddy, we must handle Hesse with extreme care in our discussion tonight."

"I know, Hubie. That damned pompous limey bastard won't agree to anything unless he's made to feel it's his idea."

Hubert nodded. "Exactly. So the trick is simply to lead him in the right direction, so that he'll decide things our way."

"What about Bill Irving?" Frederic asked.

Hubert snorted, "Oh, William is just a midlevel manager for his investors back in Omaha. He'll do whatever we tell him to do, since it's his butt on the line if his ranch doesn't make a profit every year."

Slightly out of breath from their climb, they finally reached the third floor and walked into the anteroom, where they saw their friends standing in small groups, with Cuban cigars in their hands and holding crystal goblets filled with brandy and Kentucky bourbon.

Teschemacher and deBillier had spared no expense in decorating the room, making use of a French decorator brought over for just that reason. There were paintings on every wall, and a twenty-five-foot gilded mirror behind a massive, ornately carved mahogany bar that ran the length of the room, stocked with thousands of dollars' worth of expensive whiskeys and wines and brandies. A billiard table was in a corner, underneath a fancy French chandelier with hundreds of small candles arrayed around the crystal glass it was made of. The polished wooden floors were covered with hand-woven rugs of the finest wool.

Hubert and Frederic had invited a group of the richest and most influential men in the county to attend the meeting, all owners or managers of the largest cattle ranches in the area.

William Irving managed a large ranch owned by millionaire backers from Omaha, and served as a director of the Cheyenne and Northern Railroad and other corporations. Fred Hesse, an Englishman, had worked (swindled, Hubert often said) his way up from foreman to manager of a ranching system that grazed tens of thousands of cattle on far-flung Wyoming ranges. Major Frank Wolcott was a former Army officer from Kentucky who still wore puttees and maintained his military bearing despite a twisted neck—acquired in a tussle with a Laramie cowboy—that left his head permanently cocked to one side. Wolcott's jaw, Frederic had observed, "closes with a snap after every sentence he utters."

Most of the plutocrats in the group had spent less time in the saddle than in the state capital, spending most of their nights in the plush and exclusive surroundings of the Cheyenne Club.

Tonight, there were forty-one members attending the club banquet arranged by Hubert and Frederic. Some were playing billiards, while others nibbled at pickled eels and French hors d'oeuvres while waiting for the dinner to be sent up. Hubert had ordered twenty bottles of wine and over sixty bottles of champagne for his guests tonight. There would be none left by night's end.

After greeting each of the cattle barons, Hubert signaled the head butler that dinner was to be served.

Later, as the men sat around with more brandy and cigars, he addressed them from his station at the head of the table.

"Gentlemen, we are at a crossroads here in Wyoming. As you know, the smaller ranchers in the area are getting more and more brazen about stealing and rustling our cattle."

Several of the men nodded in agreement, while others scowled and sniffed their disapproval of the subject.

Hubert continued. "We are suffering unacceptable losses to our herds from the depredations of these thieves, and some drastic measures may have to be undertaken."

Even as he spoke, Hubert knew that most of the losses of the big ranchers were due to poor management practices such as overstocking the range, unpredictable whims of nature in the form of prairie fires and plagues of feed-destroying grass-hoppers, and sieges of bad weather. But he also knew that whenever lean dividends had to be explained to far-off inves-tors, rustlers provided the best excuse.

William Irving spoke up. "But Hubert, what about our cow-boy blacklist, where we agreed not to hire cowboys who owned their own spreads and cattle. Isn't that working?"

Hubert shook his head. "No, in fact our scheme has actually backfired on us, and has driven many of these cowboys who can't find work with us to strike out on their own with small ranches that further eat into our profits."

Fred Hesse stood and adjusted his vest before speaking. "How about the law we arranged to be passed by the legisla-ture, the 'maverick' law, making every unbranded stray calf on the range the property of the Wyoming Stock Growers Asso-ciation, which we control? In my annual report, I see that we are making huge profits on the cattle that we auction off under the law."

Hubert nodded. "Yes, we're making a profit, but most of that is being spent to hire stock detectives and pay them two hundred and fifty dollars for every rustler convicted or killed." He paused to relight his cigar, then continued. "Furthermore, the small ranchers are calling these detectives bounty hunters and assassins and are making a lot of noise in the legislature to get the maverick law repealed."

He pointed down the table at Albert Bothwell, one of the wealthiest and most arrogant of the cattle barons present. "And it didn't help matters any when Al lynched those two home-steaders on the Sweetwater range last summer."

Bothwell stood up, his face red and flushed from several bottles of wine. "Dammit, Hubie, you know Jim Averell and Ella Watson were squatting on my land illegally, and that whore Watson was known to take her pay in cattle rustled off my range."

Hubert nodded and held up his hand. "I know, Al. That's why we spread the rumor in the newspapers that her name was Cattle Kate and that she was a gun-toting rustler queen. But it's harder to explain to people how Jim Averell, who owned not a single cow, was a rustler."

Bothwell waved his hand. "Doesn't matter," he slurred. "He deserved to die for tryin' to settle on my land."

Hubert shook his head, trying hard not to laugh. He knew the land Bothwell claimed as his own was actually free range, owned by the state of Wyoming, and was open to anyone who chose to settle on it. Of course, since all of the men present did much the same thing, he wasn't about to quibble over small details.

"All right, Al," Hubert said, holding his hands up to soothe the big man's temper, "but what I'm trying to say is all of these things have not served to stop the rustling. I want to propose something a bit more . . . severe."

Fred Hesse called out, "I'm sure for anything that'll stop those damn rustlers from stealing me out of house and home!"

He looked around at the others, waving his cigar in the air. "And now they've had the effrontery to form their own association, calling it the Northern Wyoming Farmers and Stock Growers Association," he said, his voice heavy with sarcasm. "Hell, I think it's just a fancy name for a den of thieves and footpads and rustlers to hide behind."

Hubert's lips curled in a small smile. The group was right where he wanted them, ready to do anything to make more money. He glanced at Frederic and gave a small wink before he continued with his talk.

"Gentlemen, what I propose is to completely wipe out that organization and exterminate the rustlers once and for all."

William Irving, who wasn't as drunk as the others, arched an eyebrow and stared at Hubert thoughtfully. "Just how do you plan to go about that, Hubie? Especially since Sheriff Red Angus in Buffalo, up where most of the rustlers operate, is openly sympathetic to the small ranchers."

Hubert took a sip of his hundred-year-old brandy and puffed deeply on his Cuban cigar, letting the smoke trail from his nostrils. This was going to be the hardest part of his scheme to get the men to accept.

He leaned forward, his knuckles on the table. "First, we must recruit a force of gunfighters from outside the state, and send them in force against Johnson County, which is the head-quarters of the rustlers . . . home to men like Nate Champion, who is the head of the Northern Wyoming Farmers and Stock Growers Association."

He paused for a moment, letting the idea sink in, then continued. "Then we cut all telegraph wires that link the county to the rest of the state, thus isolating the citizens while our attack gets under way. Next, we take over the town of Buffalo, which is the county seat, and assassinate the sheriff, his deputies, and the three county commissioners, thereby stripping the county of its leadership."

He had their full attention now, as talk of a full-scale range war usually did. "And finally, we dispose of all the men on this 'death list' I've got here that our WSGA detectives have put together." He held up a fistful of papers with over seventy names printed on it.

At first, as the idea sank in, there was stunned silence from the men sitting before Hubert. It wasn't the fact that they would be breaking the law; they did that most every day. It was the sheer magnitude of the thing that gave them pause. None of the others had thought on such a grand scale before.

Slowly, they began to talk excitedly among themselves, and Hubert knew he had them. He sat down and leaned back, enjoying the double bite of brandy and cigar smoke on his tongue as he watched them assimilate his grand scheme.

After a moment, Mike Shonsey, a local rancher who was talking quietly to Charley Ford, foreman of the TA ranch, looked up and said in a loud voice, "Hubie, your idea sounds good on the surface, but just who do you have in mind to lead this expedition against the Johnson County rustlers, and where are you going to find enough gunfighters to carry out your plan?"

Hubert stood up and signaled the head waiter to his side, whispering in his ear.

The man left the room and returned a few minutes later with two men in tow. They walked over to stand at the head of the table next to Hubert Teschemacher.

Hubert put his hand on the first man's shoulder. He stood a couple of inches over six feet tall, had a wide moustache curled around the corners of his mouth, and wore a grim, serious expression.

"I'm sure most of you know Frank Canton, former sheriff of Johnson County and now one of WSGA's best stock detectives," Hubert said.

Several of the men at the table nodded and smiled at Canton, knowing him to be a stone killer who had already murdered several rustlers in his duties for the Association.

Hubert pointed to the other man, somewhat shorter than Canton, also sporting a dark moustache. He was broader, with a stocky body, and wearing a black coat, with twin Colt .45s strapped to his belt.

"This is Tom Smith, another of our fine stock detectives, ex-deputy U.S. marshal from Texas, who is going to lead our recruiting drive by going back to his old stomping grounds and finding us some of the toughest men in the country to help us in our war against the rustlers in Johnson County."

Robert Tilsdale, another rancher, called out, "Tom, just how are you going to convince these men to come all the way up here in the dead of winter to fight our war for us?"

Smith stepped to the head of the table, a small smile on his face. "I'm going to offer them wages of five dollars a day, a bonus of fifty dollars to every man for each rustler killed, no matter who kills him, and a three-thousand-dollar accident policy for each volunteer. I figure I'll need between twenty and thirty hardcases to get the job done."

"Jesus," Charley Ford said, "that's going to come to a lot of money, Hubie."

Hubert nodded. "That's right, and I'm going to ask each member of the WSGA to donate one thousand dollars to the war fund. With over a hundred members, that'll be more than enough to get the men and equipment we need."

He glanced over at William Irving. "Bill, I'm going to need the cooperation of the Cheyenne and Northern Railroad to send Tom and Frank down to Texas and to bring the Texicans back up here. There's no other way to get them here with the weather so bad right now, and we need to get this done before the spring calving or we're going to lose a lot more head to the rustlers."

Irving nodded. "That'll be no problem. I'll arrange for a couple of cars to be added to the southern run. But what about horses and weapons for the gunmen?"

Hubert said, "I plan to send a couple of our men over to Colorado to buy what we need there. If we try to round up that many extra mounts from our local ranches, it would raise too many questions and the rustlers might get wind of our plans. I've already arranged to buy three heavy freight wagons, and I've placed orders for tents, bedding, guns, pistols, and ammunition enough to see us through this war."

He waved the men toward the parlor. "Now, if any of you have any further questions, Tom and Frank will be glad to answer them over coffee and cigars."

As they made their way to the elaborate bar at the other side of the room, Canton and Smith looked around at the expensive furnishings. This was quite a change from the saloons they used to frequent when they were deputy U.S. marshals.

Four

Big Rock, Colorado

Smoke stood on the porch and watched lazy snowflakes dance and weave as they fell from a leaden sky while he had his morning coffee. He heard a noise and turned. Sally stood in the bedroom doorway, her hair tousled and her face sleep-puffy. Smoke thought he'd never seen a lovelier woman in his life.

Sally rubbed her eyes and smoothed back her hair. "Smoke, I hate saying good-bye to you in a train station. Why don't you come back in here and let me tell you how much I'm going to miss you in private?"

She didn't have to ask him twice.

A while later, Cal and Pearlie accompanied Smoke into Big Rock, the town he had founded a few years back after the Tilden Franklin affair. He had packed his buckskins and moccasins and most of his guns in a large valise, and was wearing his traveling clothes—a flannel shirt, corduroy pants tucked into knee-high leather boots, and a rawhide coat with fur on the inside to protect against the harsh winter of northern Wyoming. His only weapons were a Colt Navy .36 carried in a shoulder holster under the coat and a bowie knife in a scabbard on his belt.

"Smoke, I sure wish you'd let one of us go with you," Pearlie said as they entered the city limits of Big Rock.

"Now don't you start on me, Pearlie. I've already hashed this out with Sally. I don't need you trying to play nursemaid to me too."

"How are you planning on gettin' those horses back here, Smoke?" Cal asked. "You can't hardly drive them here by yourself over those mountain passes in the winter."

"I'm not going to drive them here at all, Cal. I'm going to hire a special boxcar on the train and ship them by rail."

"Hell, Smoke, it's just not gonna be the same around here without you," Pearlie said.

"Pearlie, I need someone I can trust to look after the Sugarloaf, and to make sure Sally's all right. I'm depending on you and Cal to keep things going until I get back."

Cal pulled his hat down tight, a serious expression on his young face. "You can count on us." He glanced at Pearlie. "At least, I'll try not to let Pearlie eat you out of house and home before you get back."

Before Smoke could answer, there came a whistle from a doorway, and a voice called, "Well looky who's comin' down the road. Is that some Eastern dude, perhaps a tenderfoot who's lost his way?"

Monte Carson, the sheriff in Big Rock, was leaning against the doorjamb of his office, a cigar in one hand and a steaming tin of coffee in the other.

Smoke and Monte Carson had become very good friends over the past few years. Carson had once been a well-known gunfighter, though he had never ridden the owlhoot trail.

A local rancher, with plans to take over the county, had hired Carson to be the law in Fontana, a town just down the road from Smoke's Sugarloaf spread. Carson went along with the man's plans for a while, till he couldn't stomach the rapings and killings any longer. He put his foot down and let it be known that Fontana was going to be run in a law-abiding manner from then on.

The rancher, Tilden Franklin, sent a bunch of riders in to teach the upstart lawman a lesson. The men killed Carson's two deputies and seriously wounded him, taking over the town. In retaliation, Smoke founded the town of Big Rock, and he and a band of famous aging gunfighters cleaned house in Fontana.

When the fracas was over, Smoke offered the job of sheriff in Big Rock to Monte Carson. He married a grass widow and settled into the job like he was born to it. Neither Smoke nor the citizens of Big Rock ever had cause to regret his taking the job.*

Smoke frowned. "There's men planted all over this country for talking to me like that, cowboy. You looking for trouble?"

Carson laughed so hard he almost spilled his coffee. "Oh, no, sir, Mr. Gunfighter, sir. I just didn't recognize the famous gunhawk Smoke Jensen in those fancy city duds." He bowed low. "I apologize if I offended your delicate sensibilities, sir."

Smoke grinned. "I'll forgive you if you've got some more of that coffee cooking on the stove in your office."

"Come on in, light and sit and talk a while, Smoke. It's been too long since we've had a palaver."

Smoke got down off Horse, and asked Pearlie and Cal if they'd like to have some breakfast over at Longmont's saloon while he talked with Monte.

Pearlie didn't even answer, just spurred his mount and galloped off in a cloud of dust.

"You know you have to be careful when you ask Pearlie if'n he wants food, Smoke, or you're liable to get trampled in the stampede," Cal said. He followed Pearlie at a more sedate pace, shaking his head at Pearlie's legendary appetite.

Smoke stepped into the sheriff's office and poured himself a cup of coffee from the pot on a corner stove. After taking a sip, he made a face. "Damn, Monte, this stuff is thick enough to float a horseshoe."

*Trail of the Mountain Man

Carson shrugged. "Hell, Smoke, nobody's forcin' you to drink it, an' you shore can't argue about the price."

The two men sat on opposite sides of Carson's desk, and Smoke began to tell his friend about his plans to travel to Wyoming in search of suitable horseflesh to replenish his remuda.

After he caught up on all the news about his friends in town, Smoke stood and stretched. "How would you like some breakfast over at Longmont's? It's on me."

Carson grabbed his hat. "You don't have to ask me twice, Smoke. Let's see if we can get Louis's fancy chef Andre to cook up some regular food for a change, none of them frog legs or whatever."

As they walked down the street toward the saloon, Cal came flying backwards out of the bat-wings, landing sprawled on his back with blood streaming from his nose.

Smoke ran and squatted next to the semi-conscious boy. "Cal, Cal, can you hear me? Are you all right?"

Cal shook his head and gently felt his rapidly swelling nose. "Uh, I guess so. Jimminy but that fellow packs a mean punch."

Smoke gently wiped blood off Cal's cheek. "Seems like every time I bring you to town, Cal, you end up bleeding on me." He sighed. "Well, at least this time you haven't been shot," he said, referring to the fact that Cal seemed to get wounded in every fracas he'd ever been in. Then, Smoke's eyes turned dark and he stood up and walked into the saloon. Pearlie was standing next to a table, twin Colts in his hands pointed at two large men with heavy beards dressed in dirty buckskins. He glanced over his shoulder at Smoke. "Is Cal all right?"

Smoke didn't take his eyes off the two men as he answered, "Yeah. What happened here?"

"These two galoots were talkin' bad 'bout you, Smoke. They was saying they heard you got your reputation by bein' a back-shootin' coward. Cal told 'em to take it back, and they walloped him without any warnin' whatsoever."

Smoke glanced over to an adjacent table where Louis Longmont sat, smoking a cigar and drinking brandy out of a large crystal snifter. The gambler had a slight smile on his face, but Smoke noticed the rawhide thong was off his Colt and his right hand was lying on his thigh, indicating Louis was ready to step in if Pearlie needed any help.

"That about the size of it, Louis?" Smoke asked.

"Yes, Pearlie has reported the events that transpired with amazing clarity and accuracy," Louis answered. "These . . . gentlemen were being very disparaging of you, Smoke, and I was on the verge of asking them to depart when Cal took them to task for their remarks."

Smoke frowned as he took a pair of black gloves, padded over the knuckles, out of the back of his belt and walked toward the two trappers. "You assholes have something to say about me, you can say it to my face instead of picking on someone half your size."

One of the men stuck out his chest and pulled up his pants, his expression belligerent. "We got a right to our opinion, Jensen. We was jest sayin' what we heared, that's all. Ain't that right, Asa?"

"Jesse's right," said the one called Asa. "It was jest a friendly little fracas. Weren't no need to git pistols involved."

Smoke shook his head. "No such thing as a friendly fight, mister. Fighting is deadly serious, especially when your opponent is only a boy."

"Well, he shouldn't oughta have called me a liar," Jesse said. "I don't let nobody, boy nor man, talk to me like that."

Smoke smiled. "Oh, is that so? Well, I don't only think you are a liar, but I think you stink. I could smell your rotten carcass from across the street."

The two men looked nervously at Pearlie and his twin Colts. "You wouldn't dare to talk at me like that if'n you didn't have those six-shooters backin' yore play," Jesse mumbled.

"Pearlie, holster your weapons," Smoke said without looking at him as he pulled his gloves on tight. "I'm going to teach these ignorant bastards a lesson in manners."

Jesse grinned and suddenly swung a meaty fist in a round-house right cross at Smoke's head, trying to surprise him. The mountain man ducked easily under the punch and stabbed a quick right jab square into the man's nose, flattening it and spreading it all over his face. The trapper grunted in pain as his head snapped back, and Smoke kicked sideways into his knee, snapping it inward where it hung for a moment at an awkward angle until the man fell over screaming.

Asa growled and rushed forward, wrapping his huge arms around Smoke's chest in a bear hug. He squeezed until his face turned red, but Smoke flexed his muscles and just smiled at the straining man. After a moment, Smoke head-butted Asa in the face, splitting his nose in two and breaking it with a loud crack.

As Asa let go of Smoke and grabbed at his ruined face, Smoke drew back and hit him in the stomach with all his might, lifting all two hundred pounds of the man off his feet and slamming him back against the bar, where he leaned bent over, moaning and gasping for breath. Smoke stepped up and threw a left cross, catching the man in the temple and knocking his lights out. He crumpled in a heap on the saloon floor, dead to the world.

Smoke turned in time to see the other trapper struggle to his feet, his face screwed up in rage and his fists doubled at his sides. "I'm gonna kill you, Jensen," Jesse snarled.

"I don't think so," Smoke said and planted the toe of his boot in Jesse's mouth, shattering his teeth and knocking him unconscious.

Smoke bent, took a gold double-eagle coin from the trapper's poke, and handed it to Louis. "This should pay for their drinks and any damage they caused."

Louis smiled and pocketed the coin. He glanced at the bartender. "Jake, drag this trash out back and pile it in the alley, will you? And open the windows and let some of their stench out, please. I'm beginning to feel a bit nauseated at the odor."

Smoke looked up as Cal stumbled in, holding a bandanna

to his face. "Where are they? I want another shot at that big bastard."

Monte Carson laughed. "You're just a tad late, son. Smoke's already taken care of that for you."

Smoke put his arm around Cal's shoulder and led him to a table. "Come on, Cal, let's have that breakfast you came here for."

Louis clapped his hands. "Andre, fresh coffee and buns for our guests, then burn five steaks and scramble some hens' eggs with chopped tomatoes and onions. These men look hungry."

As Cal and Pearlie and Monte Carson sat at their table, Smoke walked over to shake Louis's hand. "Thanks for the backup, partner, I appreciate it."

"You noticed?" Louis answered as he put the rawhide hammer thong back on his Colt.

"Even if I hadn't, I always know you've got my back, *compadre.*"

Louis nodded and raised his brandy glass in a salute to his friend of many years. The gambler owned this saloon and considered it his home. It was where he plied his trade, which he called teaching amateurs the laws of chance.

Louis was a lean, hawk-faced man, with strong, slender hands and long fingers, nails carefully manicured, hands clean. He had jet-black hair and a black pencil-thin moustache. He was, as usual, dressed in a black suit, with white shirt and dark ascot—something he'd picked up on a trip to England some years back. He wore low-heeled boots, and a pistol hung in tied-down leather on his right side. It was not for show, for Louis was snake-quick with a short gun, and was a feared, deadly gunhand when pushed.

Louis was not an evil man. He had never hired his gun out for money. And while he could make a deck of cards do almost anything, he did not cheat at poker. He did not have to cheat. He was possessed of a phenomenal memory, could tell you the odds of filling any type of poker hand, and was one of the first to use the new method of card counting.

He was just past forty years of age. He had come to the West as a boy, arriving with his parents from Louisiana. His parents had died in a shantytown fire, leaving the boy to cope as best he could.

He had coped quite well, plying his innate intelligence and willingness to take a chance into a fortune. He owned a large ranch up in Wyoming Territory, several businesses in San Francisco, and a hefty chunk of a railroad.

Though it was a mystery to many why Longmont stayed with the hard life he had chosen, Smoke thought he understood. Once, Louis had said to him, "Smoke, I would miss my life every bit as much as you would miss the dry-mouthed moment before the draw, the challenge of facing and besting those miscreants who would kill you or others, and the so-called loneliness of the owlhoot trail."

Sometimes Louis joked that he would like to draw against Smoke someday, just to see who was faster. Smoke allowed as how it would be close, but that he would win. "You see, Louis, you're just too civilized," he had told him on many occasions. "Your mind is distracted by visions of operas, fine foods and wines, and the odds of your winning the match. Also, your fatal flaw is that you can almost always see the good in the lowest creatures God ever made, and you refuse to believe that anyone is pure evil and without hope of redemption."

When Louis laughed at this description of himself, Smoke would continue. "Me, on the other hand, when some snake-scum draws down on me and wants to dance, the only thing I have on my mind is teaching him that when you dance, someone has to pay the band. My mind is clear and focused on only one problem, how to put that stump-sucker across his horse toes down."

* * *

Smoke tipped his hat and went back to join his friends at their table, where Pearlie was telling Cal how Smoke had whipped the two trappers.

Five

Johnson County, Wyoming

Nate Champion tugged gently at the reins of his big dun stallion and stopped in the shade of a copse of piñon trees. He pulled a pair of battered binoculars out of his saddlebags and began to look over the herd of milling cattle spread out in the valley below him.

Sure enough, he didn't have to search for very long before he found what he was looking for. There, mixed in with the other cattle, were over fifty of Nate's own beeves.

He put the binoculars back in the saddlebag, pulled out his old Winchester Model 1873, and levered a round into the chamber. He shoved the carbine in the saddle boot and then flipped open the loading gate on his Colt Army and checked his loads. He knew Shonsey was going to be plenty pissed when he braced him about the cattle, and he wanted to be ready for anything.

Nearing thirty years of age, Nate Champion had been born in Round Rock, Texas, and was considered a top cowboy by all who knew him. With a fierce moustache, he was a solid, good-looking man, noted for his honesty and forthrightness. He had many friends among the punchers and small ranchers in northern Wyoming.

Until he was blacklisted six months ago by the Wyoming Stock Growers Association for starting his own small herd, he'd been the kind of cowboy every ranch owner wanted. Now that he was persona non grata to the big ranchers of the Association, it was a different story. Nate was not a man they could scare. He was handy with a gun and was never far from his weapons.

He didn't plan to back down from Shonsey, or any of the other cattle barons for that matter, no matter how many hired guns they had riding for their brands.

Nate slipped his Colt in his holster, but left the rawhide hammer thong off, and rode down the slope of the hill toward the group of men tending Shonsey's herd below.

Johnny Garfield slapped the rump of a cantankerous steer with the end of his lariat, and had leaned to the side to spit tobacco juice when he noticed Nate Champion riding over.

He settled back against the cantle of his saddle and waited to see what Champion had to say.

"Howdy, Johnny," Nate said as he pulled his horse to a stop in front of the wrangler.

Garfield spat again, then nodded. "Howdy, Nate. What're you doin' over here? I thought your spread was 'bout ten mile the other side of the crick over there."

Nate crossed his leg over his saddle horn, pulled a bag of Bull Durham tobacco out of his shirt pocket, and began to build a cigarette.

He struck a lucifer on the hammer of his Colt and lighted the butt, then left it in the corner of his mouth as he spoke, the smoke trailing up to make his eyes squint.

"Well, Johnny, it's true my spread's over to the east, but damned if about a fourth of my beeves aren't right here with yours."

Garfield narrowed his eyes, shifting his butt in his saddle just a bit. "You don't say?"

He looked out over the herd for a few moments, then nodded and spat again. "Now that you mention it, I did see some beeves that didn't look familiar to me this mornin'. I just put it down to some mavericks having drifted into the herd during the night."

Nate took a deep drag of the cigarette and tilted his head to let the smoke out. "Yeah, Johnny, 'cept mavericks don't generally have brands on 'em, and these do . . . my brand."

"I can see that, Nate, now that you point it out."

"How about I ride on in there and cut my cattle out of yours, and then I'll drive 'em back to my place?"

Garfield's face screwed up in a frown. "I don't know, Nate. Ever since you been blacklisted by the Association, Mr. Shonsey been talkin' bad 'bout you something fierce."

Garfield hesitated, glancing at Nate out of the corner of his eyes, as if afraid to look him in the face. "Matter of fact, he's kind'a spreadin' the word that you were blacklisted for rustlin' cattle."

"That so?" said Nate, his lips and jaws tight.

"Yeah. He said that's how you managed to put your herd together, by takin' mavericks off the range that belong to the Association and puttin' your brand on 'em."

Nate took a deep breath, trying to control his temper, which typically had a short fuse anyway.

"Johnny, how long you been punching cows here in Wyoming?"

" 'Bout five year, why?"

"Then you know that most of the land around here is owned by the government, and mavericks have always belonged to whoever took the trouble to round 'em up and brand 'em. Just because the Stock Growers Association bribed the legislature to write a nonsense law sayin' they belonged to the Association don't make it so."

"That may be, Nate, but it's still the law."

Garfield pointed at Nate's clothes. "Mr. Shonsey says that sash you're wearin' is the mark of your gang of rustlers, even says it's called the Red Sash Gang."

Nate, who was something of a "dude" in his dress, was

wearing black corduroy pants, a red and black checkered flannel shirt, and a red sash tied around his waist.

He laughed and shook his head. "Now I've heard everything. Hell, half the cowboys I know wear these things, Johnny," he said, pointing to his sash. "They get 'em from the Sears and Roebuck catalog and wear 'em 'cause the ladies seem to like 'em."

Garfield shifted his cud of tobacco from one cheek to the other. "Well, anyways, Mr. Shonsey won't like it much if I let you cut some beeves outta his herd." He paused a moment before adding, "I'll tell you what, Nate. We're gonna be movin' this herd tomorrow, an' I'll have the boys cut any beeves with the KC brand on 'em out and leave 'em here for you. How's that?"

Nate shrugged. "I'll take your word on it, Johnny, an' I'll be back just after dawn with a few of my men to pick 'em up."

The next morning, Mike Shonsey was out on the range with his men when Garfield and the others culled Champion's beeves from his herd. After Garfield and the other drovers drove Shonsey's cattle over the hill toward another range to feed, Shonsey turned to the two men with him.

"Bob, I want you and Curly to scatter those cattle all over the range."

Bob Cartwright looked at his boss in disbelief. "But Mr. Shonsey, those are Nate Champion's cattle. If'n we do that, it'll take him two days to round 'em up."

Shonsey gave him a hard look. "Bob, I don't recall askin' your advice on the matter. I'm foreman of this spread, an' long as you ride for this brand you'll do what I say. Is that clear?"

"Yes, sir, Mr. Shonsey," Bob replied.

He pulled his hat down tight, pulled his pistol out, and put the spurs to his mount. He and Curly charged toward the small group of cattle, then fired into the air and whooped and hollered, causing the grazing cattle to stampede off in several directions.

Ten minutes later, as Shonsey and Bob and Curly were riding toward Shonsey's herd, Nate Champion came riding after them, leaning over his saddle and raising a cloud of dust.

Shonsey pulled his mount to a stop and waited. He looked at the two men with him. "All right, boys, here he comes, and he looks madder than a wet hen."

Nate pulled his horse to a stop next to Shonsey's.

"Why'd you scatter my beeves, Shonsey?" he asked, his face red as a beet.

"Because they were grazing on my land, eating feed that belongs to my cattle, that's why."

"This ain't your land, asshole," Nate said, his voice low and hard. "This is free range, in case you've forgotten, and it's open to anybody's cattle that wants to use it."

Shonsey gave a nasty grin. "Well, Champion, seein' as how there's three of us an' only one of you, just what do you intend to do about it?"

Nate cut his eyes to the two men with Shonsey. He straightened in his saddle and let his hand hang near his Colt.

"You boys want some of this?" he asked, his eyes cold as the water in the nearby stream.

Bob and Curly looked at each other, then at Shonsey, their eyes wide. They both knew Champion's reputation as a fast gun.

"We ride for Mr. Shonsey, Nate, but he don't pay us for no gunplay. This is between you and him."

Nate glanced back at Shonsey. "Looks like it's you and me, Mike. You want to make your play?"

Shonsey's face began to gleam with sweat, though the temperature was barely above freezing. "Now wait a minute, Champion. I don't intend to draw on you," Shonsey said, his voice rising into a whine. "You can't shoot a man down in cold blood over a few head of cattle."

Nate shook his head, his expression disgusted at Shonsey's

cowardice. "No, you're right, Mike. I can't shoot a coward who won't back his play."

Without another word, Nate swung a backhanded blow and knocked Shonsey out of his saddle, to land on his butt on the frozen ground with a loud grunt.

Nate swung out of his saddle and walked over to stand before the man on the ground.

"Get up, you spineless cow flop," he said.

Shonsey rubbed his reddening jaw and shook his head. "I'm not gonna fight you, Champion."

Nate, who stood a couple of inches over six feet and had broad shoulders and wiry muscles from years riding the range, reached down and grabbed Shonsey by the front of his shirt, lifting the man to his feet as if he were a child.

He held his shirt with his left hand and began to slap his face with his right, back and forth, snapping his head with each blow.

Finally, Shonsey tried to fight back, swinging a wild punch at Nate's head. Nate ducked the blow, twisted his shoulder to the side, and swung with all his might, catching Shonsey flush in the face with a fist hardened by years of hard work.

Shonsey's nose cracked with a noise like a rifle shot, flattening over his face, sending blood and teeth flying in the chilly air. His eyes crossed and he dropped like a stone to the ground, unconscious.

Nate rubbed his fist, his first two knuckles already beginning to swell. Then he bent, picked Shonsey up, and threw him face-down across his saddle.

"Take this piece of crap back to his ranch and get him doctored up," Nate said to Bob and Curly.

As he stepped into his saddle, he pointed a finger at the two punchers. "And spread the word that the next time any of your men touch or mess with any of my beeves, I'll kill 'em."

He touched the brim of his hat. "If any of your men have a problem with that, you know where to find me."

After Nate rode off, Bob glanced down at Shonsey where he lay over the saddle.

"Jesus, Curly. Look at his face. It looks like he's been kicked by a mule."

Curly watched Nate's back as he rode off to round up his strays. "You know, Bob, I think I may just mosey on down south an' see if there's any work down there. Mr. Shonsey don't pay me enough for this. That Champion's meaner'n a two-peckered billy goat, an' I don't want to be on the receiving end of that fist of his."

Bob nodded. "Yeah, an' unless I miss my guess, things around here are gonna get a whole lot worse 'fore they get better."

Six

Nate Champion pulled his dun to a halt on a ridge overlooking a wide, flat range that stretched as far as the eye could see.

He nodded at his friend, George "Flat Nose" Curry, sitting on a horse next to him.

"George, see those beeves down there?"

Curry inclined his head before leaning to the side to spit a wad of Bull Durham onto the ground. "Yep."

"Those are the cattle Bob Tilsdale stole from my herd the other day."

Curry pursed his lips. "Let me get this straight, Nate. Tilsdale put two thousand cattle onto a range where you was already grazing your herd, then had the balls when you braced him about it to drive his cattle and yours over to this range?"

"That's about the size of it," Nate answered.

"That sumbitch is too dumb to know who he's messin' with, ain't he?"

Nate grinned. "Tell me, George, what would your old pals in the Wild Bunch or the Hole in the Wall Gang do about something like that?"

Curry—who wore two pistols on his belt, butt first for cross-handed draws, and a double bandolier of Winchester rifle shells across his chest—pulled his rifle out of its saddle boot and levered a shell into the chamber.

"They'd probably do what we're gonna do in a few minutes."

Nate glanced back over his shoulder at the twelve hardcases riding with him and Curry.

"Load 'em up six and six, boys," he called as he pulled a Colt from his holster.

A few minutes later, the fourteen men put the spurs to their horses and charged down the hill in a cloud of dust toward the cattle milling below.

Robert Tilsdale's men minding the herd looked up and saw them coming. Joshua Barlow, Tilsdale's foreman, almost swallowed his chewing tobacco when he saw the group of heavily armed men riding down on him.

He cupped his hands around his mouth and shouted, "Rustlers comin'! Draw your guns, boys!"

The other six men riding herd glanced at each other, then pulled their reins around and headed their horses away from the fracas, wanting no part of gunplay to save a few cattle that didn't belong to them.

Barlow, seeing he was standing alone against the men, held up his hands as Nate and his group approached.

He relaxed a little when he saw it was Nate Champion riding down on him.

"Howdy, Nate," he said as the gang reined to a halt next to him.

"Howdy, Josh," Nate replied, holstering his pistol and signaling his men to put their guns away.

"What're you boys doin' way out here this mornin'?" Barlow asked, breathing a bit easier with all the firearms out of sight.

"We come to get my beeves, Josh."

"The ones your boss stole from Nate the other day," Curry added, his heavily bearded face screwed up in a scowl.

Barlow shook his head, but couldn't bring himself to look Nate in the eyes. "We didn't mean to take your cattle, Nate. But Mr. Tilsdale wouldn't give us time to cut them outta the herd. He said to drive 'em all over here and he'd make sure you got yours back later."

"That's bullshit, an' you know it, Josh," Nate said angrily. "You know as well as I do he never intended to give me my cattle back."

Barlow shrugged. "Hey, Nate. I'm just a hired hand, doin' what I'm told. I don't never mix in politics nor other people's business."

"Good," Curry said, "then you can just ride on over to that stand of trees over yonder and sit your butt down and take a little siesta while we get Nate's beeves."

Barlow hesitated just a moment, as if weighing his chances against Curry, before he nodded and jerked his horse's head around to ride away.

"Mr. Tilsdale ain't gonna like this very much, Nate," he said over his shoulder.

"Good," Nate growled, "I hope he chokes on it."

Nate turned to the others. "Okay, boys, round 'em up and move 'em out."

Billy Black, a youngster of no more than sixteen years, yelled back, "You want us to just take the ones with your brand on 'em, or you want us to get the calves too?"

Nate pursed his lips, thinking for a moment, then called back, "Take everything with my brand on it, an' everything without any brand on it, and scatter the rest all over the range."

Curry grinned. "We're gonna get a lot of calves that belong to Tilsdale then."

"Maybe it'll teach him not to mess with the other small ranchers around here," Nate said. "Especially ones that belong to the Northern Wyoming Farmers and Stock Growers Association."

"You a man after my own heart, Nate, tough as nails and hard as steel."

Nate spurred his horse. "Only way to be and still survive out here, George."

* * *

Early the next morning, Nate was having coffee and pan dulce in his cabin with an old friend, Ross Gilbertson.

"How do you feel about the men electing you president of the Northern Wyoming Farmers and Stock Growers Association the other night, Nate?"

Nate smirked. "Other than the fact that it's kind'a like hanging a bull's-eye on my shirt, I guess it's all right."

Gilbertson frowned. "You don't really think the other cattlemen's association will try and do anything against you, do you?"

"I think it's only a matter of time, Ross. The big ranchers can't allow us little ranchers and independents to organize. Otherwise they won't have any power over the cattle business in Wyoming."

"What do you mean?"

"Well, for instance, if enough of us gather together, we can get the legislature to repeal the maverick law, an' that's where the WSGA gets the money to finance their stock detectives and hire the bounty hunters to shoot down innocent ranchers."

Gilbertson was about to reply, when suddenly the door crashed open, splinted by a man wielding a sledgehammer.

As Nate slapped at his thigh, he realized his pistol was hanging on a post next to the wall, behind his head. He was unarmed.

Three men, wearing bandannas over their faces, stormed into the room, pistols in their hands.

"Put' em up," one of the men called, aiming his gun at Nate.

Nate and Gilbertson raised their hands.

"What do you men want here?" Nate asked, seemingly cool as a cucumber under the circumstances. "I don't have no money nor valuables for you to rob."

"We ain't robbers, Champion. We came to drill you through and through for all the rustlin' you been doin' of the Association's stock."

Nate nodded slowly, staring at what he could see of the men's faces over their kerchiefs. He saw one of the men had a crooked scar over his right eye, running through his eyebrow, and knew he was Joe Elliot, a stock detective for the Association.

"I ain't no rustler, an' you boys know it."

One of the men with Elliot turned to the detective. "What 'bout this other feller? They didn't say nothin' 'bout killin' anybody else."

"Shut up, you idiot!" Elliot said.

He pointed his pistol at Gilbertson. "Who might you be, mister? You a rustler like your friend here?"

"My name is Ross Gilbertson, and neither one of us is rustlers."

"Are you a rancher?" the third man, who had remained silent until now, asked.

Gilbertson shook his head. "No, I'm not. I own a general store over in Buffalo. Me and Nate been friends since we was pups."

"Well," the man Nate recognized as Elliot said, cocking his pistol, "you're gonna die with him anyway."

The third man put his hand on Elliot's arm. "Just a minute. We ain't got no call to be killing innocent shopkeepers."

While Elliot was distracted, Nate pretended to yawn and stretch, extending his hands back over his head toward the post holding his holster and Colt.

When Elliot turned his eyes to the third man, Nate grabbed his pistol and drew and cocked in one fluid motion. He swung the Colt Army down and pulled the trigger, his slug taking the second man in the upper chest, next to his shoulder and spinning him around.

When Nate's gun exploded, blowing smoke and flame out into the room, the other two intruders ducked and dove through a door into another room in the cabin, just as Nate fired two more rounds, chipping wood from the door frame.

Gilbertson dove to the floor, while Nate flipped the table over and the two friends got behind it, using it as partial cover.

Elliot stuck his head around the door and fired into the room, drilling holes in the thin wood of the table.

Nate didn't bother to duck, but aimed and shot back, his slug hitting Elliot in the forehead, burning a shallow furrow along his scalp and piercing his hat.

"Goddamn," he shouted, grabbing his head and ducking back out of sight, "I'm hit, Frank, I'm hit!"

"Come on," the third man yelled, "let's get out of here."

He stuck his hand around the corner of the door without looking and fired off three or four shots.

While Nate hid behind the table, the two men scrambled on hands and knees into the front room, all three, including the wounded man, ran out the front door.

When the door slammed, Nate bounded up and ran out the side door, aiming and firing as fast as he could at the retreating figures as they jumped into their saddles and rode away.

He saw Elliot grab at his shoulder as if one of his shots had hit home, but he couldn't be certain just how bad the man had been wounded.

"Holy Mary, Mother of Christ!" Gilbertson said as he walked out of the cabin, unconsciously crossing himself as he spoke. "That was a close call, Nate."

"Yeah, it was," Nate replied.

"You think that was men from the WSGA come to kill you?"

"I know it was, Ross. The man doing most of the talking was Joe Elliot, one of the men the Association hired as so-called stock detectives. Hired killers is more like it."

"What about the other two?"

Nate wagged his head.

"I don't know. I didn't recognize either one of them."

"Cowardly bastards," Gilbertson said, "bustin' in on a man's house, wearing masks like common stage robbers. They ought to be hanged."

"Yeah, they should, but you and I both know with the power

of the WSGA behind them, there's slim chance anything will ever come of it."

"What are you gonna do now, Nate?"

"First off, I'm going into Buffalo and file a formal complaint with Sheriff Red Angus. He's pretty much on our side in this range war, but even his hands are tied, especially since we can't testify we saw any faces on the men."

"Then what's gonna happen?"

"Then, I'm going to call for a roundup by our Association, and we're gonna start rounding up mavericks on our own, and we'll just see what the WSGA tries to do about it."

Seven

Smoke boarded the train, stuffed his valise under his seat, and leaned out the window to wave good-bye to his friends on the platform.

"Ride with your guns loose," Pearlie said.

"Keep 'em loaded up six an' six," Cal added as he tipped his hat.

Smoke smiled to himself, thinking, *It's hell getting old. Everyone starts worrying about your hide all of a sudden like you can't take care of yourself.*

With a rush of steam and a series of small jerks, the train pulled out of Big Rock, heading north, straight into the face of a chilly wind blowing southward from the arctic regions of Canada.

Smoke shivered and pulled his coat tight. The railroad passenger cars were unheated, and the temperature in the drafty coach was barely above freezing. He cracked his window, pulled a long stogie out of his pocket, and sat back in his seat to relax and enjoy his journey northward. As ice crystals formed on the window and wind-driven sleet and snow pounded the glass, he was grateful he wasn't trying to make the trip on horseback.

After lighting his cigar, he took out a small map and used

his finger to trace his path to where he'd heard the Nez Percé had been sighted.

It was about 125 miles straight north from Big Rock to Casper, Wyoming, and then another eighty miles or so up to Buffalo, where the Indians were supposed to be camped. His trip would take him through Boulder, cut back south to Denver, then head north to Greely. From there, it was a short hop to Cheyenne and then Laramie. From Laramie, the Union Pacific ran north to Medicine Bow and finally Casper, where he would change trains for a ride up into the Big Horn Mountains and Buffalo on a spur line.

He knew he was traveling in the worst of the winter weather, and expected many delays as tracks would have to be cleared of snowdrifts at times, especially in the higher elevations of the many mountain passes they were to traverse.

He wondered briefly if he was, as Sally had hinted, being foolish to head north this time of year. Sally, an ex-school-teacher, was exceptionally smart, and Smoke had found she was not often wrong about such things. No matter. He loved Sally deeply and had never regretted giving up his traveling ways to marry her and settle down. But lately, he had been feeling hemmed in by civilization, crushed by the weight of humanity all around him.

Since his teen years, when he had lived with Preacher, Smoke had loved the high lonesome of the mountains. He was more used to going months without seeing another human being than being in their company on a daily basis.

Old Hoss, he thought, *you just need to get up into the high country for a while, stretch your legs, and get away from people before you explode like dynamite too close to a campfire.* He had a feeling Sally understood more of his motives than she let on, but loved him enough to give him free rein when he felt he needed it. Not many women were that understanding or insightful about their mates.

He flipped his cigar out the window, pulled his hat down over his face, stuck his hands in his coat pockets, and settled back for a nap as the iron horse pulled him through the blizzards toward a much-needed adventure in the mountains.

The trip was uneventful until he reached Denver, where the conductor announced there would be a layover due to the heaviness of the snowfall. The passengers were told the train would leave at dawn with a snowplow engine preceding them through the mountain passes north of the town.

Smoke took his valise and walked two blocks down the main street to check into the Alhambra Hotel. He had need of a hot bath to get the cinders and ash from the engine off his clothes and out of his hair and skin after traveling all day.

Once in his room, he unpacked fresh clothes and took them, his money belt holding two thousand dollars in greenbacks, and his Colt Navy pistol with him to the room where the hotel had several tubs set up and an attendant keeping water heated on a wood-burning stove.

Smoke set his clothes, gun, and the money belt on a chair next to the tub, and eased down into the steaming, soapy water with a sigh of relief. He lay back and let the heat soak some of the soreness out of his muscles.

Smoke smiled as he thought how ironic it was that he could ride horseback for days at a time and never get stiff or sore, but twelve hours in a rocking and rolling passenger car and he felt like someone had beaten him with ax handles.

After ten minutes, the young boy acting as attendant poured more hot water off the stove into Smoke's tub. Smoke opened sleepy eyes to thank him, and heard footsteps approaching outside the door. He realized with a start he could also hear the jangle of spurs on boots. *Damn,* he thought, *men coming for a bath seldom wear their spurs.* He sat up a little in the bathtub and reached over to pick up his Colt and slip it under the suds, resting it on his knee just above the water while he waited.

Seconds later, the door opened and three rough-looking men stepped into the room. They were all wearing trail clothes that looked and smelled as if they hadn't been washed for weeks.

The attendant muttered, "Uh-oh," as his face paled at the sight of the men.

Smoke gave a lazy smile. "Come in, gentlemen. The water is hot and soapy and just right to take that stink of the trail off you."

The man in the middle, who seemed to be the leader of the trio, narrowed his eyes and glared at Smoke. He took a few steps forward and leaned over to pick through Smoke's clothes, cutting his eyes at his friends when he fingered the money belt. "Say, boys, look what we got here. A bunch of fancy city duds and a big ole thick money belt."

One of his friends said with a sneer, "Maybe you ought'a ask real polite-like if the gent soakin' over there minds you pawin' through his stuff, Carl."

"Yeah, that's a good idee, Johnny," Carl answered. "Say, mister, you don't have any objection to my lookin' at your clothes, do you?"

Smoke's smile faded and his eyes grew cold as ice. Evidently the men were too stupid to notice Smoke's empty holster lying on the floor next to the chair. "As a matter of fact I do mind. Your hands are filthy and you stink. Please put my things down and leave the room."

"And what if I don't?"

"Then I'll just have to get out of my nice hot bath and make you, and I promise you won't like that one bit," Smoke replied, his voice low and hard.

Carl, too dumb to notice the warning signs, ignored him and opened the belt, his eyes widening at the sight of thick stacks of bills lying inside. "Jesus," he said, "Johnny, Sam, come here and take a look at what the dude is carryin'."

As the two men rushed over, the attendant tried to sneak out the door behind them. Carl drew his pistol and pointed it at the young man. "Hold on there, ace. You ain't goin' anywheres, just stay put where you are."

Johnny reached down and fingered the greenbacks, his

mouth hanging open in wonderment. "Jeez, Carl, I ain't never seen so much money in one place at a time!"

Smoke shifted in the water, steam rising from his bare shoulders. "Gentlemen, I worked hard for that stake. Do you really think I'm going to sit here and let pond scum like you take it from me?"

Carl stepped back, still holding the belt in one hand and his pistol in the other. Johnny and Sam drew their Colts and waved the attendant over to stand next to the tub with Smoke in it.

"Well, Mr. City Dude," Carl snarled, "I don't see you have much choice in the matter. I think we'll just tie you and the boy up and head on out of town. By the time somebody finds you, we'll be long gone."

Smoke grinned, but the smile didn't reach his eyes. "I want you to think on it real hard, Carl. Is that money worth dying for? 'Cause I'm giving you one last chance to put it down and walk out of here. Otherwise I'll see that you're carried out on a board."

The words were spoken softly but rang with tempered steel.

Carl threw back his head and laughed, along with Johnny and Sam. Carl eared back the hammer on his Colt. "Maybe I won't tie you up after all, pilgrim. Maybe I'll just drill you instead."

Smoke sighed and glanced at the attendant. "Boy, you can see they just don't give me any option."

Without another word, he let the hammer down on his Navy and it exploded, blowing suds and gunsmoke out of the tub all over the men standing in front of him. His first slug took Carl high in the forehead, blowing his scalp and half his head off and throwing him backward to land sprawled on his back, a pool of blood forming under his ruined skull.

Before Johnny or Sam could react, Smoke fired twice more, the shots sounding like dynamite in the confined room. One bullet punched a hole in Johnny's chest; the other tore through Sam's neck, almost tearing his head off. Johnny bounced on the floor, holding his hands over the hole in his chest, his eyes hurt and surprised at the turn of events. He groaned once, then died quietly, bloody froth on his lips.

Sam was dead before he hit the floor.

The attendant stood there, his hands over his mouth, his eyes wide and tearing from the acrid gun smoke in the room. He stared at the dead men for a moment, then looked at Smoke, his face paling as if he might faint.

Smoke carefully wiped his pistol on a towel before placing it gently on his clothes. Then he sighed and lay back in the water.

"Boy, open that window over there and let some of the smoke out of the room. Then get me some more hot water. All this jawing has let my bath cool down." He laid his head back and closed his eyes, relaxing again, as if nothing had happened.

As the smoke whirled out the open window and the room began to clear, a man wearing a sheriff's star on his vest came running into the room, his gun in his hand. "What the hell's goin' on in here?" he shouted.

A younger man, carrying a shotgun and sweating in spite of the cold, ran into the sheriff's back as he stopped short just inside the doorway, staring at the carnage lying around him. The sheriff glared at Smoke, turning his pistol to point at him. "Are you responsible for this, mister?"

Smoke opened his eyes and sat up a little to look over the edge of the tub, as if noticing the dead bodies for the first time.

After a moment, he shrugged and lay back in the water, his expression calm. "No, Sheriff, those men are. They started the dance, and I just reminded them someone had to pay the band. As you can see, it ended up being them."

The attendant nodded his head rapidly. "That's right, Sheriff Thomas. This man was just sittin' there in his bath when those three tried to rob him of his money. Said they was gonna tie us up and take it all."

The sheriff walked over to stand before Smoke, his pistol still pointing at his chest.

"What's your name, mister?"

"Smoke. Smoke Jensen."

The sheriff took a step back, his mouth open. *"The* Smoke Jensen?"

Smoke smiled. "I wasn't aware there was more than one. And Sheriff, would you mind pointing that hogleg away. I get a mite nervous when someone aims a gun at me."

Thomas hastily holstered his pistol. "Yes, sir, Mr. Jensen." He looked over his shoulder at his deputy. "Dewey, git somebody in here to clean up this mess so Mr. Jensen can finish his bath."

Dewey glanced at Smoke, his mouth open, his eyes wide, his knuckles white where they gripped his shotgun.

"Dewey, dammit, git a move on!" the sheriff shouted, finally spurring the young man into action.

Sheriff Thomas turned back to Smoke, spreading his arms wide. "I'm sorry about all this, Mr. Jensen. Ever winter we git a bunch of white trash come into town when the blizzards blow. It's hard to keep a handle on things when the town's full like this."

"No problem, Sheriff Thomas."

"Uh, Mr. Jensen," the sheriff asked, rubbing his chin and staring at Smoke from under bushy eyebrows, "you plannin' on stayin' in town long?"

Smoke grinned. He knew his presence in their towns usually made lawmen nervous, because there always seemed to be a surplus of gunplay and dead bodies wherever he went. Such was the price of fame, of being known as the deadliest gunfighter in the West. Someone was always trying to build a reputation on Smoke's back.

"Just long enough to get a steak in the dining room and grab a few hours shut-eye until the train to Wyoming pulls out in the morning, Sheriff. I'd appreciate it if you'd keep the fact that I'm here quiet until then. Otherwise you're liable to have more bodies to clean up."

The sheriff said to the attendant, "Jeremiah, go tell the cook to get Mr. Jensen's steak ready so's he don't have to wait in the dining room too long."

"Tell him to just cook it long enough so it doesn't crawl off the plate, and it'll be just fine," Smoke told the boy as he stood to get out of the tub.

The sheriff's eyes widened at the sight of Smoke's body. He stood six feet two inches tall, with broad shoulders and huge, heavily muscled arms. His waist was lean and his ash-blond hair was cut short and neat. The sheriff couldn't help but notice the many scars covering Smoke's skin, mementos of hundreds of fights with guns, knives, and fists.

The sheriff shook his head. "You shore look like you been to the river and back again, Mr. Jensen."

Smoke glanced down at the scars as he pulled on his pants. "Just one of the many prices of fame, Sheriff, just one."

As he tucked in his shirt, Smoke asked Thomas, "Are there any Indians in town?"

The sheriff laughed. "In Denver? There are dozens, especially in the winter."

"Would you do me a favor, Sheriff Thomas? Would you ask around to see if any of them know anything about a small tribe of Nez Percé, supposed to be camping up near Buffalo in northern Wyoming?"

Thomas nodded, and said to the attendant just as he was leaving the room, "Jeremiah, after yore done talkin' to the cook 'bout Mr. Jensen's steak, head on over to the cantina at the other end of town and do what Mr. Jensen asks. If any of the braves or breeds knows anything, bring 'em on back to the hotel. You'll have to stay with 'em or they won't let 'em in to talk to him."

Smoke smiled. "Mighty obliged, Sheriff."

"Least I can do, Mr. Jensen, after you helped clean some of the trash out of my town for me."

Eight

Smoke was half through with his steak when the bath attendant, Jeremiah, appeared in the hotel dining room, followed by a rail-thin Indian dressed in dirty buckskin rags. From the way the brave licked his lips and eyed Smoke's plate, Smoke knew he hadn't eaten for some time.

Smoke flipped a coin to the young man and said, "Thanks, Jeremiah."

Jeremiah grinned and pocketed the money as he walked out of the hotel, his chest stuck out as if he was proud to have helped the famous gunfighter Smoke Jensen.

Smoke gestured for the Indian to take a seat next to him and called to the waiter, "Bring my friend a steak, some potatoes, and a pot of coffee."

The waiter looked flustered, glancing over his shoulder at the dining room manager, who was standing next to a table with several local men eating, giving the Indian and Smoke a hard look. "Uh, Mr. Blake don't allow no Indians in here, sir."

Smoke turned cold eyes on the boy. "He's with me. Now bring him some food, or call your boss over here and I'll deal with him myself."

The young man's face blanched, and he walked quickly over to the manager, speaking to him in low tones while looking over his shoulder at Smoke.

The manager scowled, hitched up his pants, and swaggered over to Smoke's table.

"I don't know who you think you are, mister, but this here is my hotel and I don't allow no dirty redskins to eat in it."

Smoke got slowly to his feet, towering over the shorter man by six inches, and leaned over to put his face right next to the manager's.

"My name is Smoke Jensen, Mr. Blake. I'm a paying customer, and this gentleman sitting with me is a friend of mine, and I intend to feed him whatever he wants. Have you got that?"

Blake's eyes widened and he took a step back, tilting his head to look up at Smoke. What he saw in Smoke's eyes must have convinced him that he was treading on thin ice.

"You be Smoke Jensen the gunfighter?"

"One and the same," Smoke answered, his voice flat and hard.

"Well, uh, I guess if you say he's a friend of yours . . ."

"He is. Now either get us our food, or I'll be forced to go back into the kitchen and get it myself, and you don't want that, do you?"

"No, sir. I'll see that it gets right out," Blake said, his head bobbing up and down with a fine sheen of sweat covering his face. He turned on his heels and walked quickly back into the kitchen, the back of his neck red and flushed.

Once he was gone, Smoke spoke to the man sitting next to him. "My name is Smoke Jensen."

"I am called Walking Bear."

Smoke took in the beads and markings on his buckskins. "You appear to be of the Kiowa people."

"Yes, I am Kiowa."

"You know anything about a small tribe of Nez Percé, supposed to be camped up near Buffalo?"

The Indian nodded. "There may be thirty . . . forty Nez Percé in the mountains just outside the town. Been there maybe four or five moons."

"Do you know if they have any Palouse with them?"

Walking Bear smiled, showing cracked, yellow teeth and reddened gums, signs that spoke to Smoke of malnutrition.

"The Nez Percé always have the spotted ponies. It is their way."

After a few minutes, the waiter put a plate of steaming meat in front of Walking Bear. The hungry man bent his head and began to tear into the steak, using a knife from his belt and ignoring the fancy silverware the hotel provided.

While he ate, Smoke poured him a mug of coffee, to which Walking Bear added large helpings of sugar from the silver service on the table.

Smoke took out his map and had Walking Bear show him where the Nez Percé were camped, just north and east of the town called Buffalo. As they were talking, a pair of cowboys who'd obviously been drinking their dinner walked up to stand next to Walking Bear.

"Hey, mister," one man said to Smoke. "We don't 'preciate havin' to eat with a dirty redskin in the room."

"Yeah," the other one added, swaying on his feet as if he was about to tip over. "They smell like dog shit an' it ruins our appetite."

Walking Bear hung his head and started to get up from the table. Smoke put a hand on his shoulder and motioned for him to continue eating. Then Smoke leaned back in his seat and looked at the pair standing before him.

"You gents just go on back to your drinking. We'll be through here in a minute."

One of the men made the mistake of putting a hand on Smoke's shoulder. "Maybe you didn't hear us, dude. . . ."

Smoke grabbed the man's fingers and bent them back, driving the man to his knees with a short scream. As the other reached for his pistol, he stopped, mouth hanging open as Smoke's Navy appeared in his hand as if by magic with the barrel two inches from his face. "I heard you just fine. I just didn't think I needed to pay any attention to what a couple of cow-flop drunks had to say."

He eared back the Navy's hammer with a loud click and pressed the barrel against the man's lips. "Now, are my friend and I going to be allowed to finish our supper in peace, or am I going to have to blow your teeth all over this room to do it?"

When the hotel manager appeared, wringing his hands and sweating at the thought of bloodshed in his establishment, Smoke said, "You'd better escort these men out of here, Mr. Blake. One of them appears to have broken some fingers and is in need of medical attention."

He narrowed his eyes and glared at the other man. "And this one may need a dentist if he doesn't shut his mouth and get on his way."

When the manager said, "Yes, sir, Mr. Jensen, I'll see to it right away," the man looking down the barrel of Smoke's Navy paled even more.

"Jensen? You be Smoke Jensen?"

Smoke nodded, his expression not changing.

"I'm awful sorry, Mr. Jensen. Me and Roy didn't mean no harm—we was just funnin' is all."

He grabbed his friend by his collar and yanked him to his feet, hustling him out of the room without looking back.

As Smoke holstered his Colt, Walking Bear began to eat again. "I have heard of Smoke Jensen, called Man Who Walks on Mountain. It is said he is friend of Kiowa."

Smoke nodded. "The Kiowa are brave warriors, men of honor."

Walking Bear used a piece of bread to sop up the last of the gravy off his plate, then stood up. "The chief of the Nez Percé is called Gray Wolf. If any braves going north, I send word Man Who Walks on Mountain is coming."

"Are there any more of your people in town?"

Walking Bear nodded. "We come in for food, but trapping not good this year. No furs to trade, so many go hungry."

Smoke took a hundred-dollar bill out of his money belt and pressed it into his hand. "Take this—it will feed your people until the spring brings the beavers out of their houses and into your traps."

"My people will sing your song around our fires."

"You're welcome, Walking Bear. Thanks for the information."

Walking Bear walked from the hotel and into the driving snow.

Smoke settled back for another cup of coffee, thinking about the spotted ponies of the Nez Percé.

He took a long cheroot out of his pocket and struck a lucifer on his boot. As he bent over the flame, he noticed a group of twenty or twenty-five men enter the hotel dining room.

A tall, broad-shouldered man, who was evidently the leader of the group, waved Blake over to them.

"My name's Tom Smith, an' me and my boys need some food. We been on that train all the way up from Texas and we haven't eaten anything worth spit in two days."

"Yes, sir, Mr. Smith," Blake said, waving his hand at a group of tables in the corner. "Tell your men to have a seat and I'll get the cook working on your food. What will you gentlemen be having?"

"Steaks for everybody, with plenty of potatoes and gravy and some sliced peaches or tomatoes if you have 'em." He hesitated a moment, then added, "An' plenty of beer, but no hard liquor 'cause we got a ways to go yet an' I don't want 'em to get too drunk to travel."

"Yes, sir, I'll get right on it."

Smoke watched the men scramble to the tables. He noticed all the men carried rifles and wore six-shooters on their belts. Most of the men he could hear talking spoke with thick Texas accents, and they were still dressed as if they were in the heat of the Texas flatlands. None of the men had coats thick enough for the Colorado winter, and several were clad only in thin shirts and worn trousers, with boots more suited for horseback than walking.

When all the available seats in the room were filled, there

was one man left standing, looking around as if confused by the lack of a seat for him. He stood a shade over six feet and must have weighed at least 250 pounds, Smoke thought.

He was clad in nothing but a summer undershirt, trousers with suspenders, and shoes without any socks. As he stood there, snow and ice melting in his hair and running down his neck to soak his shirt, Smoke waved him over.

"Looks like you need a place to light and set, partner," Smoke said, liking the good-natured smile the man had.

"Thank ye kindly, stranger," the man said, holding out his hand. "My name's Jim Dudley, an' I'm from Texas. What's yore handle?"

Smoke smiled again, thinking, *This man is obviously from the deep backwoods of Texas, and this is probably the first time he's ever traveled outside his county, much less across several states.*

"My name is Smoke Jensen, and you're welcome to sit here while you eat your supper."

Smoke was relieved when the Texan's expression didn't change at the mention of his name. *Perhaps there's still some people in the country,* he thought, *who haven't heard of my reputation.*

Dudley nodded his thanks and pulled out a chair and sat down. As he crossed his arms and shivered from the cold, Smoke poured him a large cup of still-steaming coffee from the pot on the table.

"Here you go, Jim, drink some of this. It'll help take the chill off."

Dudley took the cup and drank half of it down in one huge swallow, moaning with pleasure at the heat of the dark liquid.

"That's mighty good. Ain't had no decent coffee for three, four days now."

Smoke took a drag from his cigar and tilted smoke out of his nostrils as he asked, "What are you boys doing way up here from Texas? Don't they have enough cattle down there to keep you busy?"

Dudley grinned in his happy-go-lucky way. "Hell, yes, we got plenty of beef in Texas, but this is a different sort'a job."

"Oh?" Smoke said as he took a drink of his coffee.

"Yep. Marshal Smith over there done hired us to come up to Wyoming and help get rid of some cattle rustlers up there."

"Marshal Smith?"

"Oh, he ain't a marshal no more, but he used to be a U.S. marshal down Texas way, an' that's where some of the boys know him from."

He leaned forward and added in a hoarse whisper, "Hell, he arrested most of 'em more'n once."

Smoke nodded and glanced over at the tables containing the men from Texas. He could see that most of them had a hard look about them, as if they had all spent some time riding the owlhoot trail. It was in their eyes, an almost-vacant look, as if there was nothing of civilization behind them.

Smoke thought Dudley seemed different from the rest of the men. "How about you, Jim? You ever been arrested by the marshal?"

"Shucks, no," Dudley replied with his ever-present grin. "I ain't no gunhawk. Me and my wife started a little spread down on the Rio Bravo, near Del Rio." His face clouded. "We didn't have enough money to buy good beeves so I got me some Mexican cattle from across the river, only they turned out to have tick fever and every one of 'em took sick and died."

The big man shrugged, his grin returning. "So I decided to join up with Marshal Smith's group an' come on up to Wyoming and earn me enough money to go back and start a new herd."

Smoke glanced at Dudley's clothes. "Well, Jim, if you plan to survive the winter up here, you're going to need some better clothes and a heavy coat."

Dudley shook his head. "I plan to buy some up in Cheyenne. That's when we'll get our first payday."

Smoke leaned over, opened his valise, and took out two

thick flannel shirts and a buckskin coat, one slightly thinner than the fur-lined one he was wearing.

He handed them across the table. "Here you go, Jim. Take these until you get some pay under your belt, then buy a coat with some fur in it."

"Shucks, Mr. Jensen, I can't take yore clothes."

"Sure you can, Jim. I've got plenty more up in my hotel room, and I'm headed up to Wyoming too, so if you see me later you can give them back to me."

The waiter appeared with a tray covered with plates of food. Jim reached up and took two plates and a knife and fork.

When he saw Smoke staring at the amount of food he took, he grinned again. "My wife tole me 'fore I left to eat plenty of food to keep up my strength."

Smoke laughed. "That much ought to take you all the way to Wyoming before you need a refill."

The next morning, on the way to board the train, Smoke found a dime novel on a chair in the hotel lobby. He picked it up, glancing at the cover with a smile. It showed a man dressed all in black, with a large handlebar moustache, menacing a cowering young girl who looked terrified. Smoke stuck the penny dreadful in his pocket. Reading about the adventures of Deadwood Dick and Hurricane Nell would keep his mind occupied on the long, slow trip through mountain passes covered neck-deep in snow.

On the way to the train, he thought about when he'd met Erastus Beadle, who wrote the dime novels under the name Ned Buntline. The adventures they'd had together rivaled anything the imaginative writer ever conjured up in his mind.*

Battle of the Mountain Man

Nine

Smoke stretched and yawned, thinking he felt like he had been beaten with a barrel stave. Every muscle in his body ached from riding for two days and nights on the hard wooden bench of the railroad car.

The trip from Denver to Greely hadn't been too bad, the mountain passes having received less snow than expected, but the run from Greely to Cheyenne was horrible. The Union Pacific engine was only able to go at a snail's pace, depending on the smaller engine with the snowplow attached to clear a way through drifts as high as ten or more feet.

To make matters worse, Smoke hadn't been able to catch much shut-eye, since the group of Texans in the next car had managed to smuggle aboard a prodigious supply of whiskey, and were using the cold as an excuse to fill their bodies with as much liquor as possible. This, of course, led to the inevitable rowdiness and fighting that went with cowboys and liquor as sure as stink went with a skunk.

Several times, Smoke was on the verge of walking to the Texans' car and pounding some sense into their heads, but then he remembered how it was to be young and away from home for the first time, and was able to laugh at the antics of the youngsters as they discovered the blinding pain of hangovers caused by too much liquor and too little food.

At one point, Jim Dudley stumbled through Smoke's car, his hand over his mouth, looking for someplace to unload his swollen, bloated stomach. Without too much pleasure, Smoke pried open a window frozen stuck with two inches of ice and stuck the big man's head out into the freezing snow and sleet.

Dudley sobered up surprisingly fast, and was kind enough to thank Smoke for his efforts before heading back for more of the same with his newfound friends.

Smoke breathed a sigh of relief when the train finally pulled into Cheyenne in the dead of night. The conductor told him he would transfer to the Cheyenne and Northern Railroad in the morning to continue northward to Laramie, Medicine Bow, and finally on into Casper. There he would change trains yet again, switching to a spur line for the ride up into the Big Horn Mountains and Buffalo.

At least, he thought, he would have a chance to get a room in a hotel, preferably one other than that chosen by Tom Smith and his Texas vigilantes, and he might be able to get some much-needed sleep.

As he climbed down off the train, his valise and suitcase swung over his shoulder, Smoke saw Dudley and the other Texans exiting their car further down the tracks. Most of the men looked like death warmed over, heads hanging, some bending over to throw up in the black snow next to the railroad car, while others walked with arms around friends' shoulders for support.

He noticed Tom Smith walk up to a man dressed in Army puttees and carrying a swagger stick, and watched as the two men exchanged what seemed to be angry words, wondering briefly who the martinet was and what he had to do with the Texans.

Smoke shook his head, chuckling softly to himself. *I sure hope they have a chance to sober up before they run into those rustlers they're looking for,* he thought. *Otherwise, it'll be Texas's worst defeat since the Alamo.*

After consuming a thick steak, sauteed in fresh-cut onions

and sliced tomatoes, with canned pears as a dessert, Smoke finally was able to slip between the covers of a hotel bed, his last conscious thoughts of Sally and the Sugarloaf and how much he missed them both.

While Smoke was sleeping, the Pullman containing Tom Smith and the Texans was shunted into the switching yard and joined to a train that included a baggage car, three stock cars, a flatcar bearing the three big freight wagons the cattlemen had equipped with camping gear, weapons, and ammunition, and a caboose.

Of the one hundred stockmen who had put up the money for the expedition, nineteen had chosen to go along with the gunfighters.

With their cattle detectives and a few guests, they boarded the Pullman for their first look at the Texans.

As a Union Pacific locomotive was readied for a fast run to Casper, a little range town at the foot of the Big Horn Mountains, the expedition's commander, Major Wolcott, issued his first order.

"Hurry up," he barked at the railroad superintendent. "Put us at Casper and we will do the rest."

Shortly thereafter, with a hiss of steam and the squeal of brakes being released, the train chugged off, due at Casper before dawn.

As the train pulled out of Cheyenne, the Texans were in the passenger car, bunched together at one end. Some of them were playing cards, while others dozed and tried to suffer through their headaches and stomach cramps.

At the other end of the car, Wolcott and Smith and the Wyoming stockmen were gathered, talking over their plans for the upcoming battle with the small ranchers. It was evident that while the cattlemen valued their hired gunfighters, they would never dream of admitting them to the society of gentlemen.

The Texans, for their part, showed no interest in pressing

the matter, content to play cards, smoke, and try to get over their hangovers.

After a while, plans having been made, Wolcott walked two cars back to the baggage car, intent on rearranging the supplies to expedite unloading at Casper.

He was surprised when Frank Canton entered the car, since he had expressly forbidden anyone else to come there.

"Canton, I thought I told you to stay out of my business. Now get your ass back to the others and stay there, like I told you."

Canton arched an eyebrow, a slight grin tugging at the corners of his mouth.

"Kiss my ass, you sawed-off little runt," Canton replied, standing a bit straighter to emphasize the difference in their heights. He knew the major was sensitive about his shortness, and he couldn't resist a chance to rub it in, especially when the man dared to give him orders like a common soldier under his command.

Major Wolcott fairly sputtered. He wasn't used to being talked to in this disrespectful manner.

"Mr. Canton, need I remind you I am in complete command of this expedition." He squared his shoulders and stuck his chest out. "Now, you'll follow my orders or I'll have you removed from the train."

Canton stared back at Wolcott with an insolent grin on his face.

"We'll see about that, Wolcott. You won't have an expedition to command without my men and me."

He turned to go, calling back over his shoulder, "Before this is over, you'll be apologizin' to me, just wait an' see."

Canton walked rapidly back to the passenger car, grabbed Tom Smith by the arm, and took him to a far corner, away from the other cattlemen. In a quiet voice, he told Smith what had transpired in the baggage car. Smith, an old cowboy like Canton, didn't appreciate the way the Army, or its officers like

Wolcott, looked down on their abilities. He slapped Canton on the back.

"I'm with you, Frank. Now, let's go on back with the Texicans and let the major stew in his own juices for a while."

He winked at Canton. "I'm sure 'fore the train pulls into Casper, he'll see the light."

During the night, Canton and Smith hung out at the end of the passenger car with the Texans, laughing and joking and playing cards with them. Every effort by Wolcott and the cattlemen to engage them in conversation or to tell them of the plans for the upcoming fight was rudely rebuffed.

Finally, at breakfast the next morning, Wolcott grandly resigned his command, and Tom Smith took charge of the Texans, while Frank Canton assumed leadership of the expedition as a whole.

While on the way to Casper, Canton had the engineer stop the train at a small junction, where he attempted to telegraph the town of Buffalo. He was delighted when the telegraph operator reported he couldn't get through. To Canton, that meant the cattlemen's allies in Johnson County had done their job and the wires to the county seat were down.

Once they arrived in Casper, the plan had been to unload their gear and pick up their horses for the 150-mile ride to Buffalo. The cattlemen had planned it this way to insure the element of surprise, rather than take the quicker and much easier ride the rest of the way by rail.

The problem was the Texans were in no shape for a long jaunt through snow-covered mountain passes. They needed some sleep and food, and most of all a couple of days without liquor.

Major Wolcott was furious when Canton hired an entire hotel in Casper and ordered the Texans to eat and then go to bed, but since he had resigned his command, there was little he could do about it.

Ten

Smoke carefully wrapped his money belt around his waist and pulled his buckskin shirt down over it after paying the man at the livery stable in Buffalo.

He'd bought a large, black stallion with plenty of muscles through his shoulders, figuring the horse would have to have lots of stamina to carry him through the deep snow up into the mountains toward the camp of the Nez Percé.

He'd also purchased a somewhat smaller, but still sturdy packhorse to carry what supplies he thought he might need on the trip up into the high lonesome.

Glancing up at a leaden sky filled with dark, roiling clouds, he knew he was only hours ahead of a fierce snowstorm. If he was going to make any time, he needed to get on the trail pronto.

Jake, the livery man, shook his head. "You sure you want to take off 'fore that storm hits, mister? It shore looks like it's gonna be a doozy."

Smoke stepped into the saddle of the stud and lightly touched him with his spurs, wrapping the dally rope to the packhorse around his saddle horn.

"If I wait for it to quit snowing, I'll be here until summertime. Thanks for your help, Jake. When I come back through Buffalo with the horses, I'll stop in and say hello."

Jake scratched an unruly beard. "You do that, mister. I'll be lookin' for you in a couple of months."

Smoke pointed the horse's head straight north and started up the trail, large, wet snowflakes already starting to fall. He wasn't worried overly much, having wintered in the higher elevations of Colorado since he was in his teens. He wondered briefly if there were any mountain men in these mountains, hoping if there were he might be able to find out about some old acquaintances among the breed he hadn't heard of for years.

It felt good for Smoke to be out of his traveling clothes and back into his mountain duds. He wore a buckskin shirt and buckskin trousers, tucked into knee-high moccasins such as the Apache wore. He carried a .44 Colt on his right hip, and a .44 Colt on his left hip, butt-first. A large bowie knife rested in a scabbard on his belt, and a tomahawk was stuck in his belt at the small of his back. He had a Greener ten-gauge shotgun in his left saddle boot, and a Winchester Model 1873 carbine in his right saddle boot.

The livery man, seeing his armament, had asked if Smoke was going to war. Smoke had laughed, saying, "You never know what you're going to come across in the high lonesome, Jake, and I've always found it's better to be prepared for the worst than to hope for the best."

Smoke made better time than he'd figured, and was twenty miles or more from Buffalo by the second day.

As he traversed a wide range between two mountain peaks, a man rode out of the mist and light snowfall toward him. Even though Smoke saw the man had his hands empty on the reins, he reached down and loosened the rawhide hammer thong on his Colt.

"Howdy, mister," the man called as he approached.

Smoke smiled and nodded as he pulled the big black to a halt.

"I hope I'm not trespassing on your property," Smoke said,

crossing his leg over the saddle horn to take a rest from his riding.

The man grinned and looked around at the range surrounding them. "Hell, no, you're not. This here is government property, free to anybody wants to make use of it."

Smoke took a pair of cheroots out of his shirt pocket and offered one to the cowboy.

As they lighted them, the man said, "My name's Nate Champion, an' I'm bunkin' at the old KC ranch, just over the hill yonder."

Smoke took a deep drag of the stogie, enjoying the bite of it on his tongue.

"My name's . . ." he started to reply as suddenly several gunshots rang out in rapid succession.

When one ricocheted off his saddle horn, Smoke dove to the side, landing in a snowdrift and immediately rolling to his knees, both hands filled with iron.

Nate jumped to the same side, grabbed Smoke by the shoulder, and pulled him out of the clearing behind a small group of Aspen trees next to the trail.

Two slugs tore holes in the bark of the trees as Smoke and Nate ducked.

"Can you see where the shots are coming from?" Smoke asked, peering around the side of the trees.

"Naw, not just yet," Nate answered, rearing back the hammer of his pistol.

As the snowfall slowly increased and the gathering dusk brought semi-darkness, a voice called out, "Come on out and face us like a man, Champion! You've rustled your last steer in this county!"

Smoke glanced at Nate. "You one of the rustlers I've been hearing so much about?"

Nate chuckled. "Only if rounding up stray mavericks on the open range is rustlin', which it ain't."

"Are those lawmen out there?"

"Not hardly. Most probably bounty hunters hired by the big

ranchers in Cheyenne. They're offerin' a reward of five hundred dollars for each of us small ranchers they can kill, claimin' we been shootin' their beeves out on the range. They've been pickin' off one or two men 'bout near every week."

"And *have* you been shooting their cattle?"

Nate shook his head. "Not this cowboy. I run a few hundred head of my own." He hesitated, grinning sideways at Smoke. "Supplemented by the occasional stray that wonders into my herd, and I don't believe in wastin' beef. If I wanted their cattle, I'd take 'em, not shoot 'em."

A rifle shot screamed as it ricocheted off a nearby rock, and Smoke said, "I got that one sighted, saw the flash of his rifle." He pointed toward a clump of trees about two hundred yards away, barely visible in the gloom of the storm and dusk.

Their horses had wandered a few yards away, frightened by the gunfire, and neither Nate nor Smoke had rifles with them.

"Give me some covering fire, and I'll see if I can't get us some rifles off those mounts," Smoke said.

Nate looked at him. "Are you crazy? They've got us pinned down here like fish in a barrel. You'll never make it."

Smoke gave a tight grin. "You have any better ideas, Nate? The temperature's dropping pretty fast, and I don't relish sitting here freezing while we wait for them to decide what to do with us."

"You got a point, mister," Nate said, and he rose up and began to fire his pistol as fast as he could cock and pull the trigger.

Smoke leaped over the rocks in front of the trees and sprinted for their horses, zigzagging as bullets began to pock the snow by his feet and buzz by his head.

When he got to the horses, he jerked his rifle out of its saddle boot and grabbed his saddlebags with his extra ammunition.

As he stepped quickly to Nate's horse, a bullet took the animal in the neck, knocking it to its knees with a terrible scream of pain.

Smoke pulled Nate's rifle out and ran back toward the trees, ducking as a slug nicked the back of his neck, burning a tiny furrow in the skin and stinging like hell.

He handed Nate's rifle to him and levered a shell into his own Winchester at the same time.

"Can't hardly see nothin' to aim at," Nate observed.

Smoke peered over the rock in front of them, laying his rifle across the top of it and sighting down the barrel.

"The trick is to wait for the flash as they shoot and aim a couple of inches over it. If you're quick enough, you might get lucky and nail one of them."

Nate cut his eyes at Smoke. "Course, that means you got to sit there with your head stuck out and let them fire first, don't it?"

Smoke nodded. "Yes, but they can't see us any better than we can see them, so I figure it's worth a try. If more than one fires, I'll take the first, you draw down on the second."

"All right, mister," Nate said, sounding as if he still wasn't sure about it.

Suddenly, there came a flash from the distance, followed a second or two later by the thunder of a rifle shot. Smoke's answering fire was almost immediate, his carbine exploding and slamming back into his shoulder just as another wink of light appeared to the right of the first one.

Nate, his ears ringing from the blasts, pulled his trigger, aiming just above the flash in the distance as Smoke had told him to.

A loud scream rang out, followed by a harsh grunt and a muttered curse.

"God damn you, Champion!" a voice called. "You kilt my partner, you son of a bitch!"

"Sounded like another one got hit, too," Smoke whispered to Nate. "Get ready—they'll probably try again in a minute."

They both levered shells into their rifles and settled down to wait, the increasing cold seeping through their clothes to make them shiver and ache with fatigue.

Twin flashes blinked in the darkness, and Smoke immediately returned fire. He had time to hear a distant yelp of pain, and the whine and crack of a bullet ricocheting back and forth between the rocks next to where he and Nate lay, before a sudden pain in the side of his head was followed by a flash of light and then all-encompassing darkness.

Nate heard the slap of the bullet striking the stranger next to him, and saw his head snap back as he dropped to the ground. Nate fired several quick rounds toward where the flashes had come from, and heard a horse nicker and then hoofbeats as someone took off.

He bent quickly and felt the stranger's head, unable to see in the darkness, but afraid to light a lucifer and perhaps draw fire.

There was a knot on the man's head as big as a goose egg, but no hole, and not much blood, considering he had taken a bullet just moments before.

When there was no further sound from across the clearing, Nate scrambled to his right and snuck up on the ambushers' hiding place as quietly as he could, ready to shoot should they still be there.

He found one man lying on his stomach, still holding a rifle, half his head blown off, face-down in a wide pool of blood as black as tar in the darkness.

To his left was more blood, so either Nate or the stranger had hit another of the men, evidently wounding but not killing him.

He struck a lucifer, shielding it from the wind with his hands as he rolled the dead man over. He recognized him as one of the stock detectives, a man called Zack Renfield, who worked for the Wyoming Stock Growers Association. There was no horse, so the others must have taken it with them as they fled.

He grabbed the man's rifle and took his pistol out of his holster, and trotted back toward where the stranger's body lay.

Striking another lucifer, he examined the man's wounds. Imbedded in his hair, just under the skin of his scalp, Nate felt a flat, metallic object. He pried it loose and looked at it. It was a lead slug, flattened out by where it had hit the rocks before striking the man in the head.

He whistled under his breath. "You are one lucky hombre, friend," he whispered to the unconscious man. "If that rock hadn't taken the point off that bullet, you'd be a goner for sure."

Working quickly, before the cold finished the job the rifle bullet started, he managed to get the man across his saddle. He covered him as best he could with a blanket from his own gear, then took his own saddle and saddlebags off his dead horse and put them on the stranger's packhorse. Finally, Nate took the reins of the big, black horse along with those of the pack animal, and started across the range toward his ranch house, leading both of the wounded man's horses behind him. It promised to be a tough walk in the storm, but he had no choice but to try.

He bent his head against the driving snow, hoping the frigid air would keep the man from bleeding to death, but not kill him on the journey.

He desperately wanted to save the stranger, for the man had certainly saved Nate's life. Nate knew if he had been alone when the detectives ambushed him, he'd be lying back there forked end up, as dead as Zack was now.

He owed the man a great debt, and he intended to do all in his power to pay him back, though he didn't even know his name or where he came from.

If he survived, and with a head wound as serious as this one he might not, perhaps he would tell Nate just what he was doing up here in this country during the dead of winter.

One thing was certain. He didn't look or act like a cowboy, at least not any that Nate had ever met. There was something about him, something that spoke of greater things.

Eleven

Nate Champion made it back to the KC ranch just as the winter storm let loose with all its fury. Visibility dropped to a few feet and the temperature plummeted deep into the minus figures, while the wind howled, blowing snow and ice almost sideways in the worst storm of the year.

Nate bundled the stranger, who was still unconscious, into bed and piled on plenty of covers, before getting the horses into the barn where they'd have food and shelter from the weather.

While he heated some beef stew on the wooden stove, Nate conjectured to himself on the stranger's background and purpose in being in Johnson County.

He knew from the way the man talked that he was well educated, and his accent was different from the people from Wyoming, but didn't have the soft, slurred vowels of a man from the Deep South either.

Fellow, Nate mumbled to himself, *you got to be from out west, or somewhere in the middle of the country, Kansas or Colorado maybe.* He spooned himself a generous portion of stew onto a plate, took a handful of cold biscuits he'd made that morning, and began to eat.

He was ravenous and felt as if he hadn't eaten for days. *Battle's like that,* he thought. *It seems fighting for your life, and winning while taking another man's living away from him, stimulates all the appetites.* During the big war between the states, he'd known men who looked for whores after large battles, while others wanted to eat or drink themselves sick. He shook his head, thinking it must be a body's way of celebrating the fact that it was alive, rather than true hunger for food or whiskey or women.

Nate jumped to his feet and ran back into the bedroom when he heard loud moaning and what sounded like talking coming from there.

The man with the head wound was thrashing about on the bed, rolling his head back and forth, talking and mumbling, though still unconscious.

Nate got his coffee from the kitchen and sat across from the bed, lighting a cigarette and sitting back to listen to what the man said. Might be there'd be some clues to who he was and why he was in the area.

He heard the stranger mention the name Kirby several times, and he even seemed to be talking to a man he called Preacher, as if he were asking advice or asking for help. Nate couldn't make out all the words, and the sentences were often garbled, not making any sense. Sometimes there were shouted warnings to look out for the Indians, or sometimes, there were tender words obviously meant for the man's wife or sweetheart that made Nate blush with embarrassment at listening in.

Nate finally shook his head and got up to fix himself a place to sleep in the other bedroom. He put extra wood in the fireplace and settled in, burrowing deep under his own covers to get warm, wondering if he'd get some answers when his new friend awakened in the morning—that is, if he awakened at all. Nate had known men in the war who'd had serious head injuries that never came out of the sleep the doctors called a coma, but stayed forever in the twilight between sleep and wakefulness.

While Nate slept, the stranger tossed and turned in bed, his body feverish, his mind reeling with sleep images and dreams that were at times real as life and at other times as blurry as images seen through a thick fog. In his dreams, he was sixteen, a gangly, skinny kid tall for his age with wide shoulders that his body hadn't yet grown into. . . .

He knew his name was Kirby, and that the man riding with him was his father, but he couldn't bring his father's name to his mind. They rode westward, edging north. Several weeks had passed since they rode from the land of Kirby's birth, and already that place was fading from his mind. He had never been happy there, so he made no real effort to halt the fading of the images.

Kirby did not know how much his pa had gotten for the land and the equipment and the mules, but he knew he had gotten it in gold, and not much gold at that. His pa carried the gold in a small leather pouch around his neck with a piece of rawhide.

His pa was heavily armed: a Sharps .52-caliber rifle in a saddle boot, two Remington army revolvers in holsters around his waist, two more pistols in saddle holsters, left and right of the saddle horn. And he carried a gambler's gun behind his belt buckle, a .44-caliber, two-shot derringer. His knife was a wicked-looking, razor-sharp Arkansas Toothpick in a leather sheath on his side.

Kirby never asked why his father was so heavily armed. But he did ask, "How come them holsters around your waist ain't got no flaps on them, Pa? How come you cut them off that way?"

"So I can get the pistols out faster, son. This leather thong run through the front loops over the hammer to hold the pistol."

"Is gettin' a gun out fast important, Pa?" He knew it was from reading dime novels. But he just could not envision his father as a gunfighter.

"Sometimes, boy. But more important is hittin' what you're aimin' at."

"Think I'll do mine thataway."

"Your choice," the father replied.

Kirby knew, after hearing talk after Appomattox, that the Gray were supposed to turn in their weapons. But he had a hunch that his father, hearing of the surrender, had just wheeled around and taken the long way back home, his weapons with him, and the devil with surrender terms.

His dad coughed and asked, "How'd you get the Navy Colt, son?"

"Bunch of Jayhawkers came ridin' through one night, headin' back to Kansas like the devil was chasin' them. Turned out that was just about right. 'Bout a half hour later Bloody Bill Anderson and his boys came ridin' up. They stopped to rest and water their horses. There was this young feller with them. Couldn't have been no more than a year or so older than me. He seen me and Ma there alone, and all I had was this old rifle."

He patted the stock of an old flint-and-percussion Plains rifle in a saddle boot. "So he give me this Navy gun and an extra cylinder. Seemed a right nice thing for him to do. He was nice, soft-spoken, too."

"It was a nice thing to do. You seen him since?"

"No, sir."

"You thank him proper?"

"Yes, sir. Gave him a bit of food in a sack."

"Neighborly. He tell you his name?"

"Yes, sir. James. Jesse James. His brother Frank was with the bunch, too. Some older than Jesse."

"Don't recall hearin' that name before."

"Jesse blinked his eyes a lot."

"Is that right? Well, you 'member the name, son. Might run into him again some day. Good man like that's hard to find."

As the days rolled past, Kirby and his father winged their way ever westward. As they rode on, across the seemingly endless plains of tall grass and sudden breaks in the earth, a pile of rocks, not arranged by nature, came into view. Kirby pointed them out.

They pulled up. "That's what I been lookin' for," his father said. "That's a sign tellin' travelers that this here is the Santa Fe Trail. North and west of here'll be Fort Larned. North of that'll be the Pawnee Rock."

"What's that, Pa?"

"A landmark, pilgrim," the voice said from behind the man and his son.

Before Kirby could blink, his Pa had wheeled his roan and had a pistol in his hand, hammer back. It was the fastest draw Kirby had ever seen—not that he'd seen that many. Just the time the town marshal back home had tried a fast draw and shot himself in the foot.

"Whoa!" the man said. "You some swift, pilgrim."

"I ain't no pilgrim," Kirby's dad said, low menace in his voice.

Kirby looked at his father, looked at a very new side of the man.

"Reckon you ain't at that."

Kirby had wheeled his bay and now sat his saddle, staring at the dirtiest man he had ever seen. The man was dressed entirely in buckskin, from the moccasins on his feet to his wide-brimmed leather hat. A white, tobacco-stained beard covered his face. His nose was red and his eyes twinkled with mischief. He looked like a skinny, dirty version of Santa Claus. He sat on a funny-spotted pony, two pack animals with him.

"Where'd you come from?" Kirby's dad asked.

"Been watchin' you two pilgrims from that ravine yonder," he said with a jerk of his head. "Ya'll don't know much 'bout travelin' in Injun country, do you? Best stay off the ridges. You two been standin' out like a third titty."

He shifted his gaze to Kirby. "What are you starin' at, boy?"

The boy leaned forward in his saddle. "Be durned if I rightly know," he said. And as usual, his reply was an honest one.

The old man laughed. "You got sand in your bottom, all right." He looked at Kirby's dad. "He yourn?"

"My son."

"I'll trade for him," he said, the old eyes sparkling. "Injuns pay right smart for a strong boy like him."

"My son is not for trade, old-timer."

"Tell you what. I won't call you pilgrim, you don't call me old-timer. Deal?"

Kirby's dad lowered his pistol, returning it to leather. "Deal."

"You pil . . . folk know where you are?"

"West of the state of Missouri, east of the Pacific Ocean."

"In other words, you lost as a lizard."

"Not really. You heard me say where Fort Larned was."

"Maybe you ain't lost. You two got names?"

"I'm Emmett. This is my son, Kirby."

"Pleasure. I'm called Preacher."

Kirby laughed out loud.

"Don't scoff, boy. It ain't nice to scoff at a man's name. If'n I wasn't a gentle-type man, I might let the hairs on my neck get stiff."

Kirby grinned. "Preacher can't be your real name."

The old man returned the grin. "Well, no, you right. But I been called that for so long, I nearabouts forgot my Christian name. So, Preacher it'll be. That or nothin'."

"We'll be ridin' on now, Preacher. Maybe we'll see you again."

Preacher's eyes had shifted to the northwest, then narrowed, his lips tightening. "Yep," he said smiling. "I reckon you will."

Emmett wheeled his horse and pointed its nose west-north-west. Kirby reluctantly followed. He would have liked to stay and talk to the old man.

When they were out of earshot, Kirby said, "Pa, that old man was so dirty he smelled."

"Mountain man. He's a ways from home, I'm figuring.

Tryin' to get back. Cantankerous old boys. Some of them mean as snakes. I think they get together once a year and bathe."

Kirby looked behind them. "Pa?"

"Son."

"That old man is following us, and he's shucked his rifle out of his boot."

Preacher galloped up to the pair, his rifle in his hand. "Don't get nervous," he told them. "It ain't me you got to fear. We fixin' to get ambushed . . . shortly. This here country is famous for that."

"Ambushed by who?" Emmett asked, not trusting the old man.

"Kiowa, I think. But they could be Pawnee. My eyes ain't as sharp as they used to be. I seen one of 'em stick a head up out of a wash over yonder, while I was jawin' with you. He's young or he wouldn't have done that. But that don't mean the others with him is young."

"How many?"

"Don't know. In this country, one's too many. Do know this: We better light a shuck out of here. If memory serves me correct, right over yonder, over that ridge, they's a little crick behind a stand of cottonwoods, old buffalo wallow in front of it."

He looked up, stood up in his stirrups, and cocked his shaggy head. "Here they come, boys . . . rake them cayuses!"

Before Kirby could ask what a cayuse was, or what good a rake was in an Indian attack, the old man had slapped his pony on the rump and they were galloping off. With the mountain man taking the lead, the three of them rode for the crest of the ridge. The packhorses seemed to sense the urgency, for they followed with no pullback on the ropes. Cresting the ridge, the riders slid down the incline and galloped into the timber, down into the wallow. The whoops and cries of the Indians were close behind them.

The Preacher might have been past his so-called prime years, but the mountain man had leaped off his spotted pony, rifle in hand, and was in position and firing before Emmett or Kirby had dismounted. Preacher, like Emmett, carried a Sharps .52, firing a paper cartridge, deadly up to seven hundred yards or more.

Kirby looked up in time to see a brave fly off his pony, a crimson slash on his naked chest. The Indian hit the ground and did not move.

"Get me that Spencer out of the pack, boy," Kirby's father yelled.

"The what?" Kirby had no idea what a Spencer might be.

"The rifle. It's in the pack. A tin box wrapped up with it. Bring both of 'em. Cut the ropes, boy."

Slashing the ropes with his long-bladed knife, Kirby grabbed the long, canvas-wrapped rifle and the tin box. He ran to his father's side. He stood and watched as his father got a buck in the sights of his Sharps, led him on his fast-running pony, then fired. The buck slammed off his pony, bounced off the ground, then leaped to his feet, one arm hanging bloody and broken. The Indian dodged for cover. He didn't make it. Preacher shot him in the side and lifted him off his feet, dropping him dead.

Emmett laid the Sharps aside and hurriedly unwrapped the canvas, exposing an ugly weapon with a potbellied, slab-sided receiver. Emmett glanced up at Preacher, who was grinning at him.

"What the hell you grinnin' about, man?"

"Just wanted to see what you had all wrapped up, partner. Figured I had you beat with what's in my pack."

"We'll see," Emmett muttered. He pulled out a thin tube from the tin box and inserted it in the butt plate, chambering a round. In the tin box were a dozen or more tubes, each containing seven rounds, .52-caliber. Emmett leveled the rifle, sighted it, and fired all seven rounds in a thunderous barrage of black smoke. The Indians whooped and yelled. Emmett's firing had not dropped a single brave, but the Indians scattered for cover, disappearing, horses and all, behind a ridge.

"Scared 'em," Preacher opined. "They ain't used to repeaters; all they know is single-shots. Let me get something outta my pack. I'll show you a thing or two."

Preacher went to one of his pack animals, untied one of the side packs, and let it fall to the ground. He pulled out the most beautiful rifle Kirby had ever seen.

"Damn!" Emmett softly swore. "The blue-bellies had some of those toward the end of the war. But I never could get my hands on one."

Preacher smiled and pulled another Henry repeating rifle from his pack. Unpredictable as mountain men were, he tossed the second Henry to Emmett, along with a sack of cartridges.

"Now we be friends," Preacher said. He laughed, exposing tobacco-stained stubs of teeth.

"I'll pay you for this," Emmett said, running his hands over the sleek barrel.

"Ain't necessary," Preacher replied. "I won both of 'em in a contest outside Westport Landing. Kansas City to you. Besides, somebody's got to look out for the two of you. Ya'll liable to wander round out here and get hurt. 'Pears to me don't neither of you know tit from tat 'bout stayin' alive in Injun country."

"You may be right," Emmett admitted. He loaded the Henry. "So thank you kindly."

Preacher looked at Kirby. "Boy, you heeled—so you gonna get in this fight, or not?"

"Sir?"

"Heeled. Means you carryin' a gun, so that makes you a man. Ain't you got no rifle 'cept that muzzle-loader?"

"No, sir."

"Take your daddy's Sharps then. You seen him load it, you know how. Take that tin box of tubes, too. You watch our for our backs. Them Pawnees—and they is Pawnees—likely to come 'crost that crick. You in wild country, boy . . . you may as well get bloodied."

"Do it, Kirby," his father said. "And watch yourself. Don't

hesitate a second to shoot. Those savages won't show you any mercy, so you do the same to them."

Kirby, a little pale around the mouth, took up the heavy Sharps and the box of tubes, reloaded the rifle, and made himself as comfortable as possible on the rear slope of the slight incline, overlooking the creek.

"Not there, boy." Preacher corrected Kirby's position. "Your back is open to the front line of fire. Get behind that tree 'twixt us and you. That way, you won't catch no lead or arrow in the back."

The boy did as he was told, feeling a bit foolish that he had not thought about his back. Hadn't he read enough dime novels to know that? he chastised himself. Nervous sweat dripped from his forehead as he waited.

He had to go to the bathroom something awful.

A half hour passed, the only action the always-moving Kansas winds chasing tumbleweeds, the southward-moving waters of the creek, and an occasional slap of a fish.

"What are they waiting for?" Emmett asked the question without taking his eyes from the ridge.

"For us to get careless," Preacher said. "Don't you fret none . . . they still out there. I been livin' in and 'round Injuns the better part of fifty year. I know 'em better—or at least as good—as any livin' white man. They'll try to wait us out. They got nothing but time, boys."

"No way we can talk to them?" Emmett asked, and immediately regretted saying it as Preacher laughed.

"Why, shore, Emmett," the mountain man said. "You just stand up, put your hands in the air, and tell 'em you want to palaver some. They'll probably let you walk right up to 'em. Odds are, they'll even let you speak your piece; they polite like that. A white man can ride right into nearabouts any Injun village. They'll feed you, sign-talk to you, and give you a place to sleep. Course . . . gettin' *out* is the problem.

"They ain't like us, Emmett. They don't come close to thinkin' like us. What is fun to them is torture to us. They call it testin' a man's bravery. If'n a man dies good—that is, don't holler a lot—they make it last as long as possible. Then they'll sing songs about you, praise you for dyin' good. Lots of white folks condemn 'em for that, but it's just they way of life.

"Point is, Emmett, don't ever let them take you alive. Kirby, now, they'd probably keep for work or trade. But that's chancy, he being nearabout a man growed." The mountain man tensed a bit, then said, "Look alive, boy, and stay that way. Here they come." He winked at Kirby.

"How do you know that, Preacher?" Kirby asked. "I don't see anything."

"Wind just shifted. Smelled 'em. They close, been easin' up through the grass. Get ready."

Kirby wondered how the old man could smell anything over the fumes from his own body.

Emmett, a veteran of four years of continuous war, could not believe an enemy could slip up on him in open daylight. At the sound of Preacher jacking back the hammer of his Henry .44, Emmett shifted his eyes from his perimeter for just a second. When he again looked back at his field of fire, a big, painted-up buck was almost on top of him. Then the open meadow was filled with screaming, charging Indians.

Emmett brought the buck down with a .44 slug through the chest, flinging the Indian backward, the yelling abruptly cut off in his throat.

The air had changed from the peacefulness of summer quiet to a screaming, gunsmoke-filled hell. Preacher looked at Kirby, who was looking at him, his mouth hanging open in shock, fear, and confusion. "Don't look at me, boy!" he yelled. "Keep them eyes in front of you."

Kirby jerked his gaze to the small creek and the stand of timber that lay behind it. His eyes were beginning to smart from the acrid powder smoke, and his head was aching from the pounding of the Henry .44 and the screaming and yelling. The Spencer Kirby held at the ready was a heavy weapon, and his arms were beginning to ache from the strain.

His head suddenly came up, eyes alert. He had seen movement on the far side of the creek. Right there! Yes, someone, or something, was over there.

I don't want to shoot anyone, the boy thought. *Why can't we be friends with these people?* And that thought was still throbbing in his brain when a young Indian suddenly sprang from the willows by the creek and lunged into the water, a rifle in his hand.

For what seemed like an eternity, Kirby watched the young brave, a boy about his own age, leap and thrash through the water. Kirby jacked back the hammer of the Spencer, sighted in on the brave, and pulled the trigger. The .52-caliber pounded his shoulder, bruising it, for there wasn't much spare meat on Kirby. When the smoke blew away, the young Indian was facedown in the water, his blood staining the stream.

Kirby stared at what he'd done, then fought back waves of sickness that threatened to spill from his stomach.

The boy heard a wild screaming and spun around. His father was locked in hand-to-hand combat with two knife-wielding braves. Too close for the rifle, Kirby clawed his Navy Colt from leather, vowing he would cut that stupid flap from his holster after this was over. He shot one brave through the head just as his father buried the Arkansas Toothpick to the hilt in the chest of the other.

And as abruptly as they came, the Indians were gone, dragging as many of their dead and wounded with them as they could. Two braves lay dead in front of Preacher; two braves lay dead in the shallow ravine with the three men; the boy Kirby had shot lay in the creek, arms outstretched, the waters a deep crimson. The body slowly floated downstream.

Preacher looked at the dead buck in the creek, then at the brave in the wallow with them . . . the one Kirby had shot. He lifted his eyes to the boy.

"Got your baptism this day, boy. Did right well, you did."

"Saved my life, son," Emmett said, dumping the bodies of

the Indians out of the wallow. "Can't call you boy no more, I reckon. You be a man, now."*

As his father talked, the dead Indian in the creek jumped to his feet and charged at Kirby's father's back, his knife held high.

"Dad, look out!" Kirby screamed, pointing at the Indian. . . .

"Wake up, mister, wake up!" Nate said, shaking the man by his shoulders as he thrashed and called out in his sleep.

The man opened his eyes, staring wildly around the bedroom of Nate's cabin.

"What . . . what happened? Where am I?"

"You're safe, friend. You're in my ranch house. You took a bullet to the head in a little fracas last night."

The stranger's eyes grew puzzled, and he looked at Nate as if he'd never seen him before.

"Who are you?" he asked.

"I'm Nate Champion. We met on the trail yesterday, but you never told me your name."

The man on the bed opened his mouth to speak. Then his eyes went vacant and he said nothing.

"Well," Nate said, smiling to reassure the man he meant no harm. "What's your handle, mister?"

"I don't know," the man said as he looked up at Nate with naked fear in his eyes. "I can't remember!"

*The Last Mountain Man

Twelve

Nate pursed his lips for a moment, staring at his new friend, then shrugged and bent to examine the wound on his head.

The bleeding where the bullet had been lodged was stopped, and the swelling seemed to be less pronounced.

"How's your head feel?"

The man gingerly explored the swollen tissue with his fingers, his frightened look gradually fading, to be replaced by a slight grin. "How do you think it feels? Like I've been hit in the head with a sledgehammer."

Nate laughed and motioned for the man to follow him. "Get up and come with me. Maybe some *cafecito* will jog your memory."

"Sounds good to me," the man muttered as he climbed out of bed, wincing as the movement made his head pound again.

In the kitchen of the small ranch house, Nate stirred the coals in the stove and added a couple of sticks of wood. He put a handful of coffee grounds in a pot on the counter, added water, and put it on the stove to cook.

He sat across the table from the stranger and began to make himself a cigarette. When he finished, he handed his cloth pouch of Bull Durham to the man, who did likewise.

When they both had their butts going, Nate asked, "So, you can't remember anything about your past?"

"Not a thing, 'cept I had a dream while I was sleeping earlier. In it, I was a boy about sixteen years old, and the man with me was my dad. He was called Emmett, and he called me Kirby."

"Now we're gettin' somewhere, Kirby. What was the dream about?"

"We were on our way out west, and had got as far as Kansas, when we met up with an old mountain man, called himself Preacher."

When the water on the stove began to boil, Nate got up and crumpled in some egg shells to settle the grounds, then poured them both cups of the steaming, black brew.

While Nate fixed the coffee, Kirby continued to tell him about the Indian attack. "You woke me up just after the Indians had run off."

"You remember dreamin' 'bout your last name?"

"Nope. Kirby is all I can recall."

Nate nodded, taking a drink of his coffee. "Then I guess we'll just have to call you Kirby until the rest comes back to you."

"You think it will?"

Nate shrugged. "Don't rightly know. I had a saddle-partner on a drive once, was kicked in the head by an old, cantankerous mule. He lost his memory for a while, till he got in a bar fight a couple of years later and was slapped upside the head by a .44."

"What happened then?"

Nate grinned. "He remembered everything from before the mule kicked him, but forgot everything in between. Pissed me off, too. I'd loaned him twenty dollars and he said he plumb didn't remember it."

Kirby fingered his head again, a wry look on his face. "So the best I can look forward to is getting my bell rung again, and maybe I'll remember my name?"

Nate laughed. "Oh, I wouldn't go that far. There's a fancy doctor over to Cheyenne, went to some school back East called Harvard. Could be maybe he'll know what to do 'bout all this."

Kirby glanced out the window at the snow that was still

falling, but not so heavily as the night before. "Maybe when the storm let's up, I can take a ride over there and let him take a look at me."

"One thing I do know," Nate added, finishing his coffee in a long swallow. "Whoever you are, you are one mean sonofabitch with a Colt in your hand. I ain't never seen nobody clear leather nor shoot as straight as you before."

As Kirby started to reply, the two men heard hoofbeats outside the cabin. They got up and walked to the door, both men taking their belts and holsters off a peg next to the door and putting them on as they peeked out a window.

"Looks like four of 'em," Nate said.

"They don't have their guns out, so maybe they're not hostile," Kirby said.

Nate's lips curled up in a half smile. "Only one way to find out," he said, and opened the door and walked out on his porch.

Without quite knowing why, Kirby reached down and unhooked the hammer thongs from his Colts as he followed Nate outside.

"Howdy, gents," Nate said to the four men sitting on their horses in front of him, a light snowfall drifting down to settle on their hats and shoulders. "What do you boys want?"

The apparent leader of the group—a short, squat man almost as wide as he was tall, and who must have weighed two hundred pounds—spoke up, "My name's Jeremiah Kidder."

As soon as the man spoke, Nate recognized his voice from the night before. He was the same man who'd called out that Nate had killed his partner.

Nate tensed, knowing that now there was certain to be gunplay.

"Oh, is that so?" Nate said. "And just who might you other men be?"

The man sitting to Kidder's left was much better dressed than the other three. He was wearing a suit coat and vest under a thick, rawhide coat with fur lining, highly polished black boots to his knees, and a derby-style hat. He touched the brim of his hat and said, "Mr. Champion, my name's John Clayburg, and I'm head of the stock detectives for the Wyoming Stock Growers Association."

He inclined his head to a man on the far right, who was tall, over six feet, and wore a large handlebar moustache, had suspenders over a white shirt, and carried a long, Sharps .52-caliber rifle in his saddle boot and a Colt in a holster on his right hip.

"That there is Tom Horn, who works for us, and the man next to him is Bobby Burrough."

Nate thought Horn's eyes were the coldest he had ever seen, and right away marked him as the most dangerous of the four men.

"Just what are you gentlemen doing out here on my ranch?"

Clayburg sat back against the cantle of his saddle and pulled a cigar from his coat pocket. After he lighted it, he pointed over his shoulder to the east. "We found one of our men lying dead on the eastern edge of your spread, a man named Zack Renfield."

He stuck the cigar in the corner of his mouth and stared at Nate. "It appears he's been dead since yesterday. You know anything about his death?"

Nate grinned, but his eyes remained serious. "You say you found this gent on my property?"

"That's right, Champion," Kidder growled, his face screwed up in a scowl. "And he was a good friend of mine."

"Just how'd you manage to find this man?"

Clayburg looked puzzled. "What do you mean?"

Nate waved his hand at the ground. "It appears to me there's been almost two feet of snowfall since the storm blew in last night. A person'd have to either be awfully lucky to find a dead man under all that snow, or know exactly where to look."

Out of the corner of his eye, Nate noticed the man named Tom Horn give a slight smile and nod his head approvingly, as if he thought this was a good point.

Clayburg took his cigar out of his mouth and stared at the

glowing tip for a moment, as if he were thinking of a suitable reply to Nate's logic. "Be that as it may, we did find him, and I'm asking you if you know anything about it."

"Nope, not a thing," Nate replied. "But"—he inclined his head toward Kidder—"you might ask Mr. Kidder there. Since they was such good friends, maybe he can tell you what this Renfield was doin' on my property in the middle of the night in a snowstorm in the first place."

Tom Horn cleared his throat. "Excuse me, Mr. Champion, but who is your friend there? We haven't been introduced."

Nate looked over his shoulder at Kirby, and decided he didn't want him to get any further involved in his troubles than he already was.

"His name's Kirby, an' he's not exactly a friend. He got lost on the range last night, an' I took him in to give him shelter from the storm. He's just passing through the territory."

"You're a liar, Champion," Kidder snarled, his hand dropping toward his right hip. "You shot my friend down in cold blood, an' I'm gonna make you pay!"

Kidder and Burrough suddenly went for their guns, both men grabbing iron as if on a prearranged signal.

Before they had a chance to clear leather, two shots rang out from next to Nate, who'd barely had time to get his hand on his pistol butt himself.

Kirby stood there, both hands filled with Colts, their barrels smoking, as Kidder and Burrough were blown backwards off their saddles. Kidder had a small black hole in the center of his forehead, with the entire back of his skull blown off, while Burrough had a hole in the left center of his chest and a rapidly spreading stain of blood surrounding it. The two men lay sprawled spread-eagled on their backs in the snow, Kidder dead as a stone, and Burrough dying, moaning and whimpering through bloody froth on his lips.

"God damn!" Clayburg yelled, holding his hands high and staring at Kirby through terrified eyes. "You murdered them in cold blood."

Tom Horn just sat on his horse without moving, his hands crossed on the saddle horn, gazing at Kirby appraisingly. "That's a mighty fast draw for a cowboy, Kirby."

Kirby's eyes, cold as a snake's after striking his prey, turned to Horn. "I never said I was a cowboy, Mr. Horn. But you're a witness. Those men tried to draw down on Nate without any cause."

"That's preposterous!" yelled Clayburg, pointing his finger at Kirby. "You drew first—you had to. Nobody's that fast with a gun. Those men didn't even clear leather."

Horn shook his head. "No, he's right, Mr. Clayburg. Kidder and Burrough made the mistake of going for their guns, without knowing just who they was up against."

Nate nodded at the bodies. "You'd better get your men and hightail it off my property, Clayburg."

Horn and Clayburg got off their horses, picked up Kidder and Burrough, and threw them across their mounts, face-down.

As Horn took the reins and started to ride off, he tipped his hat at Nate and Kirby. "Just want you boys to know, I'm not near as dumb as these two were, and now I know what I'm up against."

Kirby holstered his pistols. "Good-bye, Mr. Horn."

Horn shook his head. "Not good-bye, Kirby, so long. We'll meet again, soon."

After the men rode off, Nate looked at Kirby, shaking his head. "I don't know who you are, Kirby, but one thing's certain. You are the fastest man with a gun I've ever seen." He clapped Kirby on the shoulder. "Come on in, an' let's have some coffee and talk about it."

As they sat drinking coffee and smoking cigarettes, Nate said, "You still don't remember nothin' 'bout your previous life?"

"Not a thing," Kirby replied. Then he said, "You'd better fill me in on what's going on around here, since it appears I'm in the middle of it now."

The pot of coffee was empty by the time Nate had finished

outlining the problems between the large ranchers and small, independent ranchers in Johnson County.

"What about those two who were here?" Kirby asked.

"Clayburg is, as he said, head of the stock detectives hired by the WSGA to kill any men they suspect of being rustlers. Tom Horn is famous all across the country, but this is the first time I've seen him."

"Tell me about him."

Nate settled back and crossed his legs, while building another cigarette. "Horn was a legendary Western scout, Pinkerton detective, and range detective. He started as a scout for the army at age sixteen and worked there for 'bout ten years. It was Horn who, after he was made chief of scouts in the Southwest, tracked Geronimo and his band to their hideout in the Sierra Gordo outside of Sonora, Mexico. Horn rode alone into the Indian camp, talked Geronimo into surrendering, and brought him and his men back to the States, where they gave themselves up to the army."

"The man has some *cojones* to take on Geronimo and his tribe all by himself," Kirby observed.

Nate nodded. "After he quit the army, he became a top cowboy, and once won the world's championship in rodeo steer roping. Then he joined the Pinkertons out of Denver, and chased down bank robbers and train thieves all over Colorado and Wyoming."

Nate lighted his cigarette, and as he exhaled a cloud of smoke, said, "My friend, Flat Nose Curry, who rode with the Wild Bunch and the Hole-in-the-Wall gang, told me a typical story of Horn's bravery. One day, Horn was on the trail of Peg-Leg Watson, a notorious outlaw and killer who had recently robbed a mail train. Horn tracked Watson to a high mountain cabin and called out to him, telling Watson he was coming for him. Watson stepped from the cabin with two six-guns in his hands. He stood there, his mouth hanging open as Horn walked toward him across an open field, his Winchester carried limply at his side. Watson was so unnerved by this display, he gave up without firing a shot. Rumor has it, Horn killed more than seventeen men while working for the Pinkertons."

"So," Kirby asked, "why is a Pinkerton man working for the ranchers here in Wyoming."

"He don't work for the Pinkertons no more," Nate said. "He just recently hired out to the WSGA to hunt down rustlers for them. Word is, they're paying him six hundred dollars for each one he kills."

Kirby nodded. "I noticed he's carrying a Sharps buffalo rifle. That how he does it?"

"Yeah. He spends several days tracking anyone he thinks is a rustler, learnin' the man's habits and watchin' him make camp and such. Finally, when he's good an' ready, Horn ambushes the man with his high-powered, long-distance buffalo gun, that Sharps you seen him carryin'."

"I see," said Kirby. "It seems Mr. Horn has lost his stomach for face-to-face encounters."

Nate nodded. "He shore has gotten strange, too. There's been dozens of men found shot to death on the range. Beneath each man's head was a large rock. Horn says it's his trademark, an' that way he'll get credit for the kill when he comes to collect his blood money from the WSGA."

Kirby stared at Nate for a moment with appraising eyes. "You afraid this Horn fellow is going to come after you next?"

Nate looked down into his coffee cup, as if he might find the answer to Kirby's question there. "Well, now that you mention it, I do know the WSGA is gunnin' for me, but whether they'll use Horn, or some other galoot like Frank Canton, I don't know."

Kirby got up from the table and flipped his cigarette butt out the window. "Why don't you just pack up and leave this area, since you know they're going to kill you if you stay?"

Nate grinned, and Kirby realized he was a man after his own heart. "I dunno, just plain stubbornness, I 'spect."

He took a drink of his coffee and stared out the window

over Kirby's shoulder. "The way I figure it, Kirby, once a man starts to runnin' when a little trouble comes his way, 'stead of facin' it and standin' up to it, he might as well keep on runnin, 'cause next time there's more trouble, it's just gonna be that much easier for him to take off again."

He shook his head. "No, this is just somethin' I got to stand up to, or I wouldn't much like the man I see starin' out at me every mornin' from my shavin' mirror."

Thirteen

Casper, Wyoming

Major Wolcott, slapping his leg impatiently with his swagger stick, jutted his chin out and tried to straighten his twisted neck as he spoke angrily at Frank Canton.

"God dammit, Canton, these lazy Texicans of yours have rested and sobered up enough! Don't you think two days lying around and eating up our entire budget for this assault is a bit excessive?"

Canton stared back at Wolcott, unintimidated by his ranting. "Major, I've tried to explain to you: It's a hundred-and-fifty-mile ride to Buffalo from Casper, an' fo₁   past two days we've had a heavy winter storm." He lookeu around at the Texans, most of whom still wore their Texas duds, which were not made for heavy winter riding. "Hell, half these boys would've froze to death had we tried to leave before today."

Unmollified by logic, Wolcott snapped, "Well, be that as it may, could you please get on with it now that the snow has stopped?"

"Why, yes, sir," Canton replied with more than a trace of sarcasm in his voice. "Tom Smith is unloading the horses from the cattle car now. Soon as we get 'em saddled up, we'll be on our way."

Canton grabbed a cup of coffee from the hotel kitchen, using it to keep his hands warm in the barely above-freezing weather, and wandered over to see if Tom was getting the boys set with their horses.

When he arrived, he saw Wolcott was already there, and was raising hell with Smith about something while the country boys from Texas stood around watching.

Just as Canton arrived, Wolcott turned to the Texans and shouted, "For heaven's sake, isn't there a one of you smaller men who will trade with him?"

Canton leaned over to whisper to Smith, "Tom, what the hell's goin' on here?"

Tom grinned and answered back in a low tone, "See that feller over there, the big, fat one with the dumb expression on his face?"

"Yeah."

"His name's Dudley. He can't find a hoss big enough or strong enough to carry his weight, an' none of his friends is willing to trade mounts with him."

Sure enough, Canton could see that the only horse left for Dudley to ride was small-boned through the chest, and was already swaybacked from being broken down in the past. Canton agreed with Wolcott. That horse wouldn't last five miles carrying the big Texan, especially through the ice and snow of the mountains between Casper and Buffalo.

Just as Canton was about to order someone to switch with Dudley, one of the cattlemen's guests, an Englishman named Wallace, offered to trade mounts with Dudley.

Finally, almost an hour after sunup, the expedition, with over fifty riders and three freight wagons full of equipment, supplies, and ammunition and weapons, left Casper and headed up into the hills toward Buffalo.

Within a couple of hours, Canton faced more problems. The heavy freight wagons began to bog down in trails left muddy after the recent snows. The entire first half of the day was spent with men hitching ropes to wagons and practically dragging them the few miles they managed to cover.

It was almost noon, and Canton decided the men had worked

hard enough to deserve some warm food, so he ordered camp be made and breakfast cooked. Wolcott, of course, wanted to press on, but Canton and Smith had begun to just ignore his outbursts, further infuriating him.

The Texans, hungry enough after all their work to eat dirt, tied their horses to a small group of sagebrush near the campfires and rushed over to grab tin plates heaping with scrambled hens' eggs, fatback bacon cut thick, and potatoes chopped up and fried with sliced onions and canned tomatoes.

A wolf howled from someplace nearby, spooking the horses, which jerked back on their reins and uprooted the sagebrush, which had much shallower roots than its cousin bushes in Texas had. It was only a few minutes until almost all of the group's horses were running out of sight. The Texans bolted their food and took off on foot after their mounts, taking almost another two hours to round up the frightened beasts.

More than five hours behind schedule now, Canton pushed the men hard to make up for lost time. When they came to a bridge over a shallow dry gulch, he hurried the drivers of the wagons to get across, causing one of the wagons to break through the flimsy boards and go crashing into the gully below. It took another two hours for the men to tie ropes from their saddle horns to the wagon below and drag it up and out of the shallow ravine.

Canton sat on his horse and watched the men dragging the wagon along the ground, shaking his head, thinking things couldn't get much worse. As if he had tempted fate, the dark, black clouds overhead, heavy with snow, opened up and the snow came down. Not just a regular winter snowstorm, but so heavy and thick he could barely see beyond his horse's head, and within minutes, the faint outlines of the trail were obliterated.

The schedule had initially called for the force to spend their first night on the trail at Robert Tilsdale's ranch, located sixty-five miles out of Casper. As it was, it took the beleaguered force almost two full days and nights to reach this place where the riders and their mounts could get out of the weather for a much-needed rest.

Though they arrived there in mid-afternoon, Canton ordered the men to unsaddle their broncs and get inside the ranch house, where some good, hot food was being prepared. Wolcott, for once seeing the necessity of Canton's decision, didn't argue with his plan.

As dusk fell on the ranch, Canton, too dog-tired to undress, threw himself onto a bunk in a room filled with his exhausted men.

I wonder what else can go wrong on this trip, he thought as he fell into a deep, dreamless sleep.

Fourteen

The man who knew himself only as Kirby tossed and turned in his sleep, dreaming of another time and another place. . . .

The man calling himself Buck West looked briefly at the wanted poster with his picture on it. It read:

Wanted
Dead or Alive
The Outlaw and Murderer
$10,000 Reward
Contact the Sheriff at Bury, Idaho Territory

Buck folded the poster and put it in his coat pocket, then looked back over his shoulder. He had yet to catch a glimpse of his pursuers, but he knew someone was tracking him; he knew it by that itchy feeling between his shoulder blades. Twice in as many days he had stopped and spent several hours checking his back trail. But to no avail. Whoever or whatever it was coming along behind him was lying way back, several miles at least, and they were very good at tracking. They would have to be for Buck not to have spotted them, and Preacher had taught the young man well.

Puzzled, Buck rode on, pushing himself and his horses, skirting the fast-growing towns in the eastern part of the state, staying to the north of them. Because of the man, or men, tracking him, Buck changed his plans and his direction. He rode seemingly aimlessly, first heading straight north, then cutting south into the Bridger Wilderness. He crossed into Idaho Territory and made camp on the north end of Grays Lake. He was running very low on supplies, but living off the land was second nature to Buck, and doing without was merely part of staying alive in a wild and untamed land.

The person following him stayed back, seemingly content to have the young man in sight, electing not to make an appearance, yet.

Mid-afternoon of his second day at Grays Lake, Buck watched his horse, Drifter, prick his ears up, his eyes growing cautious as the stallion lifted his head.

Buck knew company was coming.

A voice helloed the camp.

"If you're friendly, come on in," Buck called. "If you want trouble, I'll give you all you can handle."

Buck knew the grizzled old man slowly riding toward his small fire, but could not immediately put a name to him. The man—anywhere between sixty-five and a hundred and five—dismounted and helped himself to coffee and pan bread and venison. He ate slowly, his eyes appraising Buck without expression. Finally, he belched politely and wiped his hands on greasy buckskins. He poured another cup of coffee and settled back on the ground.

"Don't talk none yet," the old man said. "Jist listen. You be the pup Preacher taken under his wing some years back. Knowed it was you. Ante's been upped some on your head, boy. Nearabouts thirty thousand dollars on you now. You must have a hundred men after you. Hard men, boy. Most of 'em. You good, boy, but you ain't that good. Sooner 'er later, you'll slip up, git tired, have to rest, then they'll git you." He paused to gnaw on another piece of pan bread.

"The point of all this is?" Buck said.

"Tole you to hush up and listen. Jawin' makes me hungry. 'Mong other things. Makes my mouth hurt, too. You got anything to help ease the pain?"

"Pint in that pack right over there." Buck jerked his head.

The old mountain man took two huge swallows of the rye, coughed, and returned to the fire. "Gawddamn farmers and such run us old boys toward the west. Trappin's fair, but they ain't no market to speak of. Ten of us got us a camp just south of Castle Peak, in the Sawtooth. Gittin' plumb borin'. We figured on headin' north in about a week." He lifted his old eyes. "Up toward Bury. We gonna take our time. Ain't no point in gettin' in no lather." He got to his feet and walked toward his horses. "Might see you up there, boy. Thanks for the grub."

"What are you called?" Buck asked.

"Tenneysee," the old man said without looking back. He mounted up and slowly rode back in the direction he'd come.

"You're not any better-lookin' than the last time I saw you!" Buck called to the old man's back, grinning as he spoke.

"Ain't supposed to be," Tenneysee called. "Now git et and git gone. You got trouble on your back trail."

"Yeah, I know!" Buck shouted.

"Worser'n Preacher!" Tenneysee called. "Cain't tell neither of you nuttin'!"

Then he was gone into the timber.

Fifteen minutes later, Buck had saddled Drifter, cinched down the packs on his pack animal, and was gone, riding northwest.

He wondered how many men were trailing him. And how good they were.

He figured he would soon find out.

The year 1874 in most of Idaho Territory was no time for the fainthearted, the lazy, the coward, or the shirker. Idaho Territory was pure frontier, as wild and woolly as the individual wanted to make it. It would be three more long, bloody, and heartbreaking years for the Nez Percé Indians before Chief Joseph would lead his demoralized tribe on the thirteen-hundred-mile retreat to Canada. There, the chief would utter, "I am tired; my heart is sick and sad. From where the sun now stands I will fight no more forever."

But in 1874, the Indians were still fighting all over Idaho Territory, including the Bannocks and Shoshones. It was a time for wary watchfulness.

It had been fourteen years since an expedition led by Captain Elias D. Pierce of California had discovered gold on Orofino Creek, a tributary of the Clearwater River. It wasn't much gold, but it was gold. Thousands had heard the cry and felt the tug of easy riches, and thousands had come. They had poured into the state, expecting to find nuggets lying around everywhere. Many had never been heard from again.

Buck rode through the southern part of the state, heading for the black and barren lava fields called the Craters of the Moon. Even there he was able to see the mute heartbreak of the gold-seekers: the mining equipment lying abandoned and rusting, the dredges in dry creek beds. Now, in early summer, a time when the creeks and rivers were starting to recede, Buck spotted along the banks a miner's boot, a pan. He wondered what stories they could tell.

He rode on, always checking his back trail. He had a vague uneasy feeling that he was still being followed. But he could never spot his follower. And that was cause for alarm, for Buck, even though still a young man, was an expert in surviving in the wilderness.

He skirted south of the still-unnamed village of Idaho Falls, a place that one man claimed "openly wore the worst side out."

Buck rode slowly but steadily, coming up on the south side of the Big Lost, north of the Craters of the Moon. He stopped at a trading post at what would someday be a resort town called Arco. Inside the dark, dirty place, filled with skins and the smell of rotgut whiskey, Buck bought bacon and beans and coffee from a scar-faced clerk. The clerk smelled as bad as his store.

Buck's eyes flicked over several wanted posters tacked to the wall. There he was.

"Last one of them I seen had ten thousand dollars' reward on it," he said to no one in particular. He noticed several men at a corner table ceased their card playing.

"Ante's been upped," the clerk/bartender said with a grunt.

"Man could do a lot with thirty thousand dollars," Buck said. He walked to the bar and ordered whiskey. He didn't really care for the stuff, but he wanted information, and bartenders seldom talked to a non-drinking loafer. "The good stuff," he told the bartender. The man replaced one bottle and reached under the counter for another bottle.

He grinned, exposing blackened stubs of teeth. "This one ain't got no snake heads in it."

Buck lifted the glass. Smelled like bear piss. Keeping his expression noncommittal, he sipped the whiskey. Tasted even worse.

"Have any trouble coming in from the east?" the bartender asked.

"How'd you know I came in from the east?"

"That's the way you rode in."

"Seen some Blackfoot two-three days ago. But they didn't see me. I didn't hang around long."

"Smart."

"You see four men, riding together?" the voice asked from behind Buck, from the card table.

"Yeah, and so did the Blackfeet."

"Crap! You reckon the Injuns got 'em?"

"I reckon so. I didn't hang around to see."

"You mean you jist rode off without lendin' a hand?"

"One more wouldn't have made any difference," Buck said quietly, knowing what was coming.

"Then I reckon that makes you a coward, don't it?" the cardplayer asked, standing up.

Buck slowly placed the shot glass of bear piss back on the rough bar. He eyeballed the man. Two guns worn low and tied down. The leather hammer thongs off. "Either that or careful."

"You know what I think, Slick? I think it makes you yellow."

"Well, I'll tell you what I think," Buck said. "I think you don't know your bunghole from your mouth."

The man flushed in the dim light of the trading post. His dirty hands hovered over his guns. "I think I'll jist kill you for that."

"Bet or fold," Buck said.

The man's hands dipped down. Buck's right-hand .44 roared. The gunhand was dead before he hit the floor, the slug taking him in the center of the chest, exploding his heart.

"I never even seen the draw," the bartender said, his voice hushed and awe-filled.

"Any of you other boys want to ante up in this game?" Buck asked.

None did.

The dead man broke wind as escaping gas left his cooling body.

"He were my partner," a man still seated at the table said. "But he were wrong this time. I lay claim to his pockets."

"Suits me," Buck said. No one had even seen him holster his .44. "He have a name?"

"Big Jack. From up Montana way. Never spoke no last name. Who you be?"

"Buck West. I been trackin' the man on that wanted poster for the better part of six months."

Big Jack's partner visibly relaxed. "Us, too. I would ask if you wanted some company, but you look like you ride alone."

"That's right."

"Don't reckon you'd give us a hand diggin' the hole for Jack?"

"I don't reckon so."

"Cain't much blame you."

"Bury him out back," the bartender said. "Deep. If he smells any worser dead than alive I'll have to move my place of business."*

Kirby awoke and sat up in bed, the dream so real he was sweating from the closed-in heat of the tavern and could still taste the bitter whiskey and the smell of death on his tongue.

So, he thought, *I was once called Buck West, and there was a reward on my head of thirty thousand dollars.* He grunted as he slipped out of bed, quickly putting his clothes and boots on to ward off the chill of the cabin. *I must've been some bad hombre to warrant that kind of reward money on my head.*

He walked into the kitchen, dipped some water out of the pail on the counter, and put it and a handful of coffee grounds in the pot, stoked the embers in the stove, added a few sticks of wood, and put the pot on the stove to boil.

A dim memory of an old man in dirty buckskins sitting across a campfire from him appeared in his mind. "The trick to makin' good *cafecito* is, it don't take near as much water as you think it do," the man was saying, grinning to show yellow teeth, worn down almost to the gums.

The name Puma Buck came to Kirby, but the memory faded almost as quickly as it came.

Nate walked into the room, buttoning his shirt and yawning prodigiously. "Mornin', Kirby," he said, rubbing his eyes.

Kirby looked back over his shoulder. "Morning, Nate."

"Coffee 'bout ready?"

"I reckon so," Kirby replied, slipping into the accent Buck West had used in his dream.

Nate raised his eyebrows at Kirby, but took the coffeepot and poured them both steaming cups without remarking on

*Return of the Mountain Man

the change in the way Kirby talked. It was amazing. The man sounded like a completely different person.

"You sleep good?" Nate asked, handing a cup to Kirby.

"I had another dream, about my past."

"Oh?"

"Yeah. At one time I went by the name Buck West. Had wanted posters out on me."

Nate stared at Kirby for a moment, then shrugged. "Hell, Kirby. Plenty of men in this part of the country had paper out on them before. That don't mean nothin'."

Kirby smiled and sipped his coffee. The more he was around Nate, the more he liked the man. They had become good friends in the few days Kirby had been staying with him. Somehow, Kirby knew he was used to riding alone, but he thought if he ever had a partner, he would hope it would be a man like Nate. He was a good cowboy, handled steers like he was born to it, but more importantly, he was a *good* man, clear to the bone.

"You feel like doin' some work today?" Nate asked. "I got some beeves need movin' from one pasture to another 'fore the next storm comes through."

"Sure, only I require my wages in advance."

Nate raised his eyebrows.

"You got to feed me some bacon and eggs before we round up any cattle. A man can't work on an empty stomach."

Nate grinned. "Tell you what. I'll cook if you'll go down to the stream in front of the house and fill up that pail of water."

Kirby shook his head and grabbed the pail. "You're not much of a friend, sending a fellow out into the cold this early in the morning."

Nate laughed. "Just be glad we don't have no cows to milk nor chickens to feed."

Kirby smiled as he opened the door, his face stinging from the bitter cold of the predawn in a Wyoming winter.

Fifteen

Robert Tilsdale, Frank Canton, Major Wolcott, and Tom Smith were sitting at the kitchen table of Tilsdale's ranch, eating supper and making plans for the attack on Buffalo. They intended to storm the town, kill the sheriff and his deputies, and take over the militia arms stored in the courthouse there. Once they had control of the town, they could proceed to move on to the neighboring Converse and Natrona Counties, eliminating those on their "dead list" as they went.

Canton knew a standing order to militia units to answer only headquarter's orders for assistance and not county officials' calls for help effectively isolated Sheriff Red Angus and his deputies in Buffalo.

Suddenly the door burst open and a man rushed into the room, his shoulders still covered with ice and snow from his evening ride.

"Mr. Tilsdale, I got some news."

"Who is this man, and what does he mean by interrupting our supper?" the testy Wolcott asked.

"He's one of my range foremen," Tilsdale said. "Go on, Johnny, what's your news?" Tilsdale asked the man, who was still standing in the doorway, his hat in his hands.

"I got word there's a band of rustlers holed up at the old KC ranch, runnin' cattle on the ranges there. Some of the boys an' me want to head on over there and kill 'em."

Several of the Wyoming stockmen from Cheyenne, who

were sitting in the other end of the room, shouted out their agreement with this plan.

Canton shook his head. "I don't think that'd be wise, boys. Time is short, and we need to get on over to Buffalo and secure the town 'fore they find out we're comin'."

"Hell," Wolcott said, seizing on any opportunity to disagree with Canton. "With the number of men at our disposal, it'd only take a couple of hours to rid the county of some of these rustling scum."

Canton eyed Tom Smith, who could usually be counted on to agree with him against Wolcott. "What do you think, Tom? I'm worried that the longer we delay getting to Buffalo, the more chance someone there's gonna find out about us comin', an' I don't relish givin' up the element of surprise."

Smith shrugged. "Like the man says, Frank, we got over fifty hands, so it shouldn't take overly long to accomplish the deed." He grinned. "And it means that many less thieves we're gonna have to kill later."

Canton turned to Tilsdale. "Just how far is it to the KC ranch?"

"It's only fifteen miles, about a hour and a half ride is all."

Reluctantly, Canton finally agreed to the assault. He ordered the Texans to saddle up and get ready to ride.

By the time the horses were saddled and the wagons made ready for the trip, it was almost midnight. Finally, after what seemed to be an eternity, Canton and Smith, with Wolcott and his Wyoming stockmen riding along, were ready to leave for the fifteen-mile trip to the KC ranch.

As Canton stepped into his stirrups and swung up into his saddle, the light snowfall of earlier in the evening had turned into a full-fledged winter storm, with driving snow mixed with sleet and temperatures dropping faster than a cowboy's pants in a bawdy house.

Canton leaned over to speak to Smith, and had to shout to be heard over the roaring wind. "I'm tellin' you, Tom, I got a real bad feelin' 'bout this little jaunt."

Smith pulled his hat down tight against the wind. "I gotta say, Frank, I'm beginnin' to agree with you."

Earlier that same evening, at the KC ranch, Kirby and Nate Champion and a cowboy friend of Nate's named Nick Ray were just sitting down to supper when a shout came from in front of the cabin, "Yo, the ranch house!"

Nate buckled on his belt and holster and pulled his six-shooter out as he went to the door. Cautiously, he opened it a crack and looked out into the gathering darkness.

After a moment, he looked back over his shoulder at Kirby and Nick. "Looks like a single man on a horse."

Nick Ray, who like Nate was on the Cheyenne cattlemen's "death list," pulled his pistol out. "You don't think it's one of those stock detectives of the WSGA been on the prowl for us, do you?"

Nate shook his head. "Naw, this guy looks older'n dirt."

Ray shook his head. "Can't be too careful, Nate. I heard they kilt Bobby Banion the other day. Said they caught him rustlin' cattle." He turned and spat, showing his disgust. "Hell, old Bobby didn't have but fifteen head to his name, and they was all mavericks from the open range."

Nate grunted. "I hadn't heard 'bout Bobby. What's that make, fifteen or twenty they killed in the last year?"

"At least that many," Ray replied, rearing back the hammer on his Colt.

Nate waved his hand at Ray. "Put that away, Nick. This looks like an old mountain man, one of the trappers that live up in the mountains. I don't 'spect he'll be any trouble."

He walked out on the porch, followed by Kirby and Ray, who still had his pistol out but kept it pointing at the ground.

Sitting on a ragged-looking horse was a man who appeared to be in his seventies at least, wearing dirty buckskins covered with a bearskin coat, a Sharps .52-caliber buffalo rifle across his saddle horn.

"Howdy, gents," the old man said, dipping his head in greeting. " 'Pears there's a hell of a storm comin', an' I got caught out here on your range without any suitable cover to make camp. I's wonderin' if'n I might bunk me an' my hoss in your barn for the night, or till the storm blows over."

Nate nodded. "Sure thing, mister—only put the horse in the barn and you can come on into the cabin here. We got plenty of room and hot coffee's on the stove."

The stranger grinned, showing a couple of stubs of yellowed teeth in an otherwise-empty mouth. He touched the front of his wide-brimmed hat and walked his pony toward the barn.

After he joined them in the ranch house, Nate asked the man his name.

"Don't rightly recollect my Christian name, been so many years since I used it, but my friends calls me Bear Claw," he said, reaching up to finger a rawhide necklace around his neck adorned with rows of bear claws hanging from it.

"What are you doin' way out here on the open range?" Nate asked, pouring the man a cup of coffee.

"I been trapping beaver and such up in the mountains, an' ran outta tobaccy. I was on my way into Buff'lo to buy me a couple'a twists of Bull Durham an' some Arbuckle's coffee when my old nose smelt the comin' storm."

He bent his head to drink the coffee, then looked up and smiled in delight. "Boy, that tastes mighty good . . . bit weak, but mighty good nonetheless. I been havin' to make do with acorn coffee, an' it do leave something of a bitter taste on the tongue."

Ray built himself a cigarette and stared at the old man. "I thought all the mountain men were dead by now."

Bear Claw chuckled. "Well, there be fewer of us than there used to be, but there still be a few of us old beavers alive and kickin' up in the high lonesome."

"I had a dream about a couple of mountain men I used to know the other day," Kirby said, dishing out some beans and fried fatback onto Bear Claw's plate.

As the old man shoveled the mixture into his mouth, he glanced up at Kirby. "Who might that be, boy?"

"They were called Preacher and Puma Buck."

The mountain man's eyes widened in surprise. Then he smiled and his gaze became far away as if he were remembering old friends.

"Gawd, I hadn't heard those names in quite a while."

"Did you know them?" Kirby asked, leaning forward, hoping he might learn something about his past life.

"Hell, boy. Everbody who lived in the mountains knew Preacher. He was one of the first men to come out here, back when there weren't no other white men for a hundred miles."

"Is he still alive?" Kirby asked.

Bear Claw pursed his lips. "Don't rightly know. He'd have to be over ninety years by now." Then he winked. "Course, he was a tough old bird. Had so many bullets and arrowheads in him, he'd sink like a rock if he ever got in the water, which to my certain knowledge he never did."

"How about Puma Buck?"

Bear Claw's eyes looked sad. "Old Puma got kilt a couple of years back, but I heared he took six or seven good men with him 'fore they got him. He was ridin' with a man Preacher raised from a pup, helpin' him out in some trouble he was havin'."

"How'd it happen, old-timer?" Nate asked.

Bear Claw leaned back in his chair. "My mouth's gittin' kind'a dry from all this jawin'. If'n you got somethin' a mite stronger than this coffee, an' some makin's fer a cigarette, I'll tell ya' the tale the way it was tole to me."

After Nate poured some whiskey into his coffee, and Ray gave him a cigarette, Bear Claw's eyes got a faraway look in them and he started to talk. . . .

Puma Buck walked his horse slowly through underbrush and light forest timber in the foothills surrounding Murdock's spread. His mount was one they'd hired in Pueblo on arriving, and it wasn't as surefooted on the steep slopes as his paint pony back home was, so he was taking it easy and getting the feel of his new ride.

He kept a sharp lookout toward Murdock's ranch house almost a quarter of a mile below. He was going to make damned sure none of those *buscaderos* managed to get the drop on his friends. He rode with his Sharps .52–caliber laid across his saddle horn, loaded and ready for immediate action.

Several times Puma had seen men ride up to the ranch house and enter, only to leave after awhile, riding off toward herds of cattle, which could be seen on the horizon. Puma figured they were most likely the legitimate punchers Murdock had working his cattle, and not the gun hawks he'd hired to take down Puma's friends. A shootist would rather take lead poisoning than lower himself to herd beeves.

Off to the side, Puma could barely make out the riverbed, dry now, that ran through Murdock's place. He could see on the other side of Murdock's ranch house a row of freshly dug graves, some of them his doing, and Smoke's way of depriving the man of water for his horses and cattle.

As Puma pulled his canteen out and uncorked the top, ready to take a swig, he saw a band of fifteen or more riders burning dust toward the ranch house from the direction of Pueblo. Evidently they were additional men Murdock had hired to replace those he and Smoke and Joey Wales had slain in their midnight raid.

"Uh-huh," he muttered. "I'll bet those *bandidos* are fixin' to put on the war paint and make a run over to Smoke's place."

He swung out of his saddle and crouched down behind a fallen tree, propping the big, heavy Sharps across the rough bark. He licked his finger and wiped the front sight with it, to make it stand out more when he needed it. He got himself into a comfortable position and laid out a box full of extra shells next to the gun on the tree within easy reach. He figured he might need to do some quick reloading when the time came.

After about ten minutes the gang of men Puma was observing arrived at the front of the ranch house, and two figures Puma took to be Murdock and Vasquez came out of the door to address them. He couldn't make out their faces at the distance, but they had an unmistakable air of authority about them.

As the rancher began to talk, waving his hands toward Smoke's ranch, Puma took careful aim, remembering he was shooting downhill and needed to lower his sights a bit, the natural tendency being to overshoot a target lower than you are.

He took a deep breath and held it, slowly increasing pressure on the trigger, so when the explosion came it would be a surprise to him and he wouldn't have time to flinch and throw his aim off.

The big gun boomed and shot a sheet of fire two feet out of the barrel, slamming back into Puma's shoulder and almost knocking his skinny frame over. Damn, he had almost forgotten how the big Sharps kicked when it delivered its deadly cargo.

The targets were a little over fifteen hundred yards from Puma, a long range even for the remarkable Sharps. It seemed a long time, but was only a little over five seconds before one of the men on horseback was thrown from his mount to lie sprawled in the dirt. The sound was several seconds slower reaching the men, and by then Puma had jacked another round in the chamber and fired again. By the time the group knew they were being fired upon, two of their number were dead on the ground. Just as they ducked and whirled, looking for the location of their attacker, another was knocked off his bronc, his arm almost blown off by the big .52–caliber slug traveling at over two thousand feet per second.

The outlaws began to scatter, some jumping from their horses and running into the house, while others just bent over their saddle horns and burned trail dust away from the area. A couple of brave souls aimed rifles up the hill and fired, but the range was so far for ordinary rifles that Puma never even saw where the bullets landed.

He fired another couple of rounds into the house, one of which penetrated wooden walls, striking a man inside in the thigh, and then Puma figured he had done enough for the time being. Now he had to get back to Smoke and tell him Murdock was ready to make his play, or would be as soon as he rounded up the men Puma had scattered all over the countryside.

Several of the riders had ridden over toward Smoke's ranch, and were now between Puma and home. "Well, shit, old beaver. Ya knew it was about time for ya to taste some lead," he mumbled to himself. He packed his Sharps in his saddle boot and opened his saddlebags. He withdrew two Colt Army .44's to match the one in his holster and made sure they were all loaded up six and six, then stuffed the two extras in his belt. He tugged his hat down tight and eased up into the saddle, grunting with the effort.

Riding slow and careful, he kept to heavy timber until he came to a group of six men standing next to a drying riverbed, watering their horses in one of the small pools remaining.

There was no way to avoid them, so he put his reins in his teeth and filled both hands with iron. It was time to dance with the devil, and Puma was going to strike up the band. He kicked his mount's flanks and bent low over his saddle horn as he galloped out of the forest toward the gunnies below.

One of the men, wearing an eye patch, looked up in astonishment at the apparition wearing buckskins and war paint charging them, yelling and whooping and hollering as he rode like the wind.

"Goddamn, boys, it's that old mountain man!" One-Eye Jackson yelled as he drew his pistol.

All six men crouched and began firing wildly, frightened by the sheer gall of a lone horseman to charge right at them.

Puma's pistols exploded, spitting fire, smoke, and death ahead of him. Two of the gunslicks went down immediately, .44 slugs in their chests.

Another jumped into the saddle, turned tail, and rode like hell away from this madman who was bent on killing all of them.

One-Eye took careful aim and fired, his bullet tearing through Puma's left shoulder muscle, twisting his body and almost unseating him.

Puma straightened, gritting his teeth on the leather reins while he continued firing with his right-hand gun, his left arm hanging useless at his side. His next two shots hit their targets, taking one gunny in the face and the other in the stomach, doubling him over to leak guts and shit and blood in the dirt as he fell.

One-Eye's sixth and final bullet in his pistol entered Puma's horse's forehead and exited out the back of its skull to plow into Puma's chest. The horse lowered its head and somersaulted as it died, throwing Puma spinning to the ground. He rolled three times, tried to push himself to his knees, then fell face-down in the dirt, his blood pooling around him.

One-Eye Jackson looked around at the three dead men lying next to him and muttered a curse under his breath. "Jesus, that old fool had a lotta hair to charge us like that." He shook his head as he walked over to Puma's body and aimed his pistol at the back of the mountain man's head. He eared back the hammer and let it drop. His gun clicked . . . all chambers empty.

One-Eye leaned down and rolled Puma over to make sure he was dead. Puma's left shoulder was canted at an angle where the bullet had broken it, and on the right side of his chest was a spreading scarlet stain.

Puma moaned and rolled to the side. One-Eye Jackson chuckled. "You're a tough old bird, but soon's I reload, I'll put one in your eye."

Puma's eyes flicked open and he grinned, exposing blood-stained teeth. "Not in this lifetime, sonny," and he swung his right arm out from beneath his body. In it was his buffalo-skinning knife.

One-Eye grunted in shock and surprise as he looked down at the hilt of Puma's long knife sticking out of his chest. "Son of a . . ." he rasped, then died.

Puma lay there for a moment. Then with great effort he pushed himself over so he faced his beloved mountains. "Boys," he whispered to all the mountain men who had gone before him, "git the *cafecito* hot. I'm comin' to meet ya."*

Kirby, with eyes full of tears, felt himself strangely affected by the story Bear Claw was telling. He noticed the mountain man staring at him, a strange look on his face.

Nate, also affected by the courage the story evidenced, nodded. "That's some tale, old-timer. Puma Buck had a set of *cojones* on him, that's for sure."

Bear Claw struggled to his feet, his ancient joints cracking with arthritis, and walked to the stove to pour himself another cup of coffee.

Kirby stood and went to stand next to him, his cup held out for a refill.

Bear Claw glanced at the others and saw they weren't paying attention, so he whispered, "I don't know what's goin' on or why yore callin' yourself Kirby, big fellah, but we need to talk . . . private-like."

Kirby straightened, his heart racing. It sounded like the old mountain man might know something of his past. "Do you know who I am?" Kirby asked, whispering, like Bear Claw.

Bear Claw nodded, winked, and said, "In the mornin'." He drank his coffee down and in a louder voice said, "It's a mite past this old beaver's bedtime, boys. If'n ya don't mind, I'm gonna lay down in that corner over yonder and git me some shut-eye."

Nate and Nick Ray both stood up, Nate muffling a prodi-

Honor of the Mountain Man

gious yawn with his fist. "Me, too, Bear Claw. I'll see you gents in the mornin'."

After the lanterns were extinguished and everyone was bedded down, Kirby lay thinking for a long time about an old mountain man named Puma Buck, whose story had caused an inexplicable ache in his heart.

Sixteen

The ride from Casper to the KC ranch was a living hell for the expeditionary force led by Frank Canton. The temperature had dropped into minus figures, and they were riding straight into the face of a howling north wind mixed with snow and ice.

As the men rode, hunched over against the cold and wind, they became coated with ice so thick they could barely move their arms and their hands froze to the reins. Several times horses faltered, falling to their knees, exhausted by the continual battle against the elements.

Finally, after four hours on a trip that was supposed to take only an hour and a half, Canton called a halt. He instructed the men to build several large campfires and try to thaw themselves and their animals out. He knew if he didn't stop and let his men and their horses warm up and eat something, he was going to lose them all.

Sitting so close to the large fire that his clothes were steaming, Canton wrapped blue, bloodless hands around a hot tin cup of coffee and enjoyed warmth for the first time in several hours. Trying to keep his teeth from chattering, he glanced at Major Wolcott next to him. "So, this little jaunt is gonna be like a walk in the park, huh?"

Wolcott, sitting with his back ramrod straight, icicles hanging from his handlebar moustache and muttonchop sideburns and whiskers, gave Canton a steely look, then dipped his head and went back to drinking his coffee without answering.

Canton leaned toward the man sitting on his other side, Tom Smith, and said, "Tommy, do you think the men will be in any shape for a fight after ridin' through this storm all night and half freezin' to death?"

Smith pursed his lips, head down as he built himself a cigarette and lighted it off a burning branch from the fire.

"Don't rightly know, Frank." He looked around at the men, standing with their hands outstretched toward the fires they had built, most with their horses next to them so they could warm up too. "I guess if we don't get in no hurry and give them plenty of time to eat some hot food and drink lots of coffee, they'll be all right. They's all tough men, hard clear to the bone. That's why we picked 'em, 'member?"

Canton nodded, still unsure. It all depended on how many rustlers were holed up at the KC ranch. At the rate they were going, it was going to be dawn before they got there and were ready to fight, so the surprise of a night attack was lost to them due to the weather. He sure didn't relish trying an assault on a well-fortified ranch filled with dangerous criminals, especially if he and his men were outside exposed to the worst winter storm in his memory.

After an hour spent filling his men's bellies with hot beans and thick slices of fried fatback bacon and gallons of steaming coffee, Canton figured it was time to move on. They were still at least two hours away from the KC ranch, and he knew if there was any chance of their attack succeeding, they had to be in place around the ranch by dawn.

They barely made it, having to stop several times to pull the wagons out of deep snowdrifts with ropes tied to saddle horns. Just as the eastern sky began to lighten, they arrived at the cabin. They were in luck, for with the dawn, the storm began to wane and as the snow slowed to a trickle, the temperature began to rise to bearable levels.

Canton had his men surround the cabin and barn, concealing

themselves in a stable, along a creek bed, and in a wooded ravine in back of the house. There were no signs of life in the cabin, and the barn, like most in the high country, was built right next to the house so they couldn't count the horses to see how many men they were facing.

Canton settled down for a cold wait to see what the dawn would bring.

In the ranch house, the men began to stir. Bear Claw, fully dressed, went to the kitchen to start a fire in the stove and make some coffee as the others pulled on their clothes. He lifted the dipper out of the tin bucket on the counter, and noticed there was only a couple of inches of water remaining.

"Boys," Bear Claw said, his voice husky with phlegm and more talking than he was used to in his lonely existence, "I'm gonna go to the crick an' git some water fer *cafecito.*"

He walked out the door and disappeared into the early morning fog.

After twenty minutes went by without his return, Kirby could wait no longer. He was desperate to talk to the old man and find out about his past, maybe even his real name. Out of long habit, without remembering why, Kirby buckled on his two pistols, stuck his bowie knife in the scabbard he wore on his belt in the back, and went to find the mountain man.

He struggled through drifts of snow almost to his waist, but had no trouble following the old man's tracks in the fresh snow.

As he entered the wooded area next to the stream running in front of the cabin, two men with drawn pistols slipped from behind trees and eared back the hammers.

"Hold it right there, mister," one of the men said.

Kirby's hand hovered near the butt of his gun, but he realized they had the drop on him. He looked behind them and saw Bear Claw, men on each arm, shake his head, telling him not to resist.

Kirby and Bear Claw were taken deeper into the woods to

the leader of the group. A tall man walked up and said, "I'm Frank Canton. Who are you men?"

The mountain man leaned to the side and spat. "My name's Bear Claw, if'n it's any of yore business."

Canton turned to Kirby. "And you?"

"My name's Kirby."

"First or last?"

"I don't rightly know," Kirby answered.

Canton narrowed his eyes. "Well, where are you from and what are you doin' here with this band of rustlers?"

"I don't know that either."

"You don't know much, do you, mister?" Canton said, glaring suspiciously at Kirby.

Kirby shrugged, his jaws tight with anger. "I may not know much, but I'm not the one askin' damn fool questions."

As Canton put his hand on his pistol, Bear Claw spoke up. "We's jest a couple 'a travelers, tooken rufuge in the cabin from the storm. We'uns don't know nothin' 'bout no rustlin' goin' on nor 'bout the men in the cabin."

Kirby looked at him, but the old man just gave a tiny shake of his head, warning Kirby not to speak.

One of the stockmen who came with Major Wolcott spoke up. "He's right, Frank. I lived here all my life an' I never seen neither of these men before. They got to be what they say they are, and neither of their names are on our list."

With a final glare at Kirby, Canton said, "All right. Take 'em out to the stable and tie 'em up good and tight. It won't be long before someone else comes out to see what happened to 'em."

About fifteen minutes later, Nick Ray walked out the door and stood there, looking around, searching for Bear Claw and Kirby.

In the stable loft, Major Wolcott nodded to a redhead called the Texas Kid, who had his rifle trained on the unsuspecting cowboy. He let the hammer down and his rifle exploded, shattering the early morning quiet.

As the rifle shot echoed through the frigid air, his slug staggered Ray, and it was followed by a sudden fusillade from the vigilantes hidden in the creek bed.

Nate Champion ran out the front door, six-shooter in hand. As Ray crawled back toward him, mortally wounded, Champion dragged his friend inside, slammed the door, and began to return fire. He arranged his weapons around the room, next to the windows, and made piles of ammunition next to each one for quick reloading.

After going to each of his windows and firing a couple of shots to keep the attackers back, Nate went to Nick and knelt by his side. The man was semi-conscious and moaning, his blood leaking from several wounds to form a pool around him on the wooden floor of the cabin. *At least there's no spurters,* Nate thought. *He's liable to live a while yet.*

Nate fetched a blanket and pillow from his bed and brought them back to the main room. He gently wrapped the blanket around Nick and put the pillow under his head.

Nick's eyes opened, and for a moment were clear. "Thanks, pardner," he mumbled through dry lips.

"Sure thing, partner," Nate answered. "Soon's I take care of these bastards, I'm gonna get you on into Buffalo and have the doc take a look at you. He'll fix you right up."

Nick groaned as a spasm of pain hit, then managed a small grin. "Don't be blowin' smoke at an old pal, Nate. We been friends too long. I know I'm fixin' to ride the long trail."

Nate, unable to answer, just held his friend's shoulder.

"Now," Nick continued, closing his eyes, "you get back to yore fightin' an' try an' kill a few of those sons of bitches."

Nate crawled toward a back window, falling flat once and covering his head as a number of bullets smacked into the side of the house, several punching through thin areas in the wood to scream through the air and embed themselves in an opposite wall.

He put his Winchester to his shoulder and aimed carefully at the copse of trees down near the creek. When he saw a flash of light from a gun firing, he squeezed the trigger. The rifle slammed back into his shoulder and belched flame and smoke. As the explosion echoed in the room, it was answered by a distant yelp of pain. *Must've winged one of them,* he thought. *Good, maybe it'll keep the bastards from rushing the cabin for a while.*

All morning long Nate held off the attackers. Intending to leave word of what had happened to his friends in Johnson County, whenever there was a lull in the fighting, he pulled a battered notebook from a drawer in the kitchen. During breaks in the fighting, he scribbled in it with the stub of a pencil, keeping a running account of the siege.

"Me and Nick was getting breakfast when the attack took place," Nate began. He described Bear Claw and Kirby's disappearance, and still early in the day he wrote, "Boys, there is bullets coming like hail. They are shooting from the stable and river and back of the house."

Two hours later, Nate looked up from reloading one of his pistols as Nick groaned and tried to sit up, throwing the blanket off. Nate scrambled on hands and knees to his side.

"Partner, you got to be still," Nate said. "You're gonna get those wounds to bleeding again if you keep moving around like this."

Nick stared up at Nate, eyes squinted against the pain. "I think it's 'bout time for me to leave, Nate." As bloody froth oozed from his lips, Nick winked. "I'll see you on the other side of the mountain, kid."

He doubled over, holding his gut as he coughed twice, and then he became limp in Nate's arms.

Nate wrote a terse note. "Nick is dead. He died about nine o'clock. I see smoke down at the stable. I think they have fired it. I don't think they intend to let me get away this time."

He continued to scrabble around the cabin, sometimes crawling, sometimes running bent over at the waist, firing a few shots from one window, then rushing to another to do the same thing. He had little hope of hitting anything—the men were too far away for a good shot—but he wanted them to know he was ready for them if they tried a frontal assault.

Toward noon, he added to his journal. "Boys, I feel pretty lonesome just now. I wish there was someone here with me so we could watch all sides at once."

Wolcott's hammer clicked on an empty chamber, and he backed away from his window in the stable and began to punch out his empties and replace them with fresh cartridges. He ambled over to stand behind Frank Canton, who wasn't shooting at the cabin but just watching the action.

"Canton, why don't you have your men rush the house? Our two prisoners tell us Champion's alone in there, so it ought to be an easy matter to storm the place."

Canton looked back over his shoulder at the major. "I'll tell you what, Major. Me and the Texicans will give you some coverin' fire, an' you can lead the other stockmen from Cheyenne in a rush on the ranch. How's that?"

Wolcott's face reddened. "But that's what we're paying the Texicans for," he snapped, his teeth almost clicking as he bit off the words.

Canton shook his head. "No, you're payin' 'em to come down here and help you kill your competitors, not to get killed in a foolish attack on one lone gunman who's holed up tighter than a tick on a coon hound. He ain't goin' nowheres long as we got him surrounded, so we'll just wait him out for a spell."

"Just how long do you intend to wait, Canton?" the major asked, jamming the last bullet into his pistol and snapping the loading gate shut.

Canton stared out the window, turning his back on Wolcott. "Until 'bout dark. If we haven't gotten him by then, I'll have the boys fire the cabin."

At about three o'clock, Nate noted in his journal, "A man in a buckboard and another on a horse went by the ranch and were fired on. I seen lots of men come out on horses on the other side of the river and take after them."

Nate's last entry was made that evening. "Well, they have just got through shelling the house like hail. I heard them splitting wood. I guess they are going to fire the house tonight. I think I will make a break when night comes, if alive. Goodbye, boys, if I never see you again."

Nate carefully signed the final entry in his journal "Nathan D. Champion," and put the notebook under the boards of the floor where it wouldn't burn if the house was fired.

As the day got later, and burning torches were thrown on the roof, Nate loaded his two pistols, kicked out the door, and made a run for it.

A man stepped from behind a tree and aimed a rifle at Nate, and was hit in the chest by a snap shot from one of Nate's pistols.

The rest of the Regulators opened fire. Two bullets took Nate in the chest, spinning him around, and another took him low in the back. As he sank to his knees, still firing, Nate pulled his triggers on empty chambers, dying the same way he lived, fighting to the end.

From behind the stable, Kirby watched his friend cut down and struggled against his ropes. "Dirty bastards," he mumbled through clenched teeth.

Sitting next to him in the snow, Bear Claw whispered, "Hush, son." His old eyes were damp from watching Nate die with such courage. "We'll git our chance, but now ain't the time. Keep your pie-hole shut an' maybe we'll live to git some revenge for your friend."

After the cabin burned itself out, the Regulators gathered around Nate's body. Canton nudged him with a boot, making sure he was dead.

He turned to Kirby and Bear Claw. "Give these two their guns back and let 'em get on their way. We're done here."

Kirby strapped on his pistols, having to resist with all his might an urge to draw and put a window in Canton's skull for what he'd done.

"You mind if we bury this man?" he asked.

"Why, I thought you said he weren't no friend of yours?"

"Any man who shares his cabin with me durin' a storm is a friend," Bear Claw said, "an' he deserves a proper buryin' no matter what else he's done."

Canton waved a dismissive hand. "I don't care what you do to his carcass." He turned to the Regulators. "Come on, boys, we got business in Buffalo an' we're already a day late 'cause of this outlaw."

As the group of men rode off, Bear Claw pulled a short-handled shovel from one of the packs on his packhorse.

Kirby stepped over and took the shovel from him. "Why don't you make us some coffee on the campfire, while I dig Nate's grave?"

Bear Claw glanced at Nate's body, took his hat off, and said, "You died real good, son. Yore daddy'd be right proud of you."

Seventeen

After Bear Claw and Kirby lowered Nate into the frozen ground, covered his body with dirt, and topped the grave with stones to keep scavengers from it, they began the grisly task of searching through the still-smoldering ruins of the ranch house for Nick Ray's body.

Surprisingly, the fire had burnt itself out before doing too much damage to the floor and lower walls. They found Nick under some roof timbers that had fallen in on him. His corpse wasn't completely burned, and still showed the numerous bullet holes where he'd been gunned down.

As Kirby walked around to the other side of Ray's body to help carry it outside, his foot fell through some floorboards.

When he pulled his boot out of the hole in the floor, Kirby saw Nate's journal lying there. He picked it up and with a glance at Bear Claw, began to read it out loud.

After he was finished, he turned sad eyes on Bear Claw. "Nate left this so the other ranchers around here would know what happened to him."

Bear Claw nodded, glancing back over his shoulder at Nate's grave. "The boy was born with lots of hair on 'im, that's fer sure."

"As soon as we get Nick buried, I'm going to take this into Buffalo and make sure Nate's friends get a chance to read it."

"You think it'll make any difference?" Bear Claw asked.

"If this notebook doesn't make the other ranchers band together to fight Canton and his men, then they deserve to lose this war," Kirby answered.

At the same time Bear Claw and Kirby were burying Nick Ray at the KC ranch, the two men in the wagon who'd ridden past the ranch were arriving in Buffalo. They'd managed to outrun their Regulator pursuers.

Oscar "Jack" Flagg, the man driving the wagon that had been fired upon, rushed into Sheriff Red Angus's office in Buffalo.

"Sheriff, they's a whole passel of men out at the KC. They got the place surrounded and they're firin' on the house."

"Isn't the KC where Nate Champion's been livin'?" Angus asked.

"Yeah, I believe it is," Flagg answered.

Sheriff Angus grabbed his hat off a post in the wall and shouted at his deputy, "Jim, get a couple of other men and ride out to the nearest ranches an' tell everyone to come on in here to town. We got a bunch of boys headed our way an' I want us to be ready for 'em."

As Angus pulled his hat down tight, he looked at Flagg and his partner. "You boys buyin' into this game?" he asked.

"God damned right," Flagg said, patting his pistol butt with his right hand. "Nate Champion was a good ol' boy, an' if'n they've kilt him, I reckon I'll do my best to see they pay for it."

A few hours later, almost a hundred small ranchers from spreads in the surrounding area, along with their hands, were gathered at the hotel dining room in Buffalo.

Sheriff Angus and Flat Nose Curry were trying to explain to them what Jack Flagg had seen, when two men rode into town at a fast clip. Sentries posted outside the hotel told the men where the meeting was, and Bear Claw and Kirby entered the room.

Everyone stopped talking as Kirby walked to the front of

the crowd. He held up Nate's journal. "I've just come from the KC ranch, where Frank Canton and a group of over fifty men have killed Nate Champion and Nick Ray."

A swelling murmur of angry voices began, for both Nate Champion and Nick Ray were popular punchers, and good friends to many of the men in the room.

Kirby handed the notebook to the sheriff. "Why don't you read this to your men, Sheriff? They deserve to know who they're up against, and how one man stood off over fifty for a night and a day."

As Angus read the report of the fight at the KC out loud, many of the men in the room had tears in their eyes, while others' faces turned red with anger at the evil deed.

Flat Nose Curry walked up to stand next to Sheriff Angus as he finished reading. "Boys," Curry said in a harsh voice, roughened by too many whiskeys and cigars, "I think we ought'a ride out and meet those so-called Regulators, an' kill every one of the murderin' sons of bitches!"

A loud shout of approval rose from the crowd, until Angus raised his hands. "All right, boys, here's what we're gonna do," he said as he began to organize the angry mob into a fighting force.

Frank Canton pushed his men as hard as he could. He'd made the difficult decision to leave their wagons behind in order to make better time, for he knew if they lost the element of surprise, it would be very difficult for them to take Buffalo under their control.

After a hard two-hour ride, his men were tired, cold, and hungry. Though there was no raging storm to fight this night, the temperature was still in the low teens and there was plenty of drift snow on the ground to contend with. At two o'clock in the morning, Canton called the vigilantes to a halt at the ranch of one of their Johnson County allies.

Wolcott rode up beside Canton. "Why are we stopping here, Canton?"

"The men are dog-tired, cold, and hungry. I plan on letting 'em get warm for a spell and gettin' some coffee and hot food into 'em."

He stepped from his horse, went to the ranch house door, and pounded on it until a lantern inside was lighted and the door opened.

A sleepy-looking man with tousled hair smiled when he saw Frank Canton standing on his porch.

"Why, howdy, Frank. What in the hell are you doin' out here this time of mornin'?"

Frank glanced back over his shoulder at the group of men sitting on horseback behind him. "Me an' my Regulators are out here after some of those rustlers been killin' your stock, Bob. Trouble is, we're cold and hungry and we got a hell of a fight ahead of us. You think you could have your cook fix us up some coffee and biscuits?"

"Why, hell, yes, Frank. Nothin's too good for you boys, 'specially if you can get those damned rustlers off my back."

"There isn't room for all of us in the house, so I'll just take 'em on out to the barn, an' we'll chow down out there."

It was about an hour and a half later when Canton told his men, "Mount up, boys. We still got some ridin' ahead of us."

As the men began to get their gear together, Jim Dudley walked up to Canton leading a ragged-looking horse by the reins.

"Mr. Canton, I need me 'nother hoss. This one's plumb worn out."

Canton looked down at the huge bear of a man standing before him, weighing 250 pounds at least, and thought, *No wonder the horse is worn out.* He said, "Check with Bob's foreman over there and see if there's not one of his horses he can loan you until this is over. Tell him I'll make good on it if anything happens."

The foreman cast a skeptical eye at Dudley, but took him

over to the corral where the ranch's remuda was herded. After trying four or five animals, Dudley still wasn't satisfied.

"None of these animals is big enough for me," whined the Texan.

Wolcott, tired of the antics of the hayseed from Texas, rode over on his horse and snarled, "Cinch up or stay behind!"

With a worried look, Dudley saddled the last horse he tried, a weak-kneed, ugly bronc who turned his head and stared at the man trying to get on his back. The horse immediately tried to buck Dudley off, but soon found itself unable to move that much weight in a hurry.

With Dudley trying his best to keep up, Canton moved the Regulators out, heading toward Buffalo. To ensure against an ambush, Canton sent two outriders ahead to scout the best trails, and to warn of anyone who might be ahead.

They hadn't ridden very long before the outriders came running back to report the presence of a large body of men camped down the road.

Canton halted the men, confused by this turn of events. "Damn," he observed to Tom Smith and Major Wolcott. "I wonder who the hell is out here in the middle of the night. I don't see how anybody could know we're comin', so they can't be waitin' on us."

Wolcott saw his chance to get back at Canton for taking his position away from him. "Hell, Frank, you been leading this group like it was out on a Sunday ride. We spent almost two days on Nate Champion. Then every time the men get a little winded, you stop and feed 'em. I wouldn't be surprised if everyone in Buffalo didn't know we're coming by now!"

He glanced at the men behind Canton and saw an old friend, one of the stockmen from Cheyenne, William Irvine. "Bill," Wolcott called, "let's you and me walk on up ahead and see what's going on."

Irvine shrugged and climbed down off his horse, following Wolcott up the trail, while Canton and the rest of the men stayed behind.

Wolcott and Irvine walked quite a ways ahead, and were just about to turn around and head back, thinking the outriders had been mistaken, when they heard a pistol discharge around a bend in the trail in front of them.

"Damn," Wolcott whispered to Irvine, "there's someone up ahead."

They quietly walked a little farther and peered around the bend from behind some trees. They could make out several campfires and what looked to be over a hundred dark shapes standing around drinking coffee and resting their horses.

"Come on, Bill. Let's get back and warn the others," Wolcott said.

On the way back, he added, "Bill, you got to back me up and get the men to let me take over. Canton is out of his depth here, and he doesn't know the first thing about how to run this outfit."

Irvine nodded. "I agree, Major. I'll talk to the boys from Cheyenne and see if they won't back your play. It's apparent we need someone with military experience if we're going up against that many men."

When they got back to the Regulators, Wolcott told the men what they had seen. "There's a sizable force up ahead, and it can only be the rustlers and gunfighters, who must know we're on the way. I think it's about time for someone experienced to take over leading this expedition."

Canton, realizing for once the major was probably right, didn't argue, and Wolcott assumed command.

He climbed on his horse and said, "Okay, boys, now it's time for you to act like soldiers, and I'm gonna drill you until I think you're ready to face those gunnies up ahead."

Wolcott lined the men up and began to drill them in the moonlight, making sure they knew how to follow his commands. He did this for several hours, to the astonishment of Canton and Tom Smith.

"I can't believe we're out here riding around in the night

while there's a force of men up ahead we need to be goin' after," Canton said to Smith.

"I got a real bad feeling about you lettin' the major take over, Frank. I don't think he knows his ass from his head."

"I didn't have no choice, Tom. The boys from Cheyenne are the ones payin' for all this, and if they want that idiot to take command, then so be it."

Finally, the major was satisfied he'd whipped his men into shape, and he ordered the men to follow him across the range to the right of the trail, explaining he wanted to try and out-flank the men up ahead of them.

After riding for another hour, they came to the TA ranch, owned by another rancher friendly to the expedition, located about fourteen miles from Buffalo.

While the major took a few men ahead to see if the other group had moved, Jim Dudley went looking for an easier horse. He convinced the ranch foreman to let him try a big gray that looked fit enough to carry the big man.

As Dudley jumped in the saddle, the gray began to buck, astonishing the foreman, for the horse had never bucked before.

As Dudley went flying through the air, his rifle slipped from the saddle boot and the gun went off when it hit the ground, shooting Dudley through the knee as he fell.

After his wounds were cleaned, the foreman had one of the hands put Dudley in the back of a wagon and sent him to Fort McKinney to see the doctor there.

The rest of the vigilantes mounted up and rode after Wolcott, intending to join him against whatever force was out there waiting for them.

As dawn was breaking in the east, a rider approached them, riding hard, leaning over his saddle horn.

"Turn back! Turn back!" he screamed. "Everybody in town is aroused. The rustlers are massing from every direction. Get to cover as fast as you can if you value your lives!"

Wolcott sat in his saddle, his back ramrod straight, as he considered the warning. Finally, he turned his horse around.

"Come on, boys, let's retreat back to the TA ranch. We can set up a defensive perimeter there."

"What the hell do you mean, retreat?" Canton asked.

"Yeah," Tom Smith added. "We came here to do a job, so let's do it. I vote we head on into Buffalo and have it out with the rustlers."

The Texans waited patiently to see which view would prevail. They'd been paid to fight, but it didn't matter much to them whether it was at the TA ranch or in Buffalo.

The members of the Cheyenne Club were of another mind. They spoke out against going into Buffalo, especially since the townspeople were armed and ready for them. They had no stomach for an adversary who wasn't going to be surprised.

Since they were paying the salaries of the fighters, the Cheyenne stockmen had their way and the Regulators retreated back to the TA ranch, to wait for an attack by their intended victims.

On the way, Wolcott rode next to Canton and Smith. "Boys," he said, "I'm going to need your support in the upcoming battle. The men need to trust their leaders, and I can't have you two questioning my every move."

Canton looked at Smith and shrugged. He knew the major was right. It was time to pull together, or they were all liable to be killed.

"All right, Major. We'll keep out mouths shut, at least in front of the men."

Wolcott nodded. "That's all I ask, boys."

Eighteen

Kirby and Bear Claw sat on their haunches near the fire, talking with Sheriff Red Angus and Nate's friend, Flat Nose Curry.

"How many men did you say the vigilantes had?" Angus asked Kirby.

"I'd say about fifty or so. Most of them hardened gunfighters, with a few ranchers thrown in."

Angus glanced back over his shoulder at the crowd of people around several other fires nearby. "Well, we got over a hundred people here, but damned few of 'em know which end of a gun the bullet comes out of. They're mostly punchers and towns-folk, and not one in ten have ever fired a pistol in anger, or been fired on."

Flat Nose Curry, his hands wrapped around a tin cup of coffee to keep warm, nodded. "That may be so, Sheriff, but this is the first time since this war started that the people of Buffalo and the small ranchers have stood together against the big-money ranchers. Whatever happens in the upcoming fight, at least we've finally come together. Those bastards from Cheyenne won't be able to ride roughshod over us anymore."

"That's true," Angus said. "One of the merchants in town has even thrown open his store and is giving away blankets, clothing, and ammunition to anyone who is willin' to fight, and the ladies of the town have set up a kitchen and are preparing wagon loads of food for the men at the front."

Bear Claw shook his head. "I jest hope the people know what they're gittin' into." He looked at the group of men gathered nearby, laughing and shouting and swaggering around like they were going to a party. "These men y'all are goin' up against are all gunslicks. This ain't gonna be no cakewalk, that's fer sure."

As he spoke, one of the young punchers was showing off his fast draw and accidently fired his pistol, shooting the toe of his boot off and making everyone nearby duck and fall to the ground.

Kirby could stand it no longer. Though he couldn't remember his past life, he knew somehow he wasn't one to join in and ride with a mob. He felt he needed to be alone, to do things his own way. Nate Champion had been a good friend, even in the short while Kirby had known him, and he planned on wreaking his own brand of vengeance on the men who had shot him down in cold blood.

Kirby stood up, emptied his cup of coffee in the fire, and said, "Sheriff, Flat Nose, I'm going to take off now. I think I'll ride on ahead and see if I can locate the vigilante force. If I find them, I'll get word back to you and your men as soon as I can."

Bear Claw struggled to his feet, grunting as he slowly stood up. "Kirby, if'n ya don't mind overly much, I'll ride along with ya."

Kirby smiled. "Suit yourself, Bear Claw," he said, glad the old mountain man was coming, for he felt sure the man knew more about his past than he had said. Maybe on the ride he could find out more about who he was.

As they rode through the moonlit night, their breaths smoking in the freezing air, Kirby said, "Bear Claw, back at Nate's cabin, just before all hell broke loose, you said you had something to tell me . . . something about my past."

The mountain man nodded, continuing to look straight ahead as he rode. "Ya tole me ya dreamed 'bout a mountain man named Preacher, and a kid and his daddy fightin' some Injuns with him."

"Yes, that was just after I got shot in the head."

"Well, more years ago than I care to 'member, Preacher an' me was holed up durin' a blizzard one winter, an' he got to talkin' 'bout this pilgrim and his son he'd met."

Kirby jerked his head to the side. "Did he tell you their names?"

"Hold your water, son. I'll git to it in good time." He pulled a twist of tobacco out of his pocket, bit off a goodly portion, and began to chew as he talked.

"Well, seems this pilgrim got himself shot, but 'fore he died, he made Preacher promise to raise his young'un, to look after him till he could fend for hisself. Preacher, though by nature a lone wolf, honored his word, an' 'fore long came to look on this pup like his own son. After some years in the high lonesome, teachin' this kid everything he knew, the boy met a woman an' got married an' even had a son of his own."

Kirby, getting more excited by the minute, asked, "You mean I have a son?"

Bear Claw shook his head. "Wasn't too long after that some bad hombres came around whilst the man wasn't to home, an' they kilt his wife an' son, after doin' terrible things to her."

Kirby, faint memories tugging at his mind, felt his stomach go cold with barely remembered fury.

"Well, this man, who Preacher had named Smoke, buried his kin an' then went after the men who done it. . . ."

Long before first light touched the mountains and the valley, creating that morning's panorama of color, Smoke was up and moving. He rode across the valley. Stopping out of range of rifles, by a stand of cottonwoods, he calmly and arrogantly built a cook fire. He put on coffee to boil and sliced bacon into a pan. He speared out the bacon and dropped slices of potatoes into the grease, frying them crisp. With hot coffee and hot food, and a hunk of Nicole's fresh-baked bread, Smoke settled down for a leisurely breakfast. He knew the outlaws were watching him; he'd seen the sun glint off glass yesterday afternoon.

"That bastard!" Canning said, cussing him from the outlaws' vantage point.

But Felter again had to chuckle. "Relax. He's just tryin' to make us do something stupid. Stay put."

"I'd like to go down there and call him out," the Kid said. His bravado had returned from his sucking on the laudanum bottle all night.

Felter almost told him to go ahead, get the rest of his butt shot off.

"You just stay put," he told Kid Austin. "We got time. They's just one of him, four of us."

"They was twice that yesterday," Sam reminded him. Felter said nothing in rebuttal.

The valley upon which the outlaws gazed, and in which Smoke was eating his quiet breakfast, as Seven, his horse, munched on young spring grass, was wild in its grandeur. It was several miles wide, many miles long, with rugged peaks on the north end, far in the distance, covered with snow most of the time, with thick forests. And, Smoke thought with a grim smile, many dead-end canyons. One of which was only a few miles from this spot. And he felt sure the bounty hunters did not know it was a box, for it looked very deceiving.

Clark had told Smoke, in the hope that he would only get a bullet in the head, not ants in the brain, that it was Canning who'd scalped his wife, Canning who'd first raped her, Canning who'd skinned her breast to make a tobacco pouch with the tanned hide.

Smoke cleaned up his skillet and plate and then set about checking out the two Remington .44's he had chosen from the pile of guns. Preacher had been after him for several years to switch, and Smoke had fired and handled Preacher's Remington .44 many times, liking the feel of the weapon, the balance. And he was just as fast with the slightly heavier weapon.

He spent an hour or more rigging holsters for his new guns, then spent a few minutes drawing and firing them. To his surprise, he found the weapon, with its sleeker form and more laid-back hammer, increased his speed.

His smile was not pleasant. For he had plans for Canning.

Mounting up, he rode slowly to the northeast, always keeping out of rifle range, and very wary of any ambush. When Smoke disappeared into the timber, Felter made his move.

"Let's ride," he said. "Let's get the hell out of here."

But after several hours, Felter realized they were being pushed toward the northwest. Every time they tried to veer off, a shot from the big Sharps would keep them going.

On the second day, Canning brought his horse up sharply, hurting the animal's mouth with the bit. "I 'bout had it," he said.

They were tired and hungry, for Smoke had harassed them with the Sharps every hour.

Felter looked around him, at the high walls of the canyon, sloping upward, green and brown with timber. He smiled ruefully. They were now the hunted.

A dozen times in the past two days they had tried to bushwhack Smoke. But he was as elusive as his name.

"Somebody better do something," Felter said. " 'Cause we're in a box canyon."

"I'll take him!" Canning snarled. "Rest of you ride on up 'bout a mile or two. Get set in case I miss." He grinned. "But I ain't gonna do that, boys."

Felter nodded. "See you in a couple of hours."

Smoke had dismounted just inside the box canyon, ground-reining Seven. Smoke removed his boots and slipped on moccasins. Then he went on the prowl, as silent as death. He held a skinning knife in his left hand.

* * *

"No shots," Kid Austin said. "And it's been three hours."

Sam sat quietly. Everything about this job had turned sour.

"Horse comin'," Felter said.

"There he is!" Austin said. "And it's Canning. By God, he said he'd get him and he did."

But Felter wasn't sure about that. He'd smelled wood smoke about an hour back. That didn't fit any pattern. And Canning wasn't sitting his horse right. Then the screaming drifted to them. Canning was hollering in agony.

"What's he hollerin' for?" Kid asked. "I hurt a lot more'un anything he could have wrong with him."

"Don't bet on that," Felter told him. He scrambled down the gravel and bush-covered slope to halt Canning's frightened horse.

Felter recoiled in horror at the sight of Canning's blood-soaked crotch.

"My privates!" Canning squalled. "Smoke waylaid me and gelded me! He cauterized me with a runnin' iron." Canning passed out, tumbling from the saddle.

Felter and Sam dragged the man into the brush and looked at the awful wound. Smoke had heated a running iron and seared the wound, stopping most of the bleeding. Felter thought Canning would live, but his raping days were over.

And Felter knew, with a sudden realization, that he wanted no more of the man called Smoke. Not without about twenty men backing him up, that is.

Using a spare shirt from his saddlebags, Felter made a crude bandage for Canning. But it was going to be hell on the man sitting a saddle. Felter looked around him. That fool Kid Austin was walking down the floor of the canyon, his hands poised over his twin Colts. An empty laudanum bottle lay on the ground.

"Get back here, you fool!" Felter shouted.

Austin ignored him. "Come on, Smoke!" he yelled. "I'm going to kill you."

"Hell with you, Kid," Sam muttered.

He tied Canning in the saddle and they rode off, up the slope of the canyon wall, high up, near the crest. There they found a hole that just might get them free. Raking their sides, the animals fought for footing, digging and sliding in loose rock. The horses realized they had to make it—or die. With one final lunge, the horses cleared the crest and stood on firm ground, trembling from fear and exhaustion.

As they rested their animals, they looked for the Kid. Austin was lost from sight.

They rode off to the north, toward a mining camp where Richards had said he would leave word, or send more men should this crew fail.

Well, Felter reflected bitterly, we damn sure failed.

Austin, his horse forgotten, his mind numbed by overdoses of laudanum, stumbled down the rocky floor of the canyon, screaming and cursing Smoke. He pulled up short when he spotted his quarry.

Smoke sat calmly on a huge rock, munching on a cold biscuit.

"Get up!" the Kid shouted. "Get on your feet and face me like a man oughtta."

Smoke finished his meager meal, then rose to his feet. He was smiling.

Kid Austin walked on, narrowing the distance, finally stopping about thirty feet from Smoke. "I'll be known as the man who killed Smoke," he said. "Me! Kid Austin."

Smoke laughed at him.

The Kid flushed. "I done it to your wife, too, Jensen. She liked it so much she asked me to do it to 'er some more. So I obliged 'er. I took your woman—now I'm gonna take you." He dipped his right hand downward.

Smoke drew his right-hand .44 with blinding speed, drawing, cocking, firing, before Austin could realize what was taking place in front of his eyes. The would-be gunfighter felt two lead fists of pain strike him in the belly, one below his belt buckle, the other just above the ornate silver buckle. The hammerlike blows dropped him to his knees. Hurt began creeping into his groin and stomach. He tried to pull his guns from leather, but his hands would not respond to the commands from his brain.

"I'm Kid Austin," he managed to say. "You can't do this to me."

"Looks like I did, though," Smoke said. He turned away from the dying man and walked back to Seven, swinging into the saddle. He rode off without looking back.*

"Smoke Jensen," Kirby mumbled into the wind as he rode alongside Bear Claw. The name, though unfamiliar, felt easy on his lips, like old boots that have been worn long enough to become soft and comfortable. He glanced to the side. "So, you think I'm this man named Smoke?"

Bear Claw nodded. "Cain't hardly be two men like that ridin' round the country. Preacher said his boy grew to be a hand over six feet tall, shoulders broad as an ax handle, and was so fast with a short-gun it was plumb scary."

He leaned to the side and spat brown tobacco juice onto the ground. "I seen you handle that six-killer, son. You be Smoke Jensen all right."

Kirby shook his head. "I believe you, Bear Claw, but knowing my name hasn't brought back any memories of just who I am."

Bear Claw shrugged. "Could be ya won't ever 'member what went before, son, or ya could wake up in the mornin' an' it'd all be jest like it was. The haid is a funny thing. Sometimes I can 'member thangs happened forty years ago like they

The Last Mountain Man

was jest yesterday, an' then again I cain't 'member what I ate fer breakfast."

Kirby was about to reply when out of the corner of his eye he glimpsed moonlight reflecting off metal, off to his left.

He stared off that way for a moment, and he noticed he could make out a force of men riding on the horizon, silhouetted against the night sky.

Kirby reached out his hand and grabbed Bear Claw's shoulder, pulling him to a halt. "Look over there. It looks like a bunch of men riding off to the south."

Bear Claw shaded his eyes against the moonlight and looked, then nodded. "That must be the vigilantes, all right. Appears to be close to fifty men, just like at Nate's ranch."

Kirby pulled his Winchester rifle from its saddle boot and worked the lever, jacking a shell into the chamber.

Bear Claw cocked an eyebrow at him. "You ain't meanin' to go after them boys by youself, is ya?"

Kirby glared at Bear Claw, and the old man could see why the Smoke Jensen he'd heard of had such a fearsome reputation. There was death lurking in those eyes for anybody who crossed the big man.

"Yes."

Bear Claw shook his head and pulled his Sharps .52-caliber from its saddle boot. "Boy, you gonna git us killed 'fore this is over."

"You don't have to join this dance, Bear Claw."

"I ain't never ducked a good fight yet, son, an' I don't intend to start now at this late age. What's yore plan?"

"There's too many for us to just ride up and start shooting, so I'm going to ride on ahead and set up an ambush. If we can fire down on them from both sides, knock a few out of their saddles, then ride like hell around them, shooting into the crowd, they'll never know what hit them."

Half an hour later, Wolcott and Canton and Smith rode along at the head of the vigilante group they called Regulators. They were in no hurry, and were discussing how they planned to combat the force of townspeople from Buffalo.

Suddenly something buzzed by Canton's head and he heard a flat slapping sound behind him, followed a few seconds later by the sound of gunfire ahead. He glanced over his shoulder in time to see a man riding behind him grab his chest and fall out of the saddle.

Before he could say anything, there was another whistling buzz and the slap of a bullet hitting home, accompanied by a grunt of pain as another man was blown from his saddle.

The booming sound of a big Sharps firing was unmistakable ahead of them, and Canton knew they were under attack.

He started to yell a warning when he felt a sharp stinging in his head as a piece of his left ear was neatly cut off by a passing bullet.

"God damn!" he screamed, grabbing the side of his head. "Look out, men!" he yelled. "We're under fire!"

As a bank of clouds began to cover the moon and the night became dark, whoops and yells could be heard from in front of the group, followed by flashes of fire as more men were shot out of their saddles.

The Regulators began to ride in all directions at once, shooting at shadows and sometimes each other, as they couldn't tell who or where their attackers were.

One of the Texans, hearing the fearsome yells of the men riding down on them, hollered, "Injuns! We's bein' attacked by Injuns!"

Canton began yelling orders, trying to get his men to form up in some semblance of order. "Line up, men!" he hollered. "Over here, make a line and stand and fight!"

Without warning, a man riding bent low over his saddle horn, his reins in his teeth and both hands filled with iron, barreled through the milling, confused group of vigilantes.

Three more men went down, and only one man managed to snap off a shot at the specter as he weaved his horse through the crowd, guiding the animal with his knees as both hands fired into the Regulators.

Two more of the vigilantes were knocked from their saddles by large-caliber Sharps bullets, and three men went down from shots fired by their comrades, who were shooting at every shadow that moved.

Finally, Wolcott and Canton were able to get the men to follow them and they rode hell-bent for leather for the TA ranch, trying their best to get away from whoever was attacking them.

The attack had only lasted five minutes, but the Regulators had lost at least ten men. Kirby sat on his horse, reloading his Colts, as Bear Claw rode up.

The old mountain man glanced at the bodies lying on the frozen ground and the horses milling about without riders.

"Gawd almighty, son! I ain't never seen nothin' like that since the time I fought some Comanch' over on the plains."

Kirby grinned, but his eyes were flat and cold, still filled with hate. "You think we got their attention?"

Bear Claw nodded. "Where'd you learn to ride like that, boy?"

Kirby shrugged. "I don't know. It just seemed like the thing to do at the time."

"I 'spect it was Preacher showed you them moves. He always was more Injun than white man anyhow."

After a few minutes, the men from Buffalo came riding up, having heard the shots.

Sheriff Angus and Flat Nose Curry rode slowly, looking at the carnage around them, the dead bodies lying sprawled in the bloody snow.

"Jesus," Angus whispered, taking his hat off and sleeving sweat from his forehead. "Did you two do this by yourselves?"

"Ya see anybody else round here, Sheriff?" Bear Claw answered, pushing cartridges into his Sharps.

Flat Nose Curry said, "Who did you say you were, mister?"

Kirby stared at him. "I didn't say. But the men we're after rode off in that direction," he said, pointing off to the south.

Angus nodded. "Looks like they're headed for the TA ranch."

"That figures," Curry said. "It won't be easy to get them out of there. That damn place is set up like a fort."

Angus turned to the side, speaking to a young boy in his teens. "Billy, you ride on into Buffalo and tell everybody we're gonna be out at the TA. They can send us some supplies out that way, 'cause we may be there a spell."

Angus twisted around in his saddle and hollered at the men grouped up behind him. "Come on, boys. They're up ahead of us, but be careful and watch out for ambushes."

Kirby watched Angus as the lawman turned back around and put the spurs to his horse, leaning over the neck as if he hoped they could catch up to the Regulators before they had time to set up in the TA ranch.

Kirby kicked his horse into a gallop following the sheriff. He knew most of the sheriff's riders were cowboys, and not professional gunfighters, and he was still uncertain of how they'd react when put up against men who made their living with a gun. *Well, hell,* Kirby thought as he charged through the frigid night on his horse, *I guess it's about time we find out.*

Nineteen

Sugarloaf Ranch
Big Rock, Colorado

Pearlie and Cal jumped from their horses and rushed into the cabin, hollering, "Miss Sally, Miss Sally."

Sally walked out of the kitchen, drying her hands on her apron. As always, when she was under stress or worried about Smoke, she tried to keep her mind busy by baking. So far today, she had baked two apple pies, a peach cobbler, and a huge batch of bear sign. She was doing all she could to try and avoid thinking of all the reasons why Smoke hadn't contacted her when he reached Buffalo.

"Yes, boys. Any word at the telegraph office?"

Pearlie, his hat in his hand, said with a serious expression, "No, ma'am. The telegraph operator said he's been tryin' to raise someone at Buffalo, Smoke's last stop on the train, for two days now, like you told him."

"And?" Sally asked, worry wrinkling her forehead.

"Nothin'," Cal answered. "He says he got through to Casper, an' the man on the wire there said there was a big shootout between some rustlers and a vigilante force."

"They're callin' it the Powder River War," Pearlie added. "The man at the telegraph says all the lines into Johnson County have been cut."

"That settles it," Sally said, and she began to walk back toward her bedroom.

"What're you plannin' on doin', Miss Sally?" Pearlie asked.

"I'm going to pack and go to Buffalo and see what's happened to Smoke. He said he would wire me when he got to Buffalo, before he headed up into the mountains." She shook her head. "Smoke wouldn't forget a promise like that. If he didn't send me a message, then something terrible has happened to him."

Pearlie glanced at Cal, who shook his head. "You can't do that, Miss Sally," Pearlie said. "That country is no place for a woman this time of year, 'specially if'n there's a range war goin' on."

"Pearlie's right, Miss Sally," Cal added. "Why don't you let me an' Pearlie head on up there? We'll find out what's goin' on with Smoke, an' why he hasn't gotten in touch, an' if he's in some sort of trouble, we'll make sure he gets out of it."

Sally stared at the boys. She knew they were right. Someone needed to stay at the Sugarloaf and keep the hands on their winter chores, and the trip would be much more difficult for a woman than for two men traveling together. Damn, but sometimes it rankled her to be a female.

She walked up to them and put her hands on their shoulders. "Men, go on up there and bring my Smoke back to me, you hear?"

They both nodded. "Yes, ma'am," Pearlie said, and they headed out to the bunkhouse to pack for the trip.

As they walked across the yard, Cal asked in a low voice, "Pearlie, what if Smoke's dead?"

Pearlie shook his head. "Can't none of those Wyoming men kill Smoke Jensen." He stared at Cal. "Can't nobody kill Smoke Jensen." He patted the Colt revolver on his hip. "But if perchance they've managed to get the drop on Smoke, they're gonna have a couple of Colorado boys to deal with."

Twenty

At the TA ranch, Wolcott began to organize his frightened Regulators back into a fighting force. The night attack had demoralized them, making them realize they were facing a formidable force of fighting men who weren't going to be easily defeated.

"Goddamn that Nate Champion," he muttered. He knew now that the time they had spent killing the cowboy had given their opponents the opportunity to get ready for them. If they ended up losing this war, he thought, it was all because of the bravery of one lone cowboy, who had fought them to a stand-still for almost two days.

He took Canton and Smith and rode around the perimeter of the TA ranch, planning on how best to defend it.

The ranch seemed well situated for defense. Its main buildings, nestled in a bend of Crazy Woman Creek, were surrounded by a log fence seven feet high, with a barbed-wire fence beyond it. The ranch house stood in a windbreak of trees, surrounded by outbuildings, a stable, an icehouse, a small henhouse, and a dugout for storing potatoes. Within this compound there was also a stack of thick timbers, recently purchased for the construction of a new building. Beyond the barbed-wire fence, the terrain stretched away in rolling hills dotted with crevices and ravines, making an approach in force difficult.

As dawn approached, Major Wolcott barked out orders for

the fortification of the ranch. On a knoll about fifty yards from the stable, he had his men build a log fort measuring twelve by fourteen feet, with openings through which sharpshooters could cover the approaches to the ranch. Trenches were dug inside the fort and breastworks were raised around the ranch house. By mid-morning the next day, the ranch was ready, and the stockmen and Texans were dug in, awaiting the appearance of the citizens from Buffalo.

As the morning fog and light snow cleared, the vigilantes could see their attackers in the distance, digging rifle pits and throwing up breastworks on every hill and hogback around the ranch. Wolcott counted fifty men who had dug in during the night, and he could see Sheriff Angus riding up with another forty or so men from the direction of Buffalo.

"Damn," he said to Canton and Smith. "It looks like the whole blamed town is coming out to fight."

Shooting started early in the morning, with sharpshooters from the town leaning their rifles over their breastworks and taking careful aim at the men dug in below at the TA ranch.

The attackers' first target was the corral. Their rifles began to pick off the vigilantes' horses. As the large-caliber bullets slapped into the animals, they screamed and began to run around the enclosure, trying to escape the slaughter.

"God almighty, Major," Canton hollered, pointing at the fallen animals. "They're shootin' our mounts. We got to do somethin'!"

Wolcott stomped around the ranch house, peering out the window as another horse went down as though he'd been poleaxed. "Frank, go send one of the Texicans out there to see if he can get what's left of the horses into the stable and under cover."

Canton watched as the deadly accurate firing knocked another horse to the ground. He shook his head. "Not me! If I remember correctly, Major, you took command of this expedition, so it's your job to give the orders . . . 'specially when it means sendin' a man out into that hail of bullets."

"How about you, Smith?" the major asked Tom Smith.

Smith looked up from making a cigarette and gave a small smile, shaking his head.

With an angry snort, Wolcott walked over and stood behind two of the Texans who were peering over the top of a pile of timbers, watching the men from Buffalo picking off the horses.

Wolcott tapped the men on the shoulder. "Okay, boys, I need two men who aren't cowards to run on over there and get those broncs into the stable."

One of the men, the one who called himself the Texas Kid, glanced back at the major. "Are you crazy? We'd get our butts blown off if we stepped out there into that fire."

Wolcott cocked an eyebrow. "So, you're awfully brave when it comes to shooting a man down from cover, like you did with Champion, but you don't have the guts to face someone who's firing back at you, huh?"

The Texas Kid shrugged. "I ain't no coward, Major, but I ain't stupid neither."

He turned back to watch the battle.

Wolcott drew his Army .44, cocked it, and placed the barrel against the back of the Kid's head. "Well, son, I'm giving you a direct order. You can obey it and maybe get shot, or you can ignore it, and I'll kill you right where you sit. You got that, soldier?"

The Kid gulped, and looked walleyed at the big pistol stuck against the back of his head. "Yes, sir," he mumbled as he got to his feet. "Come on, Jimmy," he said to the young man next to him. "Let's go get them hosses."

Bending low and running in a zigzag pattern, the two boys made a run for the corral. With bullets pocking the ground around them, they finally managed to bring the panicked, jostling surviving horses into the stable.

As they made a run back toward the ranch house, the boy named Jimmy was hit in the shoulder and spun around to land sprawled on his face in the snow and mud. The Texas Kid stopped long enough to grab him by the shirt, jerk him to his feet, and half drag him into the house, just as a fusillade of bullets splintered the doorway.

Wolcott smiled as the two men scrambled into the room. "Now, that wasn't so bad, was it?"

"No worse'n hell," the Texas Kid mumbled as he wrapped his bandanna around his friend's bleeding shoulder.

With no horses left to shoot at, the attackers soon turned their attention to the cattle, and after that anything that moved.

They soon found the range of the doors to the ranch house and began to pour lead into the building, forcing those inside to crawl when they needed to move about within the rooms.

A boy of about sixteen, who had been at the ranch when the vigilantes arrived, was pestering all of the men to give him a gun so he could join in the battle. He finally managed to find an old shotgun in the loft, and was sitting in a corner cleaning it, telling all around him how he was going to blow hell out of those rustlers.

A bullet smashed though the wooden wall next to him and creased his neck, burning a shallow furrow in the skin and causing a considerable amount of blood to flow, though the wound wasn't at all serious. After that, the boy shut his mouth, put the shotgun down, and lay on a blanket in the corner, pressing a cloth to his neck, his eyes wide with fear.

On a hill overlooking the TA ranch, Smoke sat next to a campfire, drinking coffee and talking with Bear Claw. Though his memory hadn't fully returned, he was beginning to have flashes of his old life. A pretty, brown-haired woman featured prominently in most of these—a woman Bear Claw said could only be Smoke's wife, Sally.

Sheriff Angus had ridden off some hours earlier to return to Buffalo, to further organize the efforts there to repel any additional firepower he was sure the cattlemen from Cheyenne would eventually send to reinforce the vigilantes.

Shortly after he left, a burly, unkempt figure arrived on the scene, and began to give orders. It was a man named Arapahoe Brown, who had twice previously been defeated for county sheriff.

Smoke didn't like the man from the first moment he laid eyes on him. To Smoke, he seemed the typical bully, a man who tried to foist his ideas on others by force rather than by logic.

By now the attackers from Buffalo had over three hundred men surrounding the TA ranch. Smoke and Bear Claw watched as Arapahoe Brown gathered the crowd in a large circle around him.

As he talked, he strutted around with his hands in his coat like a peacock, filled with self-importance. "Here's my plan, men. We'll close in on the TA by short dashes, using covering fire from above; then we'll burn the bastards out by firing the ranch."

Smoke glanced at Bear Claw, and saw the mountain man's expression was as disgusted as his own was. Smoke got to his feet and approached Brown.

"Have you given any thought to giving the men down there a chance to surrender?" he asked.

Brown glared at him through narrowed eyes. "And just who are you, mister, to be givin' orders around here?"

Smoke shrugged, his eyes flat and burrowing into Brown's. "I'm a friend of Nate Champion's, and I was there when those men burned him out, and then shot him down in cold blood. I didn't much like it when they did it, and I don't much like it now that you're advocating doing the same thing."

Brown, who was several inches shorter than Smoke but outweighed him by fifty pounds, stepped up close, his face next to Smoke's. "I'm tellin' you to butt out of this affair, stranger, an' mind your own business!"

As he finished talking, he put a hand on Smoke's chest and gave a shove, trying to push Smoke back. He might as well have tried to move a boulder.

Smoke looked down at the hand and spoke low. "Take your hand off me, Brown, before I break it."

Brown looked around at the crowd, his face burning red, and curled his hand into a fist and drew it back.

Before he could move, Smoke threw a short right jab, his broad, work-hardened knuckles smashing Brown's nose almost flat. As blood and mucus splattered and Brown blinked at the sudden pain, Smoke followed up with a left cross to the jaw, knocking the big man out cold and sprawling him in the snow on his back.

"Anyone else want to try and push me?" he asked.

When there were no takers, he nodded. "Now, I'm going to ride down to the ranch and see if those men will surrender. Any objections?"

There were none, but quite a few men nodded, as if they agreed with Smoke's plan.

He fixed a white shirt to the barrel of his Winchester and, holding it aloft, rode slowly down toward the ranch house.

As he approached, Major Wolcott, Frank Canton, and Tom Smith appeared at the front door, all with pistols drawn and aimed at Smoke's chest.

"What do you want?" Wolcott asked, his head cocked to the side from his neck injury.

"I hear you're a military man," Smoke said.

Wolcott nodded. "Yes. So what?"

"Then you must know you're in an untenable situation. Your men are surrounded by a superior force and you have no hope of escape." Smoke pointed over his shoulder. "Sheriff Angus has over three hundred men on those hills up there, and they're planning on burning you out and killing you to the last man."

Canton and Smith looked at each other. They evidently had no idea their situation was so desperate.

"What of it?" the major asked. "We're dug in here pretty good, and they'll lose plenty of men if they try to rush us."

Smoke wagged his head. "Why should they do that? You've got nowhere to go, and you can't have many supplies stored up. All they have to do is wait until dark, sneak up on the ranch like you did to Nate Champion, and pick you off when you come out."

"So, just what are you proposing, mister?" Canton asked.

"If you and your men surrender, I will promise you a fair trial."

Wolcott shook his head. "There is no way we could get a fair trial if we surrendered to that mob. They'd shoot us down like dogs."

"They're going to shoot you down like dogs anyway, Major. At least this way some of your men might live through this."

Wolcott considered his options for a moment, then shook his head. "No, I won't chance it. We're expecting reinforcements from Cheyenne, and we've sent a runner out last night to the U.S. troops at Fort McKinney and to Governor Amos Barber, asking them for help."

Smoke gave a small smile. "Well, Major, for the sake of your men, I hope they respond soon, or you'll all be dead before they get here." Smoke looked back over his shoulder, then back at Wolcott. "I'll try to hold those men up there off until the authorities arrive, if I can."

"Why should you help us after we killed your friend Champion?" Canton asked, recognizing Smoke as the man they had taken from Champion's cabin.

Smoke shrugged. "Strange as it may seem to a man heading up a bunch of vigilantes, I believe in the rule of law, when it's available. If it was up to me, I'd shoot you down like the murdering cowards you are, but then I'd be no better than you are. No, if it's possible, I'll let the law decide what to do with you."

With that final word, he reined his horse around and trotted back up the hill toward the attackers from Buffalo.

Twenty-one

When Smoke got back to the top of the hill, Sheriff Angus was waiting for him.

"What did they say?" he asked Smoke.

"They're considering the offer to surrender," Smoke said, electing not to mention what Wolcott had said about possible reinforcements on the way.

Angus glanced at Arapahoe Brown, standing on the edge of the crowd of men, his hand holding a bandanna to his still bleeding nose, a look of pure hatred in his eyes as he glared at Smoke.

"Well," Sheriff Angus said, "I'll give them until tomorrow. Then we'll attack and burn them out if they're still undecided."

"Good," Smoke said. "That sounds fair to me."

"Fair has nothing to do with it," Angus answered, his voice rough. "As long as I'm wearin' this badge, I'll do my best to work within the law, and that don't include shootin' men like they was fish in a barrel."

Smoke inclined his head toward Arapahoe Brown. "Maybe you ought to tell that to Brown over there."

Sheriff Angus fixed Brown with a baleful stare. "Brown ain't runnin' this operation. I am." He paused and then spoke louder, playing to the crowd. "All of you get that?"

There was murmuring among the crowd of onlookers, but none questioned Angus's authority.

Smoke, satisfied that he had at least bought the vigilantes

some time and the possibility of a trial instead of a slaughter, walked back to his campfire, where Bear Claw sat watching him with a slight smile on his wrinkled face.

Smoke stood in front of the fire, taking the cup of coffee Bear Claw offered, and enjoyed the smell of the fire, the cold, crisp mountain air with a touch of pine scent to it, and the view of the snowcapped mountains in the distance.

He took a deep draft of his coffee and knelt on his haunches, facing Bear Claw. "You know, partner, I'm getting mighty tired of all this," Smoke said. He looked around at the men behind the breastworks, some still firing occasionally down into the ranch house as if they were afraid they might not get a chance to kill someone before the vigilantes surrendered.

Bear Claw nodded, a look of distaste on his face. "I know what you mean, son. Hell, I ain't been around this many people since the last gatherin' of mountain men four year ago." He shook his head, staring down into his coffee cup. "Mankind ain't all that bad when you take 'em one at a time, but when you git more'n a couple together . . ." He paused, then spat into the fire, making it hiss.

Smoke stood up and dumped the rest of his coffee onto the ground. "I think I'll take a little ride over to Fort McKinney."

Bear Claw stared at him, a questioning look on his face. "Oh?"

"Yeah. Major Wolcott told me he sent a courier through the lines last night to see if he could get the commanding officer there to send some soldiers to try and bring an end to this mess. I want to make sure his man made it, and see if there are some soldiers on the way."

"Why are you so all-fired determined to help those men down there out, 'specially after they killed Nate Champion?"

"It's like I said to the sheriff, I don't much cater to mob rule, or to killing fifty men when they're pinned down and helpless." Smoke paused, thinking of the man named Jim Dudley he'd met on the train. "Some of 'em sure as hell deserve what they get for the murder of Nate, but most of those boys down there are just up here to try and earn some money by tracking down rustlers, and have just been doing what their leaders tell them to do." He shook his head. "To me, that doesn't necessarily mean they ought to die for following orders."

Bear Claw used his Sharps to lever himself to a standing position. "You hankerin' for some company on this little jaunt?"

Smoke grinned. "Sure. On the way, maybe you can tell me some more about this Smoke Jensen that I'm supposed to be."

As they mounted up and rode out of camp, neither man saw Arapahoe Brown gather several cowboys around him and stare after them, his pig-eyes glittering hate.

Several hours later, as they rode at an easy trot down the trail, Bear Claw cleared his throat and pulled his Sharps out of its saddle boot.

"Don't look now, Smoke, but I just saw a reflection off somethin' up on the side of that hill over yonder." He cut his eyes to the right without turning his head.

Smoke glanced ahead to an area where the trail narrowed and passed between two hillocks on either side.

He pursed his lips, thinking. "That'd be a right dandy place for an ambush, wouldn't it?"

"My feelin's exactly. How do you want to handle it?"

Smoke looked around, noticing there was no cover between them and the narrow pass, and saw that the snow was piled too high off the trail for any fast horseback riding.

"There's no place for us to go, so I figure if we just pull up here and wait, they'll eventually have to come to us."

Bear Claw nodded. "An' right now we're outta rifle range, 'less they have a Sharps like I do."

The two men reined their mounts to a stop and sat there, Bear Claw with his Sharps across his saddle horn, and Smoke with his Winchester resting on his thigh.

As they waited, Smoke built himself a cigarette and Bear

Claw cut a long piece of tobacco off a twist he pulled from a pocket and stuck it in his mouth.

After a wait of twenty minutes, four men rode out of cover and began to ride up the trail toward them.

Smoke gave a low laugh. "It looks like Arapahoe Brown and some of his cronies. He must think we have some unfinished business between us."

Bear Claw leaned to the side and spat a brown stream into the snow as he eared back the hammer on his Sharps. "It don't never pay to humiliate a bully, Smoke. They's all cowards at heart."

When the men riding toward them got within pistol range, Smoke booted his Winchester and slipped the rawhide hammer thongs off his Colts.

Brown reined his men to a halt twenty yards from Smoke and Bear Claw. "Where do you gents think you're goin'?" he asked with a belligerent tone to his voice.

Smoke raised his eyebrows, a slight grin turning up the corners of his mouth. "Why do you ask, Mr. Brown, not that it's any of your business?"

Brown snorted. "I figure you're on your way to try an' get help for those bastards that kilt our friends, Nate Champion and Nick Ray."

Smoke laughed out loud. "You know, Arapahoe, I only knew Nate and Nick for a few days, but I doubt very seriously if either one of them would have ever called a scurrilous son of a bitch like you a friend."

Smoke's jibe must have struck home, for one of the men with Brown gave a short laugh, as if it were true. Brown's face reddened and he leaned forward in the saddle. "Never mind your smart-ass comments, stranger—just answer my question."

Bear Claw cocked his head to the side, "By the way, just where did you get the name Arapahoe anyhow? It cain't be 'cause you a half-breed out of some Arapahoe squaw, 'cause I know for a fact the Arapahoe never bred with no donkeys."

Brown became so furious he began to sputter, spittle forming at the sides of his mouth as he and his men went for their guns.

In the blink of an eye, Bear Claw swiveled his Sharps around and let the hammer down, the big .52-caliber rifle exploding and blowing a fist-sized hole in the chest of the man on Brown's left.

As he flung his arms out and flew backward out of his saddle, Smoke's right-hand Colt blasted smoke and fire from its barrel, sending a .44-caliber slug into Brown's neck, dead center, blowing a hole in his spine and dropping him like a sack of potatoes to slump forward over his saddle horn.

The second bullet from Smoke's pistol took the third man in the center of his forehead, shredding his skull and tearing a chunk of his scalp off.

The fourth man, his gun still in leather, shouted, "God damn!" and quickly raised his hands as Smoke's Colt turned toward him.

"Jesus," he whispered, "I ain't never seen nothin' like it! I never even saw your hand move."

"If'n you know which way the stick floats, lil' beaver," Bear Claw said, his voice husky with rage, "you'll head on back down the trail the way you came, an' maybe you'll live to tell your kids you tried to draw on Smoke Jensen an' survived."

He chuckled at the expression on the man's face as it blanched white at the mention of the name Smoke Jensen. "Not many hombres can say that!" Bear Claw added.

"Yes . . . yes, sir!" the cowboy said as he jerked his horse's head around and spurred it into a gallop. He leaned low over the saddle horn, glancing back as if he expected Smoke or Bear Claw to shoot him in the back as he rode away.

Smoke watched him ride away, a thoughtful expression on his face. "I can see by that puncher's reaction that the name Smoke Jensen carries some weight around here."

Bear Claw laughed out loud. "Son, you got that right! You're only the most famous gunfighter in the country, bar none."

Smoke holstered his pistol and said, "Come on, Bear Claw, we got some miles to ride yet and we're burning daylight."

"What about these bodies?" Bear Claw asked.

Smoke looked down at the bloody remains for a minute, then leaned to the side and spat. "Let the wolves have them—it's only fitting."

Twenty-two

The giant steam engine pulled into Buffalo with a screech of breaks and a hiss of steam.

Cal and Pearlie climbed down out of the passenger car, stretching to get the kinks out after their long ride. As they walked up the boardwalk toward the small station, five men with rifles and shotguns at the ready blocked their way.

"Howdy, gents," one of the men said, levering a shell into his rifle.

Pearlie looked at Cal, a puzzled expression on his face. "Howdy," he replied to the man with the rifle.

"Where you boys comin' from?" the man asked.

"We're from Colorado," Pearlie answered, "but just what business is it of yours?"

The man shifted a chaw of tobacco from one cheek to the other, then spat a stream of tobacco juice onto the ground.

"We're deputy sheriffs, an' we been havin' a spot of trouble with some vigilantes from Cheyenne. We're here to make sure no more of the dirty scum try to come up here an' cause more trouble."

"We don't know nothin' 'bout that," Cal said, scowling. "We're here to look for a friend of ours that arrived last week. He was supposed to wire us back home that he made it all right, only we ain't heard nothin' from him."

One of the other men asked, "What be your friend's name?"

"Smoke Jensen," Pearlie replied.

"Smoke Jensen, the famous gunfighter?" the first man asked, a surprised expression on his face.

"One and the same," Cal replied.

The man shook his head. "Nobody like that's been through here."

The second man added, "We have been havin' some trouble with the telegraph, though. Mayhap the lines were down when he came through and he just kept on goin'."

"What's he look like?" the first man asked.

Cal smiled. "I don't think you could've missed him. He's a hand over six feet tall, shoulders wider'n an ax handle, clean-shaven, and has light-colored hair, cut short."

The man raised his eyebrows and looked at the others. "There was a man like that, only he called hisself Kirby. Got into a little fracas with the vigilantes, only he left town yesterday, travelin' with an old mountain man name of Bear Claw."

Pearlie, recognizing the name Kirby as Smoke's given name, decided to keep his mouth shut until he figured out the lay of the land and just what had been going on up here.

"Naw, that don't sound like Smoke." He paused, then said, "I 'spect we'll just head on up into the mountains an' look for him there. You got anyplace that serves food around here? We're a mite hungry after three days on the train."

"Sure, there's Mary Sue's place, on over to the hotel. She serves a mean breakfast."

Pearlie nodded. "Then that's for us. Thank you kindly."

The deputies shouldered their weapons and walked on down the train, checking to make sure there were no reinforcements for the vigilantes in the other cars.

As they sat down to eat, Cal asked, "Why didn't you tell 'em Kirby was Smoke's Christian name?"

Pearlie shook his head. "No need to tip our hand just yet, Cal. If'n Smoke was usin' another name, he must've had good reason. We'll nose around here for a day or so and see what's been goin' on. Then if we don't find nothin' out, we'll hire a coupl'a broncs and head on up toward where the Nez Percé are camped an' see if Smoke's up there."

Smoke and Bear Claw were shown into the commanding officer's office at Fort McKinney.

"My name is Colonel Cartwright," the man behind the desk said, without rising or offering to shake hands. "What can I do for you gentlemen?"

"There's a range war going on over at Buffalo, in Johnson County, Colonel. The townspeople have about fifty or sixty men trapped in a ranch there and plan on killing them all for murdering some cattlemen friends of theirs. I was hoping you might be able to send some troops to restore order, and save those men's lives."

Cartwright studied Smoke for a moment, then picked up a telegram from his desk. "It's funny you should be here, Mr. Jensen. I just got this wire from President Benjamin Harrison. It seems Governor Amos Barber wired some senator friends of his and they got the President out of bed to send me this wire you see here. The President requests I send troops to Buffalo immediately to 'quell an insurrection' by the citizens there."

He looked up at Smoke and Bear Claw. "That doesn't exactly square with what you're telling me, now does it?"

"Colonel," Smoke said, an expression on his face as if he'd tasted bad meat, "there are two things I never put much stock in. One is anything a lawyer says; the other is anything a politician tells me." He shrugged. "I don't much care why you send troops to Buffalo, as long as you do something to help keep those men from being slaughtered."

"Just what's your stake in all this, Mr. Jensen?"

"Those men killed a couple of friends of mine in cold blood, and I'd like nothing better than to see the ones responsible for it punished. Trouble is, a lot of those men up there are just boys from Texas who didn't do nothing they deserve to die for."

Colonel Cartwright sat thinking, curling the ends of his moustache as he considered what to do.

Finally, after a few moments, he said, "Well, I sure as hell can't disobey a direct order from the President of the United States, so I'll send three troops of cavalry to Buffalo, with orders to stop the fighting and bring those men in for trial."

He looked up at Smoke. "That suit you, Mr. Jensen?"

"Sure does, Colonel."

After they left Colonel Cartwright's office, Bear Claw asked, "What're you gonna do now, young beaver?"

Smoke yawned and stretched. "I think I'm going to get some shut-eye. It's been a busy few days. Then I'm going back to Buffalo and make sure things get settled there. They may need my testimony about the killing of Nate Champion and Nick Ray. Then I'm going to get my supplies and head on up into the mountains and see if I can't get some Palouse studs for my ranch down in Colorado. What about you?"

The old man shook his head. "I've had 'bout all of humanity I can stand for a while. I'm goin' up into the high lonesome and see if there's any beaver left up there to trap." He smiled, showing yellow stubs of teeth. "It's time I got my camp ready for the winter."

Smoke took his hand. "It's been a pleasure meeting you, Bear Claw. I thank you for telling me about my past."

The mountain man stared into Smoke's eyes. "Maybe, if'n you give it some time, you'll recollect the rest, Smoke."

"Maybe," Smoke said as he turned and went looking for a hotel to get some sleep.

He waved as Bear Claw climbed on his pony and rode off toward snow-covered peaks in the distance, wondering if the man named Preacher was still up there, trapping his own beaver.

* * *

Soon after he fell asleep, images began to appear in Smoke's mind. He was sitting in a cafe eating, and one table over from him was a beautiful young lady with brown hair. In his dream, he knew her name was Sally Reynolds and she was a schoolteacher. He was going by the name Buck West at the time, and they were the only customers in the cafe.

Buck ordered the lunch special and coffee. He felt eyes on him, and looked up into her hazel eyes. He smiled at her.

"Pleasant day," Buck said.

"Very," Sally replied. "Now that school is out for the summer, it's especially so."

"I regret that I don't have more formal education," Buck said. "The War Between the States put a halt to that."

"It's never too late to learn, sir."

"You're a schoolteacher?"

"Yes, I am. And you?"

"Drifter, ma'am."

"I . . . don't think so," the young woman said, meeting his gaze.

Buck smiled. "Oh? And why do you say that?"

"Just a guess."

"What grades do you teach?"

"Sixth, seventh, and eighth. Why do you wear two guns?"

"Habit."

"Most of the men I've seen out here have difficulty mastering one gun," Sally said. "My first day out here I saw a man shoot his big toe off trying to quick-draw. I tried very hard not to laugh, but he looked so foolish."

Buck again smiled. "I would imagine so. But I should imagine the man minus the toe failed to find the humor in it."

"I'm sure."

Conversation waned as the waitress brought their lunches. Buck just couldn't think of a way to get the talk going again.

Deputy Rogers entered the cafe, sat down at the counter, and ordered coffee.

Rogers glared at Sally as she said to Buck, "Will you be in Bury long?"

"All depends, ma'am."

"Lady of your quality shouldn't oughtta be talkin' to no bounty hunter, Miz Reynolds," Rogers said. "Ain't fittin'."

Buck slowly chewed a bite of beef.

"Mr. Rogers," Sally said. "The gentleman and I are merely exchanging pleasantries over lunch. I was addressing the gentleman, not you."

Rogers flushed, placed his coffee mug on the counter, and abruptly left the cafe.

"Deputy Rogers doesn't like me very much," Buck said.

"Why?" Sally asked bluntly.

"Because . . . I probably make him feel somewhat insecure."

"A very interesting statement from a man who professes to have little formal education, Mr. . . . ?"

"West, ma'am. Buck West."

"Are you a bounty hunter, Mr. West?"

"Bounty hunter, cowhand, gunhand, trapper. Whatever I can make a living at. You're from east of the Mississippi River, ma'am?"

"New Hampshire. I came out here last year after replying to an advertisement in a local paper. The pay is much better out here than back home."

"I . . . sort of know where New Hampshire is. I would imagine living is much more civilized back there."

"To say the least, Mr. West. And also much duller."

Hang around a little longer, Sally, Buck thought. *You haven't seen lively yet.* "Would you walk with me, Miss Reynolds?" Buck blurted out. "And please don't think I'm being too forward."

"I would love to walk with you, Mr. West."

The sun was high in the afternoon sky, and Sally opened her parasol.

"Do you ride, Miss Reynolds?" Buck asked.

"Oh, yes. But I have yet to see a sidesaddle in Bury."

"They ain't too common a sight out here."

"Ain't is completely unacceptable in formal writing and speech, Mr. West. But I think you know that."

"Yes, ma'am. Sorry."

She tilted her head, smiling, looking at him, a twinkle in her eyes. As they walked, Buck's spurs jingled. "Which line of employment are you currently pursuing, Mr. West?"

"Beg pardon, ma'am?"

"Bounty hunter, cowhand, gunhand, or trapper?"

"I'm lookin' for a killer named Smoke Jensen. Thirty-thousand-dollar reward for him."

"Quite a sum of money. I've seen the wanted posters around town. What exactly did this Jensen do?"

"Killed a lot of people, ma'am. He's a fast gun for hire, so I'm told."

"Faster than you, Mr. West?"

"I hope not."

She laughed at that.

A group of hard-riding cowboys took that time to burst into town, whooping and hollering and kicking up clouds of dust as they spurred their horses, sliding to a stop in front of one of the saloons.

Buck pulled Sally into a doorway and shielded her from the dust and flying clods.

As they stepped out on the boardwalk again, a grand carriage passed, driven by a coachman all gussied up in a military-looking outfit. Four tough-looking riders accompanied the carriage. Two to the front, two to the back.

As the carriage passed, Buck removed his hat and bowed gallantly.

Even from the boardwalk, Sally could see the woman in the carriage flush with anger and jerk her head to the front. Sally suppressed a giggle.

"Oh, you made her mad, Buck."

"She'll get over it, I reckon."

He took her elbow and they began to walk toward the edge

of town. They had not gone half a block before the sounds of hooves drumming on the hard-packed dirt came to them. Two of the bodyguards that had been with the woman in the carriage reined up in the street, turning their horses to face Buck and Sally.

Buck gently but firmly pushed Sally to one side.

"Stand clear," he said in a low voice. "Trouble ahead."

"What . . . ?" she managed to say before one of the gunhands cut her off.

"You run on home now, schoolmarm. This here might git messy."

Sally stuck her chin out. "I will stand right here on this boardwalk until the soles of my shoes grow roots before I'll take orders from you, you misbegotten cretin!"

Buck grinned at her. Now this lady had some sand to her.

"Whut the hell did she call me?" the cowboy said to his friend.

"Durned if I know."

The cowboy swung his eyes back to Buck. "You insulted Miss Janey, boy. She's madder than a tree full of hornets. You got fifteen minutes to git your gear and git gone."

"I think I'll stay," Buck said. He had thumbed the thongs off his .44's after pushing Sally to one side.

"Boy," the older and uglier of the bodyguards said, "do you know who I am?"

"Can't say I've had the pleasure," Buck replied.

"Name's Dickerson, from over Colorado way. That ring a bell in your head?"

It did, but Buck didn't let it show. Dickerson was a top gun. No doubt about that. Not only was he mean, he was cat-quick with a pistol. "Nope. Sorry."

"And this here"—Dickerson jerked a thumb—"is Russell."

Buck hadn't heard of Russell, but he figured if the fella rode with Dickerson, he'd be good. "Pleased to meet you," Buck said politely.

Dickerson gave Buck an exasperated look. "Boy, are you stupid or tryin' to be smart-mouthed?"

"Neither one. Now if you gentlemen will excuse me, I'd like to continue my stroll with Miss Reynolds."

Both Dickerson and Russell dismounted, ground-reining their ponies. "Only place you goin' is carried to Boot Hill, boy."

Several citizens had gathered around to watch the fun, including one young cowhand with a weather-beaten face and a twinkle in his eyes.

"Stand clear," Buck told the crowd.

The gathering crowd backed up and out of the line of impending fire. They hoped.

"I've bothered no one," Buck said to the crowd, without taking his eyes from the two gunhands facing him. "And I'm not looking for a fight. But if I'm pushed, I'll fight. I just wanted to make that public."

"Git on your hoss and ride, boy!" Russell said. "And do it right now."

"I'm staying."

"You a damn fool, boy!" Dickerson said. "But if you want a lead supper, that's up to you."

"Lead might fly in both directions," Buck said calmly. "Were I you, I'd think about that."

Some odd light flickered quickly through Dickerson's eyes. He wasn't used to being sassed or disobeyed. But damn this boy's eyes, he didn't seem to be worried at all. Who in the devil were they up against?

"That's Buck West, Dickerson," the young cowboy with the beat-up face said.

"That don't spell road apples to me," Russell said. He glared at Buck. "Move, tinhorn, or the undertaker's gonna be divvyin' up your pocket money."

"I like it here," Buck said.

"Then draw, damn you!" Dickerson shouted. He went for

his gun. Out of the corner of his eye, he saw Russell grab for his .45.

Buck's hands swept down and up with the speed of an angry striking snake. His matched .44's roared and belched smoke and flame. The ground-reined horses snorted and reared at the noise. Dickerson and Russell lay on the dusty street. Both were badly wounded. The guns of the two men lay beside them in the dirt. Neither had had time to cock and fire.

"Jumpin' jackrabbits!" the young lady said. "I never seen nothin' like that in my life."

Buck calmly punched out the spent brass and dropped the empties to the dirt. He reloaded and holstered his .44's, leaving the hammer thongs off.

Sheriff Dan Reese and Deputy Rogers came at a run up the wide street. Many townspeople had gathered on the boardwalks to crane their necks.

"Drop those damn guns, West!" Reese yelled before arriving at the scene. "You're under arrest."

"I'd like to know why," Sally said, stepping up to stand beside Buck. Her face was very pale. She pointed to Dickerson and Russell. "Those hooligans started it. They ordered Mr. West to leave town. When he refused, they threatened to kill him. They drew first. And I'll swear to that in a court of law."

"She's right, Sheriff," the young cowhand said.

Reese gave the cowboy an ugly look. "Which side are you on son?"

"The side of right, Sheriff."

Dickerson cried out in pain. The front of his shirt was covered with blood. The .44 slug had hit him squarely in the chest, ricocheted off the breastbone, and exited out the top of his shoulder, tearing a great jagged hole as it spun away.

Russell was the hardest hit. Buck's .44 had struck him in the stomach and torn out his lower back. The gunhand was not long for this world, and everybody looking at him knew it.

"Any charges, Sheriff?" Buck asked, his voice steady and low.

There was open dislike in Reese's eyes as he glared at Buck. He stepped closer. "You're trouble, West. And you and me both know it. I hope you crowd me, gunfighter. 'Cause when you do, I'll kill you!"

"You'll try," Buck replied in the same low tone.

Reese flushed. He stepped back. "No charges, West. It was a fair fight."

Buck turned and took Sally's arm. "Shall we continue?"*

Smoke smiled in his sleep, his mind picturing the woman who would later come to be his wife.

Just before dawn, the beautiful woman in his dream faced him with her hands on his shoulders and looked him straight in the eye. "Smoke Jensen," she said, "you ride with your guns loose, and you be sure and come back to me, because I love you."

At those words, something clicked in Smoke's brain, connections were made, and suddenly he was Smoke Jensen again, with all his memories intact.

He sat upright in bed, looked around as if he wasn't sure how he got to be here, then grinned in the darkness.

"Sally," he whispered, "once again you saved me. Don't fret, darling, I'll be home soon."

With that, he climbed out of bed and began to get dressed. He had some business in Buffalo.

Return of the Mountain Man

Twenty-three

Back at the TA ranch, the cattlemen had just about given up hope that their friends back in Cheyenne were going to send help. As they became more discouraged, there began to be friction between the cattlemen from Cheyenne and the Texas gunfighters.

As bullets continued to strike the building, occasionally penetrating the wall to scream across the room and slap into the opposite wall, tempers became short.

At noon, Frederic deBillier stretched and yawned, then, crouched over, calmly walked toward a back room, blandly announcing he always took a nap at noon and requesting that no one disturb his sleep.

The Texas Kid snorted, looking over his shoulder as deBillier, still dressed in expensive city clothes, disappeared into the other room. "I tell you, boys," he said, speaking to the other Texans lying in front of windows, occasionally returning fire just to show the attackers they were still alive, "I cain't believe we come all the way up here to try an' help these men, an' then find out they nothin' but a bunch of candy-assed dandies."

Frank Canton and Tom Smith looked at each other, worry in their eyes. They both knew if they lost the Texans, or the gunfighters elected to give themselves up, there was nothing to keep the men from Buffalo from riding in and killing all of them.

"Now, Kid, take it easy," Canton said, trying to make peace. "He don't mean nothing by it. You got to remember, he ain't as young as you boys are."

Another Texan, who went by the name Bronco, laughed. "Yeah, Kid. It's jest that he needs his beauty sleep a lot more'n we do, ain't that right, boys?"

This last was greeted with catcalls and hoots, relieving Canton's mind. As long as the Texans were laughing at the Cheyenne cattlemen, they wouldn't be leaving them to die.

A while later, Wolcott, oblivious to the mounting tension between the two groups, stood up and pointed at one of the Cheyenne cattlemen. "Hey, Carl."

"Yes, sir, Major. What do you want?" answered Carl Robinson, who owned a large ranch just outside Cheyenne.

"Pick out some of the gunmen from Texas to go with you and run up the hill behind the house and relieve the men stationed at the outlying fort we built."

"Yes, sir." Robinson moved in a crouch around the room, tapping men on the shoulder until he had seven men getting ready to go with him. He looked over at Bronco and said, "You, Bronco, you're coming too."

Bronco glanced back over his shoulder at Robinson and laughed. "Like hell I am. It's too damn light out there. We'll be killed for sure if'n we try an' run up that hill now."

Wolcott exploded, forgetting where he was and standing up in the middle of the room. He pulled the big Army .44 from his holster and cocked the hammer, pointing the gun at Bronco's back.

"Which do you prefer, being killed going up the hill or being killed right here? You white-livered son of a bitch, you will either do as ordered, or I'll kill you myself!"

The other Texans all turned and aimed their guns at Wolcott, cocking the hammers with a multitude of metallic clicks.

Bronco smirked. "Oh, I don't think you gone be killin' anybody today, Major. Not unless you want about a pound of lead in your belly."

Wolcott's face turned fiery red, and he was about to fire and be damned, when Robinson called out, "That's all right, Major. I got enough men as it is."

He gestured at the others, and they followed him out the door and up the hill, without sustaining a single casualty.

Less than an hour later, Canton yelled out, "Look what's happening now, Major!"

Major Wolcott looked out the window and saw an immense ark of heavy timbers and bales of hay slowly moving toward the ranch compound.

"Damn," the major exclaimed, "the bastards are using our very own wagons against us."

Canton shook his head, calling from his post across the room, "I told you not to leave those wagons and supplies behind, Major."

"It couldn't be helped. They were slowing us down."

"You fool," Canton said, "do you remember what is in those wagons?"

Wolcott nodded. He remembered very well the amount of extra ammunition, weapons, provisions, and worst of all, dynamite that was now in possession of the Buffalo attackers.

He was about to call for the men in the compound to lay down a heavy fire, when he saw a man ride up from the north to halt his horse in front of the ark. He seemed to be trying to stop the attackers. . . .

Smoke reined his horse to a halt directly in front of the large, rolling fortress, forcing the men pushing it to stop.

Sheriff Red Angus stepped from behind the ark and yelled, "Kirby, what the hell do you think you're doin' out there? Get out of the way and let us do our job. We're gonna dynamite those bastards to hell and back."

"I can't let you do that, Sheriff."

Angus cocked his head to the side, an incredulous look on his face. "You can't *let* us do that? Boy, look around you. We got almost three hundred men here, primed and ready for some killin', an' you think you can stop us?"

"Sheriff, my name's not Kirby—it's Smoke Jensen."

The sheriff stopped, his mouth hanging open for a moment. Then he asked, *"The* Smoke Jensen?"

Smoke grinned. "I'm the only one I know about, Sheriff. But the main reason you can't go ahead with your plan is the United States Cavalry troops that are about five minutes behind me. They're coming up here to maintain law and order, and to arrest those men responsible for Nate Champion's and Nick Ray's deaths."

"You young fool," Angus called. "Once the soldiers take over, those men will never go to trial. They've got all the politicians bought and paid for."

As he finished speaking, from a short distance across the range there came a loud bugle call, and as the men from Buffalo turned at the sound, they could see dust and waving cavalry flags in the near distance.

All the shooting stopped as the soldiers arrived, circling their horses around the attacking force, with Sheriff Angus in the center.

Colonel J.J. Van Horn, the commander of the cavalry detachment, stepped off his horse to confer with Sheriff Angus.

"Sir," the colonel said, bowing formally, "I have an order from President Harrison to assist in quelling this disturbance. Will you cooperate and have your men stand down?"

Angus chewed on his moustache as he thought. After a moment, he answered, "Yes, sir, I will. On one condition."

"What is that, sir?"

"Your troops can have all the men we have trapped, but the vigilantes must later be turned over to civilian authorities for trial."

Colonel Van Horn didn't hesitate. "That is acceptable, Sheriff."

He made an about-face and marched down to stand just in front of the compound. "Gentlemen," he called, "are you willing to surrender quietly?"

Major Wolcott, holding a rifle with a soiled white rag on it, walked out of the building. "We are," he answered, "but only to the military, not to that man over there." He pointed at Sheriff Angus.

The colonel said, "Then by order of President Harrison, I hereby place you under military arrest."

In less than thirty minutes, the Cheyenne cattlemen along with the Texas gunfighters were stripped of their weapons and led away under military escort toward Fort McKinney.

As they began to ride away, Smoke walked over to stand next to Sheriff Angus. He stuck out his hand. "No hard feelings, Sheriff."

Angus glared hate at Smoke. "These people came in here with murder and destruction in their hearts and hands. They have murdered and burned and defied the law, and it was my duty to arrest them. They were mine. I had them in my grasp and you took them away from me."

Smoke looked down at his empty hand and lowered it, then glanced up at Angus, speaking in a low, firm voice. "You had no intention of arresting those men, Sheriff. You were going to dynamite them out of the building and then shoot them down in cold blood."

As Angus's eyes dropped and he stared at the ground, Smoke continued. "In my mind, that don't make you a whole lot different from the men you were planning to kill."

When Sheriff Angus refused to meet his gaze, Smoke turned and walked to his horse, stepping into the saddle. He looked up and found two young cowboys sitting on horses, watching him with small grins on their faces.

"Miss Sally was right, Smoke," Pearlie said in his soft drawl, "you just can't manage to stay out of trouble without Cal and me to watch out for you."

Smoke threw back his head and laughed. "Boys," he said, riding toward them, "you don't know how good it is to see familiar faces."

Twenty-four

Smoke reached across his horse's neck and shook hands with Cal and Pearlie, a smile of real welcome on his face.

"Smoke," Cal said, "would you mind tellin' us just what the heck's been goin' on up here?"

Smoke nodded. "Later, boys. Give me a few minutes. I want to say something to those men being taken away."

He wheeled his horse and rode off after the cavalry detachment. When he caught up to Colonel Van Horn, he said, "Colonel, do you mind if I have a word with your prisoners before you leave?"

Van Horn eyed the Colts on Smoke's hips. "You aren't gonna try anything foolish are you, Mr. Jensen?"

"No, sir."

"Well, go ahead then."

Smoke spurred his horse until he was riding next to Major Wolcott and Frank Canton and Tom Smith, who rode at the head of the procession of prisoners.

Wolcott glanced over at him. "Mr. Jensen, the colonel tells me we have you to thank for getting the army here to rescue us."

"Major, let me make this clear. I apprised the troops of your situation in order to make sure that you received a fair trial for the killing of my friends, Champion and Ray." He jerked his head at the group of Texas gunfighters riding behind them. "And I didn't want some of those young men back there to be killed for something that was your responsibility, and yours alone."

"Well, be that as it may, I want to thank you for saving our lives, all of our lives."

Smoke nodded, his eyes flat and dangerous as he stared at Wolcott, Canton, and Smith. "The colonel has assured me that you will stand trial for what you've done, and I believe him to be a man of his word. But if I find out that you somehow manage to buy your freedom from the politicians your rich friends have in their pockets, I'll consider it a personal affront."

Wolcott grinned, his lips curling in a nasty smirk. "So?"

"If that happens, and we ever cross trails again, I will shoot you down like the mad dogs you are." He tipped his hat, his own lips curling in a similar grin. "You have the word of Smoke Jensen on it, sir."

Wolcott found himself looking into eyes as cold and dangerous as a rattler's about to strike. His face drained of color, and he quickly looked around to make sure Colonel Van Horn was nearby.

"I'll be following your trial with a great deal of interest, Major. You can count on it."

He glanced at Canton and Smith to make sure they understood what he was saying, then jerked his horse's reins around and rode off back toward where Cal and Pearlie were waiting for him.

Wolcott took his hat off and sleeved sweat off his forehead, watching Smoke's back as he rode off. "Damn fool," he muttered.

Canton chewed on the end of his moustache. "I don't know about you, Major, but I almost hope we do stand trial. I don't relish spendin' the rest of my days lookin' back over my shoulder to see if Smoke Jensen's there."

Back in Buffalo, Smoke took Cal and Pearlie to the hotel dining room and ordered them all a big meal.

Pearlie rubbed his stomach. "Boy howdy, Smoke, but I been

lookin' forward to this. I'm so hungry, my stomach thinks my throat's been cut."

Cal shook his head. "Yeah, Smoke, ol' Pearlie there only ate enough for two men this mornin' 'fore we headed out to see if we could find you."

As Smoke chuckled, Cal added, "For him, that's like bein' on half rations."

"It's sure good to see you boys," Smoke said. "How's Sally, and the Sugarloaf?"

Pearlie looked up from cutting his steak. "Sally and the ranch are doin' fine, Smoke. Only she was awful worried when she didn't hear from you when you got to Buffalo."

Smoke nodded. "When I first arrived, the telegraph lines had been cut by the Cheyenne ranchers. They were hoping to catch the town by surprise and take over the county, then follow up by killing all the men on their 'death list' of cowboys who were trying to start their own spreads."

Cal shook his head. "How did they ever hope to get away with somethin' like that, Smoke?"

Smoke shrugged. "They damn near did, Cal. In this country, at this time of year, the only connection with the outside world is through the telegraph line. They figured if that was cut, they and their hired guns from Texas could do just about anything they wanted, and by the time anyone found out about it, it would be all over."

Pearlie grinned. "They just neglected to figure on Smoke Jensen gettin' involved, huh, Smoke?"

Smoke shook his head. "Don't give me the credit, Pearlie. They failed because of the bravery of one man, Nate Champion."

As they ate, Smoke told them about how Champion held off fifty gunmen for two days, long enough for word to get to Buffalo and the populace to arm themselves and set up a defense.

Cal's forehead wrinkled in puzzlement. "I still don't understand why you went to all the trouble to get the Army to rescue those men, after they took you and Bear Claw hostage, and killed your friends."

Smoke took the last bite of his steak, leaned back in his chair, and pulled a long, black cigar from his pocket. "Cal, I always think the law ought to be given a chance to work, if it's possible. This country's growing fast, and the more it grows, the more the rule of law has to take over from the rule of the gun."

Pearlie belched, rubbed his stomach, and leaned forward, his elbows on the table. "But Smoke, what if that Sheriff Angus is right? What if those boys get their politician friends to buy their way outta trouble?"

Smoke took a deep drag of his cigar and tilted smoke from his nostrils, watching as the ceiling fans blew it away. "Then the rule of law has failed, and it's back to the rule of the gun. I made those men a promise as they rode off, that they were going to be judged for what they did, one way or the other, either by the law or by me."

Cal asked, "Now that the war is over, what are your plans?"

Smoke stubbed out his cigar and took a final drink of his coffee. "I'm going to get some provisions and a couple of packhorses, and head on up into the mountains to see if I can find that tribe of Nez Percé. I still need to get some good Palouse stock to breed into our remuda back at the Sugarloaf."

Pearlie rubbed his lips, glancing back over his shoulder. "Just when are you plannin' on doin' that, Smoke?"

"Right away. Why?"

"Oh, I's just wonderin' if we have time for some of that apple pie I smell back in the kitchen." He rubbed his stomach. "Now that I've taken the edge off my appetite, I figure I can relax and enjoy a piece or two."

Smoke shook his head and waved at their waitress. "Hell, might as well get the whole pie. We don't want Pearlie going off half-starved, do we, Cal?"

"No, sir," the young man said, a grin on his face. "But I might oughta eat a piece or two also, 'cause I wouldn't want Pearlie to eat it all and get stomach cramps on our trip."

Twenty-five

By the time they had finished filling Pearlie's belly, it was getting late, and another winter storm had blown in. With visibility down to twenty feet and the temperature in minus figures, Smoke decided to take a couple of rooms at the hotel and start their journey in the morning.

Dawn found the snowfall down to manageable levels, and they bought supplies and packhorses and got ready to leave. They stopped at the hotel for what Pearlie said was to be their last "civilized" meal before taking to the trail.

As they ate heaping plates of scrambled hens' eggs, thick slices of smoked bacon, and sliced potatoes fried with slabs of sweet onions, some men at a nearby table glared at them, hatred in their eyes.

Cal glanced nervously over his shoulder at the men, then leaned forward and asked Smoke, "What do you think them men are starin' at, Smoke?"

Smoke continued to eat, seemingly unconcerned. "Don't pay them no mind, Cal. They're just pissed-off that they didn't get to kill the vigilantes from Cheyenne. They'll get over it."

Jack Curry, one of the cowboys at the table, finally called in a loud voice, "Hey, Jensen. How does it feel to set the men free who killed Nate Champion?"

When Smoke ignored him and continued to eat, Curry stood up and headed toward Smoke's table.

"Are you deaf, as well as a coward, Jensen?" he called,

strutting across the room, his hands near the butts of his pistols.

Smoke sighed and pushed his plate away, leaning back in his chair to look for the first time at Curry.

"I heard you, cowboy. I just didn't think it necessary to answer a damn-fool question. By the way, what is your name anyway?"

Curry glanced over his shoulder to make sure his friends were all watching as he backed down the famous gunfighter Smoke Jensen. "My name's Jack Curry. Why?"

Smoke shrugged. "I just wanted to know what name you wanted carved in the cross over your grave."

Curry's face flamed red and he squared his shoulders. "You think you got the sand to take me on, gunslick?" He gave a short laugh. "Folks around here say you're a famous gunman, but I ain't never heard of you afore."

Smoke pushed back his chair and got slowly to his feet. He walked over to stand a few feet from Curry. He glanced over the man's shoulders at his friends, still sitting at their table. "Any of you gents want to ante up in this game, or is this fool playing a lone hand?"

Curry grinned and looked back over his shoulder. Then his smile faded when the other men shook their heads and looked down at the table, clearly wanting no part in the upcoming fight.

Curry stared at Smoke, licking his lips, his hands trembling as they hovered over his weapons when he realized he might have bitten off more than he could chew.

"I hate killing a man before lunch, Curry. You want to reconsider your play?" Smoke's voice was low and almost bored, as if he had played this game too many times in the past.

"I'm gonna drill you, Jensen, and then I'm gonna spit on your body," Curry said with false bravado.

"Then let's dance, hombre," Smoke said, his eyes flat and dangerous, no longer bored, but glittering with anger.

Curry took a deep breath and went for his pistol, his hand grabbing iron.

Before he could clear leather, Smoke's .44 appeared in his hand as if by magic, leveled and cocked and pointing at Curry's face, two inches from his nose. Curry's gun was still in its holster, and his eyes were wide, sweat beginning to bead on his forehead.

"You really want me to let the hammer down and scatter your brains all over your friends, or are you gonna go back over there and finish your breakfast?" Smoke asked.

"Gawd damn!" one of the men at the table whispered, awe in his voice. "I never even seen him draw."

Before Curry could answer, Sheriff Red Angus stalked into the room, a shotgun leveled in his hand.

As he eared back the hammers, he glanced over at Smoke's table and saw two pistols aimed at his head, Cal and Pearlie grinning over the barrels. "Take it easy there, Sheriff," Pearlie said, his voice hard. "That gent drew first."

Angus lowered his shotgun, easing the hammers down. "It don't appear that way from here. Curry's gun's still in leather."

"That's 'cause he's slower'n molasses in January, Sheriff," Cal said.

"He's right, Sheriff," one of the men at the other table said, holding his hands out in plain sight. "Jack forced the play. Jensen didn't have no choice in the matter."

Curry released his pistol and slowly raised his hands, sweat running off his face to drip on his vest. "I . . . I guess I was wrong in what I said, Jensen," he mumbled, his shoulders slumped and his head hanging down.

Smoke spun his pistol and dropped it in his holster, still staring at Curry. "I'll take that as an apology, Mr. Curry."

He spun on his heels, dropped a gold double-eagle on the table, and said, "Come on, boys. Let's hit the trail."

As Smoke and Cal and Pearlie walked from the room, Curry stumbled over to his table on legs made of rubber, flopping in his chair and sleeving sweat off his face. "Damn! That Jensen's faster'n a rattlesnake with that short-gun."

The sheriff walked over to stand staring down at Jack Curry. "You're a lucky man, Jack . . . stupid, but lucky!"

Smoke and his friends got on their horses and slowly walked them out of town through a light snowfall toward the Yellowstone Mountains.

They didn't look back, and so they didn't see four men mount up and ride out of town, leaning over on their horses to follow their tracks in the snow.

After a five-hour ride, Pearlie removed his hat and brushed accumulated snow off the brim as he glanced around at the magnificent scenery along their journey. "I can see why you love the high lonesome, Smoke," he said. "It's pretty as a picture up here."

Smoke nodded. "It's something I've never tired of seeing, Pearlie, and I've been living up in the mountains off and on for more than twenty years."

"It's so quiet up here," Cal said. "The only sound is the wind whistlin' through the pines."

Smoke gave a short laugh. "It's anything but peaceful, Cal. You're looking but not seeing. You've got to learn to open your eyes and see everything going on around you."

He paused and pointed off to the side. "See those tracks there—the small ones with larger ones alongside? That's a rabbit, being trailed by a fox, and if you follow the tracks, you can see a little batch of red-colored snow where the fox made his kill."

After a moment, Smoke halted his pony and pointed to a tall pine tree next to the trail. It was easy to see where the bark had been rubbed off to a height of eight feet. "And there's where a bear, probably a grizzly from the size of him, has been scratching his back on that tree." He looked at Cal. "It is anything but peaceful up here, Cal boy. In the winter, there's a constant battle going on, a battle for survival, and only the strongest, or the smartest, will survive."

"Speakin' of survival, Smoke," Pearlie said, glancing back down the trail the way they had come. "I think somebody's back there on our back trail."

Smoke smiled and nodded. "Good, Pearlie. I've been wondering when you'd notice. They've been back there since we left town."

Cal looked nervously back over his shoulder. "You think they mean to attack us?"

Smoke pursed his lips. "I can't see no other reason they'd be following us, Cal. Weather's too bad to be doing any cattle driving today, and if they were friendly, they'd of let their presence be known by now."

"What do you plan to do about it, Smoke?" Pearlie asked as he took his pistol out of his holster and opened the loading gate to check his loads.

Smoke glanced up at the sky, watching the gathering darkness. "It's getting on toward dusk. I think we'll make us a camp up there near that grove of poplar trees," he said, pointing ahead to a small group of trees near the trail. "We'll make us a nice, warm fire, and put some beans and bacon on to cook."

Cal looked surprised. "That's all?"

"Yeah. They won't be able to build much of a fire without giving themselves away. When the temperature starts to drop, I figure that's when they'll make their move."

"But we'll be easy targets near that fire," Cal protested.

Smoke grinned. "No, we won't. I'm gonna show you something Preacher taught me when I was just about your age, Cal."

They spurred their horses and rode into the grove of trees. "While Pearlie and I gather some wood for the fire, I want you to strip some branches off those trees, ones with plenty of leaves still on 'em," Smoke told Cal.

As darkness fell and their fire caught and began to burn brightly, Smoke made a trestle, hung a pot of beans with thick chunks of bacon in it over the fire to cook, and placed a pot of coffee on coals near the edge of the campfire.

He took a handful of the branches Cal had gathered, walked over about thirty feet from the fire, and scooped a shallow depression in a snowbank there. "Lie down in there, Cal, with your Winchester cocked and ready."

Cal gave him a disbelieving look, but climbed down in the hole in the snow, and Smoke covered him with the branches, then sprinkled snow on top of the limbs until Cal was completely hidden, with only a short section of the barrel of his rifle sticking out.

Keeping out of the light shed by the fire, he walked to the other side of their camp and did the same thing, covering Pearlie up until he couldn't be seen. He leaned over and whispered, "Don't worry, Pearlie. The branches and snow will keep you warm as toast."

After he had Cal and Pearlie situated to his satisfaction, Smoke slung his double-barreled ten-gauge Greener shotgun over his shoulders on its rawhide strap and climbed up one of the poplar trees until he was ten feet off the ground, hidden among the leaves there. Then he settled down, his back against the trunk of the tree. He didn't figure he had long to wait, for the smell of food and coffee and the inviting warmth of the fire would bring their attackers out soon.

Smoke was right. In less than thirty minutes several shadowy figures could be seen slipping through the darkness up to the edge of the light from the campfire.

Smoke had laid out their ground covers and sleeping bags, stuffing them with leaves and branches and putting their hats on their saddles as if they were lying in them near the fire.

Smoke heard a hoarse whisper almost directly under his tree. "Jack, are you ready?"

A low voice answered, "Yeah. Let 'em have it, boys."

The darkness exploded as four men opened fire on the sleeping bags, shooting into them without warning, then running into the light for closer shots.

After a moment, one of the men bent over and threw the covers back, aiming his pistol to fire again.

He looked up, his eyes wide, and muttered, "Oh, shit!"

Smoke leveled his Greener and let both hammers down, making sure he was braced against the tree trunk so the recoil wouldn't throw him out of the tree.

The shotgun exploded, sending fire and smoke and molten lead pellets into the man next to the sleeping bag, blowing him almost in two, and the slugs shredded his head and shoulders, spinning him around to land half in the fire.

Cal aimed his rifle at another figure standing off to the side and slowly squeezed the trigger, as Smoke had taught him. The rifle fired, kicking back and rolling Cal slightly to the side as the man in his sights grabbed his chest and doubled over to sprawl face-down in the snow.

The other two men, seeing their ambush fail, turned and tried to run away. As one was stomping through knee-deep snow, trying to run, Pearlie rose up out of the ground in front of him, his rifle at his hip, a grin on his face, his teeth gleaming in reflected firelight like some demon from hell.

The gunman, seeing this apparition arise from the earth, screamed in fright and held his hands out in front of him, as if they could somehow protect him from evil.

Pearlie's bullet passed through the man's palm and entered his chest, exploding his heart and ending his fear and his life simultaneously, blowing him backwards in a crumpled heap in the snow. He lay there, his eyes staring upward sightlessly, filling slowly with melting snow flakes.

The fourth man threw his gun to the ground and held up his hands, screaming, "I give up! Don't shoot me! Please, Mother of God, have mercy!"

Smoke jumped from his tree, landing on cat-feet directly in front of the hollering man, almost scaring him to death.

"Jack Curry, if I'm not mistaken," Smoke said, his voice hoarse with fury.

"Jensen . . . I'm sorry. I didn't mean. . . ." the man cried, tears running down his face, terrified.

As Cal and Pearlie walked up, Smoke said, "Cal, pull that galoot out of the fire. He's stinking up our camp."

After the bodies had been piled in a heap, away from the camp, Smoke threw Curry a shovel. "Here, asshole, bury your friends."

Curry looked at Smoke in disbelief. "I can't dig in this ground. It's frozen solid."

"You'll bury 'em, or I'll kill you where you stand," Smoke growled.

Curry took the shovel and began to hack at the ice-covered ground, slowly making a shallow hole.

While he worked, Smoke and Cal and Pearlie went over next to the fire and began to eat the beans and bacon, washing it down with steaming-hot coffee from the pot.

Cal glanced over at Curry, digging furiously as if that might somehow save his life.

"What are you gonna do with him, Smoke?"

"I haven't decided yet. What do you propose?"

Cal stared into the fire. "I don't rightly know." He cut his eyes up at Smoke and said, "Can I sleep on it and decide in the morning?"

Smoke nodded. "I'll leave it up to you, Cal. It'll be another lesson in life in the high lonesome."

After Curry finished burying what remained of his friends, Smoke invited him over to the fire and gave him food and coffee.

As he ate, Curry glanced around at the men watching him. "What are you gonna do with me, Jensen?"

Smoke yawned, finished his cup of coffee, and threw the dregs in the fire, making it hiss and crackle. "We'll decide in the morning. For now, we're all gonna get some shut-eye."

He took a rope from his packhorse and tied Curry's hands and feet, covered him with a blanket, and patted him on the cheek. "But if I were you, Curry, I'd spend what time I have left making your peace with God, 'cause I have a feeling you're gonna see Him before too long."

In the morning, they restarted the fire and cooked a breakfast of scrambled eggs, bacon, and coffee. Cal remained quiet, thinking on what they should do with the killer they'd captured. Though he was still in his teens, Cal was trail-hardened from his life on the frontier and had killed men before, but it had always been in the heat of battle, never in cold blood.

After they broke camp and gathered the ambushers' horses from where they'd been picketed, Smoke stood in front of Cal.

"Well, Cal, it's time to decide."

Curry, white-faced, looked from one of the trio to the other. "You mean you're gonna let that boy decide what happens to me?"

"You got a better idea?" Smoke asked.

Curry nodded vigorously. "Yeah, let me go and I promise not to ever bother you again." He jerked his head at the fresh graves nearby. "You've already killed three of my friends. Isn't that enough?"

"Cal?" Smoke asked, looking at his young friend.

"I think he's right, Smoke. I don't think I can kill a man in cold blood." He paused. "And I don't think you or Pearlie can neither."

Smoke nodded, his eyebrow cocked, wondering what Cal was leading up to.

"I thought about what you told him last night, about making his peace with God, so I'm gonna let God decide if he lives or dies."

"What?" Curry asked, his mouth hanging open.

Cal walked to his horse, took a long bowie knife out of his saddlebags, and flipped it end-over-end to land sticking in the snow in front of Curry's feet.

"Take the knife—you're free to go."

"You mean you're lettin' me go free?" Curry asked, a grin starting to form on his lips.

"That's right," Cal answered, his expression serious.

Curry grabbed the knife and started to get on his horse.

"Uh-uh," Cal said, shaking his head. "No horse. You're gonna have to walk back to town."

Curry stared at him. "That's a three-day walk, an' the temperature's below freezing!"

Cal nodded. "We're gonna let God an' the high lonesome decide if you're worth savin'."

"But I'll freeze to death!"

Cal shrugged. "Maybe. But this way you have a chance, which is more'n you gave us when you thought we were sleepin' an' you fired on our sleepin' bags."

Curry looked at Smoke. "Jensen, try an' talk some sense into that boy. This is crazy!"

Smoke grinned. "No, I agree with Cal. It's only fitting we give you a chance to survive. I've done it with less, so if you're man enough, you can too. You're starting off with a full belly and a weapon, which is more than fair. Now, get moving!"

Curry stuck the knife in his belt and pulled his coat tight around his shoulders. He looked into their eyes, but saw no mercy, so he turned and began to walk back toward the direction of town, his shoulders hunched against the freezing wind.

Cal glanced at Smoke. "Them horses of theirs will make a good present for the Nez Percé when we go to tradin' for the Palouse you're lookin' for."

Smoke grinned. "Damn if I don't believe you've got some mountain man in you, Cal."

Pearlie clapped Cal on the back. "That's 'cause he's learned from the best mountain man around, Smoke. Now, let's get movin' 'fore my feet freeze to the ground."

Twenty-six

When they stopped for a nooning later that day, Smoke pulled out his maps of the region and took some sightings off nearby peaks to ascertain which direction to go to find the Nez Percé camping area.

"What's that X marked there on the map?" Cal asked, pointing with his finger.

"That's where the Kiowa brave I told you about, Walking Bear, said he thought the Nez Percé might be," Smoke answered.

He looked up, found his landmark, a ridge on the side of one of the mountains that looked like a bear's head and snout, and pointed up to a notch cut in the mountains.

"He said they usually head for a small valley near that notch this time of year. According to him, it's got a stream that runs fast enough not to freeze over and plenty of nearby beaver and deer and elk for the Indians to hunt to keep them eating throughout the winter months."

Cal pulled his fur-lined coat tight around him and moved a little closer to the fire, shivering in the frigid wind. "I guess if you intend to spend the winter in the high lonesome, you got to plan ahead."

Smoke nodded. "That's right, Cal. There's plenty of bones bleaching up in the mountains from men who neglected something as simple as pitching their camp near a stream, or where there was plenty of wildlife to feed off of." He looked around at the snow-covered land stretching as far as the eye could see. "It's mighty hard, when the temperature is twenty below and the snow is chest high, to travel very far looking for water or food."

Pearlie followed Smoke's gaze, feeling the cold eat right into him down to his bones. "Any other tricks we ought'a know about, Smoke?"

Smoke grinned. "You planning on becoming a mountain man, Pearlie?"

Pearlie's face remained serious. "Well, the more I'm around people like that Jack Curry and his friends, the more I like my horse."

Cal laughed. "Come on, Pearlie. The way you put the chow away, if you spent the winter up here there wouldn't be no animals left at all come spring."

"And it'd be a long time between bear sign and apple pies, my friend," Smoke added.

Pearlie nodded. "Yeah, there is that to consider." He glanced at Smoke. "Guess I'd have to try and find me somebody like Miss Sally to winter with."

"No chance, Pearlie," Smoke said, his eyes far away.

Smoke's mind drifted back to the woman he had left in Colorado. Of all the things he'd seen and done in his entire life, there were only three people he thought unforgettable. *No wonder it was so easy for you to lose your memory, old hoss,* he thought to himself. *There wasn't all that much you wanted to remember.* He thought about his dreams while his mind was confused. It was significant that the three people in his night-time memories were his father, his substitute father Preacher, and the love of his life, Sally Reynolds Jensen. He mused on this for a few minutes, thinking it extraordinary that a man could live as long as he had and go through as much and still, when push came to shove, have only three people who meant everything to him.

He forced himself to return to the present, and glanced over at Pearlie. "There isn't but one Sally Jensen, and they broke the mold when they made her," he said.

He leaned over, picked up the coffeepot, and poured them all another cup, finishing off the pot. "Better drink up, boys. It's gonna be a while 'fore we get anything else warm in our bellies."

When they finished their coffee, they broke camp and climbed onto their horses, Pearlie holding the dally rope to the two packhorses, while Cal took charge of the rope attached to the four horses Curry's men had donated to their expedition.

Smoke pointed his horse's nose directly north, into the wind coming over the mountains from Canada, and pulled his bandanna up to cover his face and prevent frostbite. He spurred his mount, and they began the long climb toward the notch in the mountain range up ahead.

When it became too dark to see where they were heading, he set up another camp in a small grove of trees to protect them from the worst of the wind and snow. He pulled the horses together, tied them to a tree so their bodies were against each other for added warmth, and fed them plenty of oats to help keep their body temperatures up against the frigid air.

After the men ate, he had Pearlie wrap their food up in a blanket and hang it from the branch of a birch tree, so it was six feet or so off the ground.

"Why are you doin' that, Smoke?" Cal asked.

"This time of year, most of the bears are trying to put on weight for their winter hibernation. They can smell food for miles, and anything they can smell they think is theirs." He grinned. "Nothing worse than having a hungry bear waking you up trying to get your food, or even worse, trying to make you his dinner."

Cal's eyes got wide, and he looked back and forth in the gathering darkness. "You think there's any chance of that happenin' tonight?"

"Always a chance up here," Smoke said. "That's why we're gonna take turns keeping that fire going strong until the morning. Bears have a natural aversion to fire." He hesitated, and before he lay down he pulled his Winchester from its saddle boot, jacked a slug into the firing chamber, and laid the rifle next to his bedroll. "Course sometimes, if he's hungry enough, a bear'll come right into camp, fire or no fire, so sleep with one eye open, boys."

Cal's face paled. "Thanks for tellin' us that, Smoke. Now I probably won't get any sleep at all."

In spite of his professed fear, two minutes after his head hit his saddle, which he was using for a pillow, Cal's snoring could be heard for twenty yards.

Pearlie raised his head and smirked. "Hell, if the fire don't keep them bars away, Cal's snoring surely will."

Two days later, they came upon the entrance to the valley below the notch in the mountains. For the first time since they left Buffalo, the ground was level, and the temperature seemed less extreme.

"Why's it gettin' warmer, Smoke?" Pearlie asked, looking around.

Smoke pointed to either side of them. "Look up there, Pearlie. We're protected on three sides by the mountains as they rise around the valley. I suspect that's another reason the Nez Percé pick this place to winter every year."

The farther they traveled into the valley, the shallower the snowdrifts became, until there were hardly any on the ground at all.

Suddenly, Cal pulled his rifle out of its boot and aimed off to the side, cocking the hammer back.

"What are you doing?" Smoke asked, reaching over to push the barrel down.

Cal pointed off toward a large buck deer, standing in the shallow snow seventy-five yards away, its head down as it pawed snow off tender green shoots of grass and grazed.

"I thought I'd shoot that buck over there and we'd have some venison for dinner tonight."

Smoke shook his head. "You see those small piles of stones every fifty yards or so along the trail, piled up to a point?"

Cal shook his head. "No, I hadn't noticed."

"Those are Nez Percé signal rocks. They show this is their territory, and I doubt they'd take kindly to us killing game on land they've claimed as their own."

"But I haven't seen an Indian yet, Smoke."

"Oh, they're there. They've been trailing us for the past six hours, keeping just out of sight on the mountainsides on either side of us."

"Damn," Cal said in frustration. "I don't think I'll ever git the hang of this mountaineering."

Smoke patted him on the shoulder. "Don't feel bad, Cal. I lived up here for several years with Preacher when I was about your age, and a day didn't go by that he didn't teach me something new about being a mountain man. There's a hell of a lot to learn, and if you don't have a good teacher, the mountain'll jump up and kill you 'fore you have a chance to learn it all."

Pearlie chuckled. "Seems like the more Cal and I learn, the more we don't know 'bout life up here."

Smoke got down off his horse and undid one of the ties to the packhorse. He pulled a bag of Arbuckle's coffee out of the pack along with the coffeepot. "Help me make a fire, boys. I think it's time we introduced ourselves before we get any closer to the Nez Percé camp. It ain't polite to go calling until we've been invited."

After they had the fire going and a large pot of coffee brewing, Smoke instructed Cal and Pearlie to sit next to the fire, hands in plain sight and away from their weapons. As they sat drinking the coffee, he set several more cups around the fire, off to the side by themselves. "That's just to let them know they're expected, and welcome," Smoke said when Cal and Pearlie looked at him with puzzled expressions on their faces.

Within fifteen minutes, two braves who appeared to be in

their early twenties, accompanied by a younger brave about twelve years old, walked their ponies into Smoke's camp.

Without getting up, Smoke waved them toward the campfire. "Coffee's brewing, and you're welcome to join us," he said in a slow voice.

Cal whispered, "You think they speak English?"

Smoke nodded. "Most of the younger braves do by now. There's been so many trappers up here, they've managed to learn enough to get by. If they don't, we'll have to use sign language, but I'm a mite rusty, so I hope these men know our lingo."

As the braves dismounted, Smoke noticed one was carrying an old muzzle-loaded rifle, while the other two had bows and arrows, one with a stone tomahawk stuck in his breeches within easy reach.

As they approached, Smoke said in a low voice, "Most of the Indians I've met have a real taste for coffee, and they don't get to partake of it very often."

The eldest of the three walked up to stand next to the fire, staring down at Smoke. He patted his chest with an open palm. "I am called Spotted Elk," he said in a deep voice.

Smoke stood up and placed his hand on his chest. "I am known as Man Who Walks on Mountain."

The brave's eyes widened and he grinned, turning to talk rapidly in his own language to his companions.

"Would you care for some coffee?" Smoke asked, pointing at the coffeepot resting on coals next to the fire.

"Cafecito?" the brave asked, making Smoke smile when he used the slang term for coffee favored by most of the mountain men Smoke had known.

As they gathered close to the fire and Smoke poured them full cups, he said over his shoulder to Pearlie, "Get the bag of sugar out of the pack. Indians have a real hankering for sugar with their coffee."

When the young brave tasted his coffee, and made a face at its bitterness, Smoke reached over and poured a generous helping of sugar into the strong, black brew.

The brave took another tentative sip, and broke into a wide grin, smacking his lips and drinking down the entire cup in one long swallow.

The two older braves laughed, along with Smoke and Cal and Pearlie.

Spotted Elk leaned over and said to Smoke, "Running Deer's first time with the black water called *cafecito."*

"It does take some getting used to," Smoke observed, grinning as the young boy held his cup out for a refill.

Spotted Elk held out his hand to stop Running Deer, trying to impart some manners to the kid, but Smoke shook his head. "That's all right—we have plenty more." He refilled the boy's cup, and watched him drink it slower this time, savoring the sweetness of the coffee.

As they drank, with the Indians sitting on their haunches around the fire, Smoke said, "We're looking for Gray Wolf." He pointed over his shoulder at the four horses tied nearby. "We have presents for your tribe, and come in peace to make a trade."

Spotted Elk finished his coffee and handed the cup back to Smoke, then walked over to run his hands down the flanks of the horses, stopping to pry open their mouths and glance at their teeth as he examined them. He looked back over his shoulder and said something in the Nez Percé language to his friends, who immediately got up and ran to their ponies. They jumped up on them and rode off with a couple of whoop and hollers, evidently on their way to let the chief know they had visitors on the way.

As Spotted Elk got on his pony, Smoke handed him the dally rope to the horses, letting him lead the animals into the village so he would get credit for the trade. In this way, Smoke knew they had at least one ally among the Nez Percé who would help break the ice in the upcoming bargaining for the Palouse ponies they were after.

Twenty-seven

Smoke and Cal and Pearlie followed Spotted Elk into the main part of the Nez Percé camp. In addition to the numerous hide huts and deerskin tepees, there were several log structures and elaborate lean-tos, showing the semi-permanent nature of this camp.

Smoke pointed out the wooden structures to Cal and Pearlie. "Evidently, the Nez Percé return to this same location every winter. Some of those cabins look like they're several years old, at least."

"I always thought Injuns roamed around, making camps wherever they happened to stop," Pearlie observed.

"That used to be true," Smoke said, "but lately, since they've become more peaceful and less warlike, and more used to the white man's presence, they seem to've become more settled in their ways."

He shook his head. "Just another part of the life up here that's passed on due to interference by white men, and will never be the same."

A brave stepped from one of the largest of the wooden cabins, holding up his spread hands in welcome. Smoke was surprised at his young age. "That must be Gray Wolf," he said in a low voice to his companions. "I would've thought he'd be older to be chief."

The Indian appeared to be in his late thirties or early forties, very young for a full chief of the Nez Percé, who, like most

Indian tribes, equated age with wisdom in choosing their leaders.

"Welcome," Gray Wolf said, his face showing neither happiness nor dismay to see them.

"Indians would make great poker players," Smoke whispered. "They don't tend to show their emotions much."

He stepped off his horse and walked up to the chief. "Hello. I am Man Who Walks on Mountain," Smoke said, lowering his head a mite showing deference to the chief's position as leader of his tribe.

"We have heard your song many times," Gray Wolf said. "One of our Kiowa brothers, Walking Bear, sent word of what you did for his people in the white-eyes camp called Denver. He said your are known as an honorable man, and a friend to all our peoples."

Smoke nodded, not saying anything, waiting to see what would happen next. He knew Indians could be very unpredictable, welcoming one minute, dangerous the next.

"Come inside. We will smoke and eat, as friends should," the chief said, turning and leading the way into his cabin.

When they entered, Smoke and Cal and Pearlie found the floor to be dirt, covered with elaborate hides of deerskin and bearskin. In the middle of the room, underneath a hole in the roof, was a small fire.

Gray Wolf waved them to be seated next to the fire, and he joined them, sitting cross-legged on the ground. Spotted Elk and the younger brave who had been with him at Smoke's camp joined them around the fire.

Gray Wolf pointed at the young brave. "This my son, Running Deer." Gray Wolf looked at the boy with undisguised pride. "He be next chief of Nez Percé someday."

Smoke nodded. "He is a fine-looking young brave. He will bring much honor to your house."

Gray Wolf picked up a wooden pipe and put it in his mouth, lighting it with a burning branch from the fire. After several puffs, he handed it across to Smoke, who also took a couple of puffs, his tongue burning from the bitter taste of the uncured tobacco, then passed it over to Cal and Pearlie.

After everyone around the fire had a taste of the pipe, Smoke took a handful of cigars from his pocket and passed them out. The chief quickly put the pipe down and lighted one of the cigars, showing he didn't much care for the taste of his tobacco either.

After a few minutes, the chief signaled a woman kneeling behind him, and she ladled liquid from a pot on the edge of the fire into small bowls and gave each of the visitors one.

Pearlie looked into his bowl with some distaste. "What do you suppose this is?" he asked Smoke in a low voice.

Smoke plucked a chunk of meat out of the stew and popped it in his mouth, chewing and smiling at the same time. "Elk stew," he said to Pearlie. "Eat it, and try to look like you enjoy it, or you'll insult our host."

Eating with their fingers, since Indians didn't use spoons and forks, they soon finished their stew, Pearlie smacking his lips as if it was the best thing he'd ever eaten.

As Gray Wolf relighted his cigar and leaned back on an elbow, he said, "Spotted Elk has shown me your gifts to the Nez Percé. What do you ask in trade?"

"I would like to take with me some of your spotted ponies, two males and two females."

"Why do you wish our spotted ponies? Your horses seem adequate for your needs."

"I have a ranch in Colorado, and I know the spotted ponies of the Nez Percé can run like the wind from sunup to sundown without tiring. I have need of such animals in my herd. They will add much to my stature among the white-eyes of my tribe."

"You have traveled far to get these ponies. You must wish them very bad, no?"

Smoke smiled and spoke out of the side of his mouth to Cal and Pearlie. "The old bastard is starting to negotiate now, making the point that I came to him, so I must give up the most in the trade."

To Gray Wolf, he said, "That is true. In addition to the horses I have already offered, I have brought white man's wampum—greenback dollars, or gold if you prefer."

Smoke opened his buckskin shirt and pulled out his money belt. He took a handful of hundred-dollar bills along with a handful of gold double-eagle pieces, and spread them on the rug in front of him.

Gray Wolf smiled and spread his hands. "Your dollars are of no use to us here on the mountain," he said, his eyebrows raised.

Smoke leaned forward. "In the spring, when you and your people travel to the south to graze your ponies and hunt the elk and deer to fill your cooking pots, these dollars can be traded for whatever you need in the white man's camps . . . tools, knives, food or grain for your ponies, beads, mirrors, blankets for your squaws."

Smoke held up a hundred-dollar bill. "Just one of these bought Walking Bear enough food to feed all his people for the entire winter."

Spotted Elk leaned over and spoke softly and rapidly to Gray Wolf in the language of the Nez Percé.

After a moment, Gray Wolf turned back to Smoke. "Spotted Elk tells me the knives of the white-eyes are much superior to ours, and that your gold can buy many knives."

Smoke nodded. "Spotted Elk speaks with much wisdom."

He took the bowie knife from his belt and held out his hand to Spotted Elk, who, after a moment, passed over his handmade knife to Smoke.

Smoke swung the bowie knife, and it cut through the blade of Spotted Elk's knife as if it were made of wood.

As Gray Wolf's eyes widened, Smoke handed the bowie knife across to him. "For you, a blade as strong as the Nez Percé's chief is."

The chief sat a little straighter at Smoke's words, a slight smile tugging at the corner of his lips.

Smoke got to his feet. "We have more on our packhorse."

He walked outside, followed by the chief and Spotted Elk and Running Deer. He stepped to the packhorse and untied the ropes holding a large canvas bag to the back of the mount, letting it fall to the ground.

When the pack hit the ground, it opened, spilling out piles of metal pots and pans, knives, woven woolen blankets in bright colors, and several packages of candies, coffee, tobacco, and flour.

Smoke bent and took a package of peppermint sticks, handing them to Running Deer, who quickly put one in his mouth, his eyes wide with delight.

Gray Wolf nodded. "Let us go to our ponies to find some suitable for your fine gifts."

They walked over toward where the Palouse herd was confined in a large corral of bushes set in a large semi-circle, leaving the tribe's squaws to paw through the pots and pans and blankets, chattering like small children at the treasure.

One of the studs immediately caught Smoke's eye. He was taller than the others, and heavily muscled for a Palouse, which tended to be slimmer than white man's horses.

The chief saw where Smoke was looking, and nodded. "Man Who Walks on Mountain has a good eye for ponies. That is one of my best, stronger and faster than others."

He turned to Spotted Elk and spoke a few words in their language. Spotted Elk quickly jumped over the bushes and walked into the herd of horses, grabbing several by the rope halters the Indians used instead of the leather ones used by white men.

Soon they had two magnificent studs, one gray with dark black spots on its rump, and another one with reddish-colored spots over a white coat. Both had the blue eyes with a circle around the iris showing the true full-blooded Palouse genes.

The mares were only slightly smaller, and both had good

lines, with strong legs and sleek muscles, showing they had been very well cared for.

Gray Wolf held out his hand. "Are these what you wish?"

Smoke walked over to run his hands over the big stud's neck and back. "These are just what I've been looking for."

Gray Wolf nodded. "Then may they carry you past your enemies in time of need, Man Who Walks on Mountain."

Smoke looked over his shoulder at Pearlie and Cal. "Throw a rope over these horses, boys, before he changes his mind."

Pearlie took the rope halters in his hand while Cal tied dally ropes to the animals. "Smoke, these are some of the finest Palouse I've ever seen," Pearlie said.

"These boys'll make old Seven a mite jealous when they're put out to breed alongside of him," Cal added.

"If they turn out to be half the horse old Seven was, they'll do just fine," Smoke said. "Excuse me for a minute, boys. There's something I want to ask Gray Wolf before we leave."

Smoke took Gray Wolf by the arm, led him off to a spot a few yards away, and began to talk to him in a low tone that Cal and Pearlie couldn't quite make out. As they talked, the chief looked over at the two young cowboys occasionally, a smile on his face as he nodded his head. After talking earnestly with the chief for about five minutes, Smoke grinned and shook the brave's hand, then returned to where Cal and Pearlie were holding the Palouse horses.

Soon, the trio had said their good-byes to Gray Wolf and Spotted Elk, and were on their way back down the mountain toward Buffalo. They made good time, since the weather had cleared and they were going with the north wind instead of against it.

"Smoke, when we breed these Palouse with those Morgans you got from John Chisum, we're gonna have the best remuda in the territory," Pearlie said.

Smoke nodded. "If we can manage to get the speed and intelligence from the Morgans mixed with the bottom and toughness of the Palouse into one animal, it'll be a tough horse to beat."

As they made their way down the mountain, Pearlie looked over at Cal, a satisfied smile on his face. "Well, Cal, I guess Miss Sally won't have to skin us alive after all."

"What do you mean?" Smoke asked.

Cal grinned. "When she sent us up here after you, Miss Sally as much as said if'n we let anything happen to you, she'd never let us forget it."

"And now that we've cleared up that little fracas down in Johnson County, an' you've got the Palouse you came after, it shouldn't be too hard to get you home with your hide in one piece," Pearlie added to Smoke.

Smoke glanced over at Pearlie. "Who said we're heading home right away?"

Cal said, "I don't like the sound of that, Pearlie."

"Well, ain't we?" Pearlie asked, a fearful expression on his face, not really wanting to hear Smoke's answer.

"Not just yet we aren't," Smoke said. "There are some things I want to do before we head back to Colorado."

"Such as?" Pearlie asked.

"When I got the cavalry involved, I was promised those boys that killed my friends Nate and Nick were going to be tried for their crimes. Once I make sure that's gonna happen, then the Johnson County War is over, and not before."

Pearlie cut his eyes heavenward. "Please God, let things go the way they're supposed to, just once."

"Smoke," Cal said, pleading, "if someone ends up shootin' a hole in you, Miss Sally'll never bake us no bear sign nor pies again."

Smoke grinned. "Well, boys, knowing how much you like Sally's cooking, I'll do my best not to let that happen."

"Besides," Pearlie added, trying to convince Cal as well as himself that everything was going to be all right, "that Colonel Van Horn looked like a right honorable man. I'm sure he was tellin' the truth when he told Smoke those boys were goin' to be tried for the killin's."

"It's not Van Horn I'm worried about," Smoke said. "It's those lily-livered politicians in Cheyenne that control things that are liable to muck things up. I never met a politician, or a lawyer for that matter, that didn't know which hand held the money. Most of 'em don't give a damn about justice, just where their next payoff is coming from."

"Smoke," Cal said, a questioning look on his face, "you said there were a couple of things you wanted to do. If one of 'em is makin' sure those Regulators get what's comin' to 'em, what's the other?"

Smoke looked over at Cal and Pearlie, a slight smile on his lips. "Well, it occurred to me when we were up there with the Nez Percé, that the only thing you boys know about the mountain men are what you've heard sitting around a campfire."

Pearlie nodded. "So?"

"I think it's about time I broadened your education a mite. What do you say to staying up here in the mountains and doing a little hunting and camping for a couple of weeks?"

Cal glanced back at their pack animal and its bare back. "But Smoke, we ain't hardly got no supplies left at all."

"That's the point, boys. You need to learn how to live up here like the mountain men did, hunting and killing your food, living off the land without relying on store-bought supplies for your life."

Cal and Pearlie stared at each other for a moment. "Does that mean eatin' bark an' such?" Pearlie asked, a worried expression on his face.

Smoke laughed. "Hell, no, Pearlie." He waved his hands at the scenery around them. "The high lonesome is God's own general store. He's put everything you need to live right here for the taking. All you got to do is learn how to take it, before it takes you."

"But Smoke," Pearlie said, giving it one last try, "you said the Indians done marked this land as theirs, an' they'd be mighty pissed off if'n we hunted it."

"That's right, Pearlie. That's why I had that little palaver with Chief Gray Wolf before we left. I told him you boys were pilgrims who needed some lessons only the high lonesome could teach. He agreed on how important that was for young men to learn, so he gave me his permission to camp up here a while and teach you what I could about living on the mountain."

Cal broke out in a wide grin and nodded his head gleefully. "Gee willikers, Smoke, I think it'd be a great adventure!"

Pearlie agreed, albeit reluctantly. "I guess so. After all, that elk stew wasn't so bad."

"Good, then it's decided," Smoke said, jerking his horse's head around and heading off in a wide sweep back up the mountain, toward areas remote from the Indians' camp.

"Wait a minute," Cal said. "What about Miss Sally? Won't she be worried?"

"No. Before we left Buffalo, I wired Sheriff Monte Carson in Big Rock, telling him to let her know we were all right and we'd be home when we got there and not to worry—you boys had the situation well in hand."

Twenty-eight

When it came time to leave the trail and head up into untraveled territory, through snowdrifts two and three feet deep, Smoke hung back. "I'm gonna let you boys take the lead and see if you remember what I told you about picking a place to make our base camp."

"No problem," Cal said, with the exuberance and cockiness of youth. "Come on, Pearlie, let's see if we can find a stream that ain't iced over, with plenty of beaver on it."

"Yeah," Pearlie said, entering into the situation with good humor, "an' we need to find someplace sheltered from the wind and snow, near a cliff or overhang or in some heavy timber so we won't freeze our *cojones* off when the next blizzard hits."

Smoke smiled to himself, thinking how much he was going to enjoy imparting some of the knowledge Preacher had given to him during his early days in the mountains.

It was getting close to dusk before they found a suitable campsite. It was situated next to the sheer stone face of a mountain wall, facing south so the north wind would be blocked during snowstorms. A gurgling, rushing stream was within twenty yards of the camp, and there was evidence of several beaver dams within easy reach, indicating an abundance of wildlife.

The site was below the timberline, so there was plenty of woodfall for making fires, and the trees had many low-hanging limbs that would be useful for forming sides and roofs on the lean-to Smoke would show them how to build to keep the worst of the weather off.

As they gathered wood for their first fire, Smoke stood in the small clearing with his hands on his hips, satisfied the boys would be apt pupils for what he had to teach them.

He helped them pick out fist-sized stones to place in a circle around the fire, explaining how the rocks were called gravel, and had been deposited by giant glaciers that had moved through the area millions of years before.

He showed them how to build a pit for their waste away from the camp, and told them it had to be covered over so it wouldn't bring predators like bears and mountain lions to their camp.

That first night, before they had their lean-tos built, they were lucky and the skies were clear, with little snowfall. They sat around the fire and made a meal of hot coffee, strong enough to float a horseshoe, and dried, jerked beef, hard enough to break a tooth if they weren't careful.

Sitting there with a roof of stars over their heads, warmed by the golden flames of a wood fire, he told them stories of the mountain men he had known and camped with, men who were legends in the lore of the early frontier.

Men with names like Preacher, Puma Buck, Huggy Charles, Dupre, Grizzly Jones, and others. Men who had lived their entire lives forsaking the company of other men to be alone in the high lonesome.

His stories were punctuated with the cries of wolves, singing to their mates in the moonlight, the occasional guttural growl of a night-hunting grizzly, and the wild scream of a mountain lion, celebrating its night-kill.

Finally, Cal and Pearlie fell asleep, with visions of buckskin-clad men, fighting bears, lions, and Indians, forging lives of happy solitude in the highest reaches of frozen mountain ranges.

When dawn came, cold and clear, Smoke began his lessons. He instructed the boys on which trees to cut to form the walls of their lean-to, how to strip the smaller branches, leaving the topmost ones for forming the roof, placing the poles at an angle against the side of the mountain cliff so as to shed the snow that was sure to come with the next winter storm.

Once they had their shelter completed, he led them on a hunting expedition, both for food and for furs to help ward off the freezing temperatures he expected in the coming days.

Cal was the first to shoot, picking out a large doe deer, after Smoke told him to ignore the buck standing nearby, since the doe's meat would be much more tender and less gamy to the taste.

Once they had skinned the deer, hanging the skin away from the camp to cure, he had them hang the meat from a tree, suspended out of the reach of hungry bears or mountain lions.

Next, they went hunting for bear, to get skins to line the walls of the lean-to and to sleep under for warmth. He showed them how to track the big animals, following spoor of bear droppings as well as tracks in the fresh snow. They passed up several shots at females, who had small cubs in tow, Smoke telling them not to kill the mothers as the cubs couldn't survive on their own.

As they were walking through dense undergrowth, suddenly a giant grizzly reared up, spreading his arms and growling in anger at their intrusion onto his hunting grounds.

Pearlie, standing firm and unafraid, raised his rifle and planted his feet.

"Through the heart, Pearlie," Smoke advised, readying his own rifle in case Pearlie missed. "You want to drop him with one shot. Can't afford to waste ammunition up here."

As the animal charged, Pearlie stood his ground and placed his shot directly in the bear's chest, dropping him like a stone only yards from where they were standing.

"Damn," Cal exclaimed, wiping fear-sweat from his brow, "that was a fine shot, Pearlie."

Pearlie, white-faced and with trembling hands now that the

danger was past, grinned. "Whew, that was close. Those bears can move faster'n I thought."

"They can outrun the fastest horse for short distances, especially through deep snow," Smoke told them as he pulled out his skinning knife. He glanced up at them. "That's something it'll pay you to remember if you ever jump one on horseback."

He handed the knife to Pearlie. "Here, son, it's your kill, so you get to do the honors."

As Pearlie approached the dead bear, he drew back, making a face. "Gawd almighty! He stinks to high heaven."

Smoke grinned. "Bears aren't partial to baths, Pearlie." He hesitated, thinking of his old friends. "And neither are mountain men, 'cept maybe once a year in the spring. A couple of weeks up here, and you won't smell much different."

As the days on the mountain passed, Cal and Pearlie soaked up the knowledge Smoke taught them like sponges. Before long they were skinning and cutting wild game as if they were born to it. Smoke was amazed at how rapidly they assimilated the lessons of living in the high lonesome, thinking they would have made admirable mountain men had they been born thirty years sooner.

The boys, for their part, mostly looked forward to the nights spent around the campfire, listening to the tales of mountain men Smoke told them each night.

When their store-bought supplies ran out, Smoke taught them to make coffee from ground up acorns and piñon nuts, how to pick grapevines to smoke instead of tobacco, and how to make a passable flour out of roots of certain trees. He taught them to hunt for and find wild onions and yams, which berries could be safely eaten and which would cause debilitating stomach cramps, and how to build traps for beaver and birds and squirrels, saving their precious ammunition, which was beginning to run low.

On this diet, the baby fat the boys had accumulated melted off, and they became lean and their muscles began to strengthen and grow wiry from the hard physical labor of surviving in the wilderness.

Smoke taught them to make needles from birds' bones and rawhide string from deer hides so they could mend and take up their clothes that were hanging loosely on their now-thin bodies.

Soon, they were all wearing homemade buckskins, much like the mountain men they had seen. Cal was even sporting a wispy, thin beard, since shaving with the frigid mountain stream water didn't much appeal to him.

Toward the end of their sojourn, Smoke took to staying in camp, getting the Palouse horses used to having saddles on their backs instead of Indian blankets, while Cal and Pearlie ran their traps and hunted for food and fresh vegetables in the woods.

Finally, Smoke decided they were ready to leave the mountain, the boys having learned enough about being mountain men to be able to survive on their own if need be.

On their last night around the campfire, Smoke took out his knife and lightly touched Cal on the shoulder. "I'm giving you a mountain man name, Cal. I'm gonna call you Deerstalker Woods, for your ability to sneak up on a deer close enough to spit in his eye without him ever hearing you," Smoke said.

As Cal beamed, Smoke looked over at Pearlie. "Your mountain name will be Hawkeye, 'cause you've become one of the best trackers I've ever known. I think you could track a field mouse through a blizzard if you had to," Smoke said, pride in his voice.

"Do we have to leave?" Cal asked.

Smoke's eyes got a faraway look in them. "Yeah. It's time we head back down the mountain and see what became of the men who killed Nate Champion and Nick Ray. I have a feeling we have some unfinished business with those boys."

Twenty-nine

When Smoke and Cal and Pearlie rode into Buffalo, they got some strange looks. They were still in their buckskins, Cal's and Pearlie's only partially cured, and all three had heavy beards and long, unkempt hair.

They took their horses to the livery stable and instructed the man there to rub them down and feed them plenty of grain. Then they headed toward the hotel. As they approached the door to the hotel, Sheriff Red Angus was walking along the boardwalk toward them from the opposite direction. When he saw them, he stopped and stared at Smoke with his head cocked to the side.

"Smoke Jensen? Is that you?"

Smoke stopped and said, "Yes, Sheriff, it is. What can I do for you?"

Angus stepped closer, put his hand on Smoke's shoulder as if to say something, then wrinkled up his nose and took a step back. "Jesus, you boys are a mite gamy."

"Three weeks in the mountains will do that to you," Smoke said.

"Well, I just wanted to warn you. Things aren't goin' so good here in Johnson County since the Army came and took the Regulators away."

"Oh? What do you mean?"

Angus looked nervously around to see if anyone was watching, then put his hand on Smoke's arm and ushered him off the street and into the hotel lobby. "It's too complicated to go into right now. Why don't you boys get cleaned up and then meet me over at my office?"

"Sheriff, I don't know what's got you so riled up, but we intend to take a hot bath, then go to the dining room for a good meal. We've been eating out of a pan for three weeks and we all want a good meal. If you need to talk to us, you can meet us here in . . . oh, about an hour."

"All right," Angus said, "only, watch your backs till I get to talk to you. You ain't exactly the most popular gent in town right now."

Smoke pursed his lips as he watched Angus walk away, wondering what was going on.

After a moment, Pearlie touched his arm. "Smoke, I think we'd better go get those baths 'fore the manager has to open all the windows in this place."

They walked up to the front desk. Smoke said, "I need three rooms and three baths, with plenty of hot water."

The desk man peered down his nose at the three men standing before him, the expression on his face showing he didn't like the way they smelled and looked.

"We don't rent to . . . men such as you. I'd suggest you take your business down the street to a . . . less expensive establishment."

Smoke opened his shirt and unbuttoned his money belt, letting the clerk see the wads of greenbacks in it. He pulled a hundred-dollar bill out of the stack and handed it to the man. "Partner, how about getting those baths ready, and you just let me know when you've gone through this one and we'll give you another one just like it, all right?"

The clerk smiled as if it hurt his face, and rang the bell on the counter. "Front!" he called, then instructed the bellboy to take their bags up to the third floor and show them where the bathroom was.

Upstairs, Smoke and the boys stripped their buckskins off and threw them in a pile. "Take these out and burn them, if you don't mind," he said to the boy in his teens working the bathroom.

As the boy bent to pick the rancid clothes up, he turned his face away, saying, "No, sir, I don't mind at all. Matter of fact, it'll be a pleasure to git 'em out of here."

Smoke laughed, and settled slowly into a tub filled with steaming-hot water. "And young man, put more water on to heat. I have a feeling we may be here a spell."

Pearlie took a long-handled brush, rubbed soap on it, and began to scrub his back, an expression of near-ecstasy on his face. "You know, Smoke, I ain't never been one to be 'specially fond of baths, but I gotta tell you, after three weeks in the high lonesome freezin' my butt off, this ranks right up there with Miss Sally's bear sign."

Cal, who was sunk down in steaming water until nothing showed but his bearded head, gave a contented sigh. "I don't know 'bout *that,* Pearlie, but this do feel right nice."

Smoke laughed. "I love the mountains, boys, but there is something to be said for civilization, too."

The attendant came back into the room after taking their stinking buckskins out to burn, and stared at the men with wide eyes. "Are you mountain men?" he said, as if he'd never seen anyone like them up close.

Smoke glanced at Cal and Pearlie, then answered, "We sure are, young fellow. Those two over there are two of the roughest, toughest mountain men I've ever had the pleasure to make camp with."

Cal and Pearlie beamed at the compliment, sitting a little straighter in their baths.

"What's it like livin' up in the mountains?" the boy asked.

"Well," Pearlie said, as if he were an expert, "other than the bears an' mountain lions an' wolves tryin' to make you their dinner, an' the Injuns wanting to take your scalp an' hang it on their lodge pole, it ain't so bad."

Cal nodded. "An' if'n the temperature don't get much under

thirty below an' the snow stays less then five feet deep, it ain't bad a'tall."

Smoke grinned, thinking how much both Cal and Pearlie had been changed by their experience in the high lonesome. Cal was no longer just a cowboy in his teens. He seemed to have matured from having to face death on a daily basis, with only his skill and brains to keep him alive. *There's nothing like knowing you're only one mistake away from being killed to make a man grow up fast and give him confidence,* Smoke thought.

Smoke climbed out of the tub and dried off, the attendant's eyes widening again at the sight of his massive body, covered with knife and bullet scars from all the scrapes he'd been in.

As Smoke stepped in front of a mirror hung on a pole and began to shave his beard off, Pearlie asked, "You plannin' on shavin', Cal?"

Cal rubbed his hands over his beard. "I ain't decided yet. You think this growth makes me look older?"

Pearlie laughed. "Uglier, if'n that's possible, not particularly older."

"You'd better shave it off, Cal," Smoke said, glancing at him in the mirror. "If I take you home looking like that, Sally's liable to shoot you, thinking you're a *bandido* or rustler come to steal our stock."

Pearlie looked at Cal's hair, hanging down over his eyes. "A little time in a barber's chair wouldn't do any of us any harm neither," he said.

Finally, when they had soaked and scrubbed until their skin was red and shining, and after they'd shaved their beards, Cal electing to leave his wispy moustache in place, they climbed into fresh clothes and headed down the stairs toward the dining room.

"I can already taste that beefsteak," Pearlie said, licking his lips.

"Smoke," Cal said, "I ain't sayin' you ain't a right good cook, but it'll sure be nice to eat some meat you don't have to cut with an ax 'fore you put it in your mouth."

Just as the waiter placed their food in front of them, along with steaming cups of real coffee, Sheriff Angus walked up and took a seat at their table.

Smoke gestured at the plates of food. "Would you like something to eat, Sheriff?"

Angus shook his head. "No. To tell you the truth, I ain't had much of an appetite lately, Jensen."

Smoke cut a piece of his steak off and stuck it in his mouth. "Why don't you tell us what's going on around here that has you all riled up, Sheriff."

Angus looked around over his shoulder to make sure no one else was listening, then leaned forward, speaking in a low tone of voice. "Jensen, since that fracas with the Regulators, this county has gone to hell. Before they came, it was a nice place to live." He shrugged. "Oh, sure, we had a little rustlin' and a little stealin', but it was on a minor scale, and was mainly directed against the large ranchers that could afford to lose a few head of stock."

"Things have changed?"

"You're damn right they have, and not for the better. I've lost all control of the county. The men around here have gone from being minor outlaws to full-fledged desperados. They're goin' around shootin' and killin' everybody they think may have helped out the Regulators."

"Well, you got to expect that."

"Yeah, but they're not stoppin' there. There's a lot of men takin' advantage of this, an' they consider anybody who has somethin' they want to be fair game." He paused long enough to build himself a cigarette, sticking it in the corner of his mouth, where it bobbed up and down as he talked. "Hell, just the other day the foreman of the Hoe Ranch, George Wellman, was gunned down in cold blood, all for about ten head of beef."

"You know who did it?"

"Sure, but there ain't no way I could get a jury in this county to convict 'em. I tell you, Jensen, it's become every man for himself around here."

"Sounds like you got yourself a problem, Sheriff."

"That's for sure, an' to make matters worse, Tom Horn and the other so-called stock detectives are still out there, shootin' up anybody they think is rustlin' the big ranchers' cattle."

Smoke's eyes narrowed. "I thought all that would stop when the Regulators and the men who led them were put on trial for the killing of Nate Champion and Nick Ray."

Angus smirked. "I guess you ain't heard 'bout that little fiasco either."

"No. Tell me."

"Soon after Wolcott and Canton and Smith and their men were taken to Fort McKinney, a sympathetic judge said they couldn't get a fair trial in Johnson County, so they were taken by train to Cheyenne."

Smoke shook his head. "As if the trial there would be fair."

"Exactly. Hell, they were transported in a private Pullman car stocked with champagne and all the whiskey they could drink."

Smoke's face clouded. "Sounds like the fix was in."

"You got that right. They were set up in a bowling alley at Fort Russell and given anything they wanted, including visits from their wives and other . . . female friends."

"What about the trial?"

"The only charges brought were for the killings of Nate Champion and Nick Ray. And since the only witnesses were you and that mountain man, and nobody made any effort to get you to testify, the prisoners were turned loose without any bond. Well, hell, by then we knew we'd never win any case against them in Cheyenne, so the charges were all dropped."

"What about the gunmen from Texas?"

"They've all gone on their way, some back to Texas, others to God only knows where."

Smoke nodded, thinking over his options.

"So, no one is going to be made to pay for killing Nate and Nick, huh?"

"Not by the law, they ain't."

Smoke leaned back and took a cigar out of his pocket. He struck a lucifer on his boot and lighted the stogie. He peered through clouds of blue smoke at the sheriff. "Well, then, maybe it's time someone other than the law took a hand in the matter."

Sheriff Angus shook his head. "I got to warn you, Jensen, to watch your back. There ain't any men on either side you can count as your friends."

"That's the way I like it, Sheriff. Then I don't have to worry about who gets in my way." Smoke took the cigar out of his mouth and stared at the glowing red end for a moment. When he spoke, it was as if he were talking to himself more than to the sheriff. "You know, Sheriff, a man's got to have a creed to live by, a set of standards that he just won't violate. Me, I'm an Old Testament kind of person, and I still believe in the old adage, an eye for an eye and a tooth for a tooth."

Angus leaned forward. "Jensen, I hope to hell you ain't plannin' on tryin' to get vengeance on your own for Champion and Ray. You won't stand a chance in Cheyenne, 'cause them boys got the law in the palm of their hands."

Smoke's lips curled up in a grin that made the hair on the back of Angus's neck stir in fear. "That may be so, Sheriff, but it doesn't matter a whole lot. By the time they know I'm coming after them, it'll be too late to do anything about it." His eyes turned flat and cold as ice. "Did you ever see a rattlesnake warn the rabbit before it strikes?"

The sheriff shook his head, not really sure he understood what this very dangerous man sitting across from him meant, but he was sure thankful he didn't have him on his back trail.

Smoke poured another cup of coffee and leaned back in his chair, crossing his legs and folding his arms across his chest as if they were old friends discussing the price of beef.

"Now, Sheriff Angus, I want you to tell me all you know about the men behind the Regulators, the men who were really responsible for what happened here in Johnson County."

Thirty

Smoke and Cal and Pearlie got off the train in Cheyenne and made arrangements for their horses to be boarded in the livery stable for a few days until they were ready to leave again.

They found a hotel in the seedier part of town, a place so low on the economic scale that Smoke was sure none of the wealthy men he was going after would find out they were there.

After eating a meal that even Pearlie wasn't too happy about, they met in Smoke's room to plan their attack.

"I wish you boys would reconsider and go on back to Colorado and let me do this on my own," Smoke said.

Pearlie shook his head. "Not a chance, Smoke. Miss Sally would cut us off at the knees if she found out we didn't back your play in this."

"Besides," Cal added, "men don't take off and turn tail when their partner's up against the kind'a odds you're facin' here. From what Sheriff Angus said, there are over a hundred members of the Cheyenne Club."

Smoke smiled, grateful for the support even though he was worried that he might be getting them all into something they wouldn't be able to get out of.

"Well, we're not going after all hundred members, just those directly responsible for the killings in Johnson County."

He leaned back on his bed on his elbow. "There's a book

Sally got me to read a while back. It's called the *Art of War,* by some Japanese man whose name I don't recollect right now. Anyway, one of the things he emphasizes if you're going to war with someone, is to learn all you can about your enemy before you try to take him on."

"Is that the book you told us about with those men who dressed all in black, the ones called ninjas?" Cal asked.

"Yes, it is. Now, what we have to do is hang around the Cheyenne Club for a day or two and find out all we can about how it operates, how to get in and out in a hurry, and then ask around and see if we can find some time when the men we're after are all going to be there together."

"Why don't we just take them out one at a time?" Pearlie asked.

Smoke shook his head. "Because after the first one or two, they'd know we were coming and would be ready for us. No, we're only going to get one chance at this, and we'd better do it right the first time. Remember, these are powerful men who have the entire law enforcement system on their side."

After talking some more about their plans, the three walked over to the more exclusive part of town where the Cheyenne Club was located.

They spent two days watching men come and go from the place, making sure no one noticed them hanging around. By spreading some money around the local saloons and stores, Smoke was able to learn all about the men he was interested in: Major Wolcott, Frank Canton, and the two men who'd planned the whole expedition, Hubert Teschemacher and Frederic deBillier.

Smoke and his band were in luck. They learned that Teschemacher, deBillier, Wolcott, and several others played poker in a weekly high-stakes game, and that on those nights the club was otherwise almost deserted since it was in the middle of the week.

Cal managed to hire on with a local whiskey merchant, and did some deliveries to the club, managing to learn about the interior layout and how best to get in and then out again without getting trapped inside. He also found out there were only two guards, one in front and one in back, the patrons evidently feeling they were secure in this high-class part of town.

When the night of the poker game arrived, Smoke took all of their baggage and their horses and loaded them on the train that was overnighting in the station. It was supposed to leave for Denver the next day at eight o'clock in the morning, and he planned that they would be on it and headed out of town before the law could be mobilized to come after them.

Smoke and the boys ate a large dinner and took their time. They wanted the poker game to be well under way and the men in it heavy into their whiskey and wine before they struck, and the later they made it, the less time the sheriff in Cheyenne would have to track them down.

It was two in the morning when Smoke walked up to the guard at the rear entrance to the Cheyenne Club.

The big man put his hand on Smoke's chest and snarled, "This is a private club. Get away from here!"

Smoke grabbed the man's hand and with a sudden downward motion, twisted and turned it back, breaking the guard's wrist with a snap and driving him to his knees. Smoke threw a short right cross that snapped the man's face to the side and put him out for the rest of the night.

Cal and Pearlie appeared out of the shadows, their arms full of weapons. Cal handed Smoke his Greener ten-gauge short-barreled express gun, while keeping a sawed-off twelve-gauge of his own. Pearlie had two pistols stuck in his belt along with the one in his holster.

Smoke opened the door and let Cal lead them into the building and up the stairs to the third-floor meeting room where the poker game was being played.

They stepped into the room, but stayed back in the shadows, wanting to get a feel for the place before they made their move.

Teschemacher and deBillier were sitting next to each other,

with Wolcott on their left, and four other men arranged around the table. Smoke recognized some of them from Angus's descriptions, and knew that all of these men bore responsibility for the Johnson County massacre of his friends.

Fred Hesse, the Englishman who managed a large ranching system for distant owners, was directly across from Wolcott, and next to him was William Irving, director of the Cheyenne and Northern Railroad. The other two men were unknown to Smoke.

As Smoke and his friends watched, Wolcott dealt the cards. They were playing five-card stud. After looking at his hole card for a few seconds, deBillier said, "Ace bets one hundred."

Teschemacher grunted. "That little bitsy old ace isn't going to win this hand, Freddy." He shoved a pile of chips out into the pot. "I'll call the hundred and raise another two hundred."

"Damn," Wolcott said, "you boys must be drunk to be betting like that after only two cards. I fold."

Smoke walked out into the light, his shotgun cradled in his arms. "Howdy, gents, mind if I ante up in this game?"

The men's faces blanched and their eyes widened at the sight of the three cowboys, loaded for bear, walking into the room.

"How did you get in here?" Teschemacher asked indignantly. "This is a private club!"

"Why, we just walked right in," Smoke answered. "We heard there was a big game up here and thought we'd join in the fun."

"Bullshit!" Wolcott growled. "You're here to rob us."

"Well," deBillier said, stifling a yawn with the back of his hand, "you're out of luck, gentlemen. We play with chips and IOUs here. There isn't any cash." He acted entirely bored with the entire matter.

Smoke stepped over to the table and in a lightning-fast movement, slapped deBillier across the face with the back of his hand, snapping the man's head around and knocking him out of his chair to land sprawled on his back on the floor.

"No, I think you're out of luck, deBillier."

"Who *are* you men, and why are you here?" Hesse said, his hand slowly moving inside his coat. Cal leaned over, put the barrel of his shotgun against Hesse's forehead, and eared back the hammers. "That better be a cigar you're reachin' for, mister. Otherwise, even your best friend won't recognize you after I let these hammers down."

Hesse brought out a derringer two-shot pistol, holding it delicately with two fingers by the barrel. "Here, take it. I wasn't going to use it anyway."

Smoke glared at Hesse, his eyes as hard as flint. "We're friends of Nate Champion and Nick Ray, the men you paid to have slaughtered in Johnson County."

DeBillier whined from the floor, "But we've already been tried for that and we were acquitted."

"In a court your cattle money bought and by a judge in your pay," Smoke said. "That don't count a whole lot with us. You see, I was there that night, and I know what you did."

Wolcott snapped his fingers, looking at Smoke with narrowed eyes. "You! You're the man who called himself Kirby that was in the cabin with Champion . . . but I don't understand. Aren't you also the one who went to Fort McKinney and got the troops that saved our lives up in Buffalo?"

Smoke nodded as he turned his attention to Wolcott. "Just one of the mistakes I've made in my life. Wasn't the first, won't be the last."

Wolcott jumped to his feet, and Smoke noticed he was wearing a side arm, a big Colt Army .44 pistol.

"I won't stand for this intimidation," Wolcott snapped, his voice trying for the force of a commanding officer in the Army. "You men are trespassing here and I demand that you leave at once!"

Smoke slowly turned and placed the shotgun on the floor butt first, leaning it against a post. He squared his shoulders and faced Wolcott, his hands hanging at his side next to his pistols. "I see you're armed, Major. Why don't you make us leave? All it takes is for you to go for that hogleg on your hip."

Wolcott licked suddenly dry lips, his eyes darting around the room to glance at Cal and Pearlie. "And have your hooligan friends shoot me down?"

Smoke wagged his head. "They won't interfere—you have my word on it. You and your friends here called the dance up in Johnson County. Now it's time someone paid the band. Fill your hand, you dirtbag."

Sweat beaded Wolcott's face and his hand was trembling where it hung by his pistol. "I've seen you draw, Kirby," he said, still calling Smoke by the only name he knew him by. "You're a professional gunfighter. I wouldn't stand a chance."

"I figure about the same chance Nate and Nick had when they were ambushed in their own home without warning," Smoke said. "Now, are you going to show some courage and draw, or not?"

Wolcott shook his head, pulling his hand out from his body and away from his gun. "I don't think so. I'll not give you the satisfaction of killing me."

Smoke walked up to the terrified man. "You are a coward, aren't you? Pretty tough when you're leading a hundred men against two lone men, but when it comes down to standing up for your honor when the odds are one to one, you don't have the sand."

Wolcott hung his head, looking at the floor.

Smoke slapped his face with an open palm, the crack of it sounding like a pistol shot, then backhanded him the same way, snapping his head back and forth.

Infuriated, his face blazing red with humiliation, Wolcott growled and charged at Smoke, his hands out as if to choke the mountain man.

Smoke leaned to the side and threw a short left jab, smashing Wolcott's nose, sending blood and mucus flying and stopping the man in his tracks. Smoke then followed with a roundhouse right cross that caught Wolcott flush on the chin, standing him up on his tiptoes and crossing his eyes. He stood balanced there on his toes for a moment, like a bloodied ballerina, then toppled face-first down onto the hardwood floors, unconscious.

With a horrified expression on his face, Hubert Teschemacher screamed out, "Guards, help! Help, come quick!"

Cal quickly stepped over and smashed the butt of his shotgun into Teschemacher's face, shattering his front teeth and splitting his lip from top to bottom. As Teschemacher shook his head, sending blood and teeth flying across the table, the door at the end of the room burst open and three men with drawn pistols charged into the room.

Smoke whirled and drew, his hand moving so fast it was almost a blur.

Cal eared back the hammers on his sawed-off shotgun and leveled it at the men, bracing the butt against his right hip.

Pearlie filled his hand with iron, drawing and cocking only a second behind Smoke.

All three friends fired at the same time, their pistols and shotguns exploding with a noise that echoed off the walls of the enclosed room like canon blasts, filling the room with billowing clouds of gunsmoke.

The three guards did the dance of death. One, almost shredded by the molten lead 00–buckshot pellets from Cal's shotgun, spun halfway around and was blown back against the wall, hanging there for a moment like some terrible painting by a deranged artist before sliding down the wall to the floor.

Pearlie's shot took his man in the chest, blowing a hole over the heart and stopping it in mid-beat. The man managed to get off one shot before he died, which went wide to the side and creased Cal's left cheek, burning a small furrow that oozed blood.

Smoke's bullet hit his target in the forehead, creating a third eye, snapping the man's head back and blowing out the back of his skull, sending hair and bone and brain splatting against the wall behind him.

As the smoke slowly cleared, and the men at the poker table could see what had happened, Frederic deBillier leaned over to the side and vomited on his two-hundred-dollar boots, retching and coughing in the sudden silence.

William Irving, himself no stranger to violence, screwed up his face and looked away from the carnage, certain that in a few moments the same thing would happen to him.

Hubert Teschemacher stared at the bloody mess of his guards with wide eyes, his ruined mouth and lips so swollen he couldn't speak, bloodstains covering the front of his expensive suit.

Tears ran down Fred Hesse's cheeks, and he could be heard quietly sobbing as he contemplated his own death, his eyes fixed on the table in front of him, as if by not looking at his attackers he could forestall their wrath.

Wolcott remained unconscious on the floor, and was spared the spectacle of the guards' deaths.

Smoke looked at the men at the table and shook his head in disgust. "Would you look at these men, boys? The most powerful men in the territory and not one of them willing or able to stand up and fight for their lives. I guess they have to have others do that for them, since they haven't got the guts to do it for themselves."

Cal and Pearlie nodded, glaring at the men as though they were something that would crawl out from under a rock, while Cal held a bandanna against his cheek to stop the bleeding from his bullet wound.

Smoke picked up his shotgun and eared back the hammers. "Well, it's clear these men aren't worth killing, but maybe we can leave them a message anyway."

He turned and aimed his Greener at the long mirror behind the fifty-foot mahogany bar that had been imported from France. He let the hammers down, shattering the mirror and twenty thousand dollars worth of wine and whiskey and brandy on the shelves underneath it.

Cal calmly reloaded his shotgun, snapped the barrel into

place, and blew the billiard table, imparted from Germany, into so much kindling.

Pearlie filled both hands with pistols and one by one, placed bullets through some of the most expensive portraits and paintings in the country that were hanging on the walls around them.

DeBillier held up his hands. "Not the Monet!" he yelled at Pearlie.

"Mon . . . who?" Pearlie said as he put one right in the center of the painting that had cost more than Smoke's entire ranch.

William Irving, unable to stand it any longer and certain he was going to be killed anyway, jumped to his feet and clawed at his pistol.

Smoke dropped his right hand, drew his Colt, and fired from the hip without taking the time to aim. His bullet hit Irving in the right elbow, shattering the joint and almost amputating the lower arm.

Irving screamed and grabbed his arm as he fell to the ground, trying to stop the spurting blood.

Smoke looked at Pearlie and nodded, and the young man quickly stepped to Irving's side and took his bandanna off. He wrapped it around the upper arm and tied it so that it cut the bleeding off.

"There you go, mister," he said to a pale-faced, sweating Irving. "That'll save your hide, but you'll never use that arm to draw a piece again."

Smoke glanced around at the shattered and ruined Cheyenne Club, then back at the men at the table. "Gents, I hope this teaches you a lesson. If it doesn't, or if I ever see any of you, or men sent by you, again, then I'll make you this promise. I will personally hunt each and every one of you down and shoot you like a dog, without warning and without mercy. You got my word on it."

He hesitated, then added, "And you can give a message from me to Tom Horn. Tell him, if he ever comes down to Colorado, he'd better ride with his guns loose, because if I see him, I'll kill him on sight."

He spun on his heels and walked out the door, followed by Cal and Pearlie, who were, incredibly, whistling as they exited. The men at the table could hear Pearlie teasing Cal about being a magnet for lead, since he seemed to get shot on a regular basis.

After their attackers were out of the building, deBillier straightened up, adjusted his vomit-stained clothes, and said grandly, "Those thugs will be sorry they did this. As soon as it's daylight, I'll have the sheriff and a posse on their trail."

Teschemacher, his eyes wide with fright, shook his head violently from side to side, though his mouth was so swollen he couldn't speak.

Hesse looked up through reddened and tear-stained eyes. "Are you crazy, Freddy? Did you see the look in that madman's eyes when he said he'd kill us if we sent anyone after him? I don't want any part of that. I vote we cut our losses and forget this ever happened."

Teschemacher and Irving, from his place on the floor, both nodded their agreement.

"Now get me a doctor, before I bleed to death," Irving said, grimacing in pain.

Thirty-one

It was almost a week later that the train carrying Smoke and Cal and Pearlie and the Palouse horses pulled into Big Rock, Colorado, just after dawn.

It was almost noon by the time they made their way on horseback to the Sugarloaf Ranch. As they rounded the final turn in the trail to the ranch, Pearlie smacked his lips loudly. "You know, fellahs, I can almost smell those bear sign of Miss Sally's already."

"Count on you, Pearlie, that the first thing you think of when you're gettin' home is food," Cal said.

Pearlie raised his eyebrows, looking surprised. "What else is more important?"

Smoke gave a small smile. "Seeing the woman you love and missed like hell, for one thing," he said to himself.

When they were almost there, Sally appeared in the yard of the log cabin she and Smoke shared, her head cocked to the side as if she had somehow sensed the presence of her man.

Smoke broke into a gallop and reined up just in front of her, jumping off his horse and sweeping her up in his arms.

Neither of them spoke for a moment, just clung together in a tight embrace, both smiling as if they were now complete.

Sally finally broke the embrace and stepped back, her hands on her hips. "I need to have a few words with you, Mr. Jensen. Something about a promise to wire me when you got to Buffalo," she said with arched eyebrows.

Smoke held out both hands. "Now wait a minute, Sally. There's a good explanation, and I'll tell you later. Right now, I want to get these Palouse into the pasture."

She turned, noticing the horses for the first time. She walked over and ran her hands down the flanks of one of the mares. "Oh, Smoke, they're beautiful. They're going to make a great addition to our remuda."

Smoke nodded. "Let's put 'em in with Seven, and see how the old man likes the company."

Pearlie opened the gate to the nearby pasture where Seven, the Palouse that Preacher had given to him, resided. He was standing in a far corner, eating the sweet, green winter grass on the high mountain plateau.

The two young studs and the two mares shook their heads and took off at a run when they were freed from their halters.

Smoke, Cal, Pearlie, and Sally leaned on the wooden fence, watching to see how the old stud would take to the new additions to his pasture.

As the newer animals ran into the open meadow, Seven perked up his ears and stood erect, sniffing the air. After a moment, he whinnied a loud challenge and raced toward the two young stallions.

The larger and more dominant of the two reared back on his hind legs and then galloped toward Seven, intending to meet his challenge. The two large Palouse ran almost into each other, then danced around for a minute, each trumpeting and screaming threats at each other. Then, in a lightning movement, Seven closed the distance between them and bent his head, biting at the jowls under the neck of the younger stud. They bumped and jostled each other briefly; then Seven spun around and gave the youngster a heavy kick in his flanks with his hind legs, almost knocking the horse off his feet.

He stumbled back, whinnied a couple of times, then turned tail and ran as Seven followed, nipping at his backside.

After Seven had shown the newcomer who was boss, he

trotted over toward the two mares, who were prancing around, their tails in the air, in obvious invitation.

"Look at those hussies," Sally said, mock indignation in her voice. "They are too stupid to play hard to get when a male comes around."

Smoke grinned. "Looks like the old stud still has the stuff in him to get them excited."

Sally put her arm around Smoke's waist and laid her head on his shoulders. "I'm kind'a partial to old studs myself," she said with a wicked grin.

As she and Smoke walked slowly off toward their cabin arm in arm, Pearlie glanced at Cal. "I guess right now might not be a particularly good time to ask Miss Sally to bake us some bear sign, would it?"

Author's Note

Creed of the Mountain Man is a work of fiction, but the events portrayed in the Johnson County War are for the most part true. The characters were true heroes and villains of the war, and while some of their actions were modified for creative reasons, the essence of what they did was preserved. After the war was over, the real-life characters continued with their lives.

Frank Canton, who became the chief detective in the vigilante war on alleged rustlers, had a past none of his employers knew about. His real name was Joseph Horner, born in 1849 the son of a Virginia doctor who moved to Texas after the Civil War. At the age of twenty-six, he was wanted for rustling, bank robbery, and assault with intent to kill. In 1874, in a barroom brawl with some soldiers, he shot his way out of town, killing one of the soldiers, and resurfaced in Wyoming under the assumed name Frank Canton. After the Johnson County War was over, Canton moved to Oklahoma Territory and resumed his career as a lawman, working for a while under "Hanging Judge" Isaac Charles Parker of Fort Smith, Arkansas. During this time, Canton helped wipe out Bill Doolin's gang, and in a stand-up gun duel reminiscent of the movies, outdrew and killed the sharpshooting outlaw Bill Dunn. Later, he followed the gold rush to the Klondike, and served for some years as a deputy U.S. marshal in Alaska. Years later, he returned to Texas and asked for and received a pardon for his earlier crimes from the governor.

Jim Dudley, the overweight Texan who shot himself in the knee when he fell off his horse, was taken to nearby Fort McKinney for medical treatment. Unfortunately, gangrene set in and he later died in agony, screaming in pain.

When the Texans were turned loose without bond by the judge in Cheyenne, they had a farewell party given by their Cheyenne employers, and then scattered out to all parts of the country. Some went back to Paris, Texas, where Tom Smith had first recruited them; others headed for Indian Territory or the wide-open towns of Oklahoma. Two of the Regulators from Texas—G.R. Tucker, nineteen years old, and Buck Garrett, twenty-two years old—moved to Ardmore, Oklahoma, where Tucker served as deputy U.S. marshal and Garrett as sheriff.

Tom Smith returned to serve again as a deputy U.S. marshal in Texas, and was killed a few months later in a shoot-out with an outlaw.

The Texas Kid, who fired the first shot at Nick Ray at the KC ranch, returned home to Texas. Soon thereafter, he quarreled with his girlfriend when she refused to marry him because he had gone off to Wyoming and left her at home. He shot her to death, and then said, just before he was hanged, he wished he'd never gone to Wyoming.

In one of the last fights of the Johnson County War, Mike Shonsey shot and killed Dudley Champion, Nate's twin brother. Though many witnesses claimed otherwise, Shonsey was released after he claimed self-defense in the shooting.

Though the war was now officially over, stock "detectives" such as Tom Horn continued killing men they claimed were rustlers for years, until Horn killed a fourteen-year-old boy by mistake, thinking the boy was his father. After bragging about the killing in a saloon, with the sheriff and others listening through a thin wall, Horn was convicted of murder and hanged.